THE DEVI IN THE DIVA

THE DEVI IN THE DIVA

MYTHS
ARCHETYPES
BRANDS
FILMS

SHYAONTI TALWAR

Vitasta

Published by
Renu Kaul Verma
Vitasta Publishing Pvt Ltd
2/15, Ansari Road, Daryaganj
New Delhi-110 002
info@vitastapublishing.com

ISBN 978-93-90961-32-0

First Edition 2022

MRP ₹525

Editor: Papri Sen Sri Raman
Layout Design: Somesh Kumar Mishra
Cover Design: Arun Talwar
Printed at Thomson Press (India) Ltd.

This book is for my son Shiv

CONTENT

Foreword *ix*

Introduction 1

Kali: The Goddess Of Excess 36

Durga: The Goddess Who Won 79

Sati: The Goddess Who Rebelled 123

Parvati: The Goddess Who Wasn't 153

Lakshmi: The Goddess On The Move 186

Saraswati: The Goddess Who Hid 222

Matrkas: The Godesses Who Are Misunderstood 256

Conclusion *293*

Glossary *299*

References *311*

Acknowledgements *315*

About The Author *319*

FOREWORD

In my decades spent understanding consumers across India, the only definite conclusion which one can derive about them is their ability to infuse their lives with a magnitude of contradictions. As Indians, we feel that we are all set to reclaim our position of glory in the centre stage of the world, yet we are so easily reconciled to our fate and our everyday struggles to make ends meet with an almost meditative fortitude.

A lot of this ability to grind along and live out our existence with forbearance comes from the deep-rooted sense of fate, influenced by the canons of religion which influence and strengthen this cosmic fortitude. After all, religion and its tenets have always been of paramount importance and which have gained increasing significance in recent times. The 2015 Pew Research Centre survey cites, eight-in-ten Indians said religion is very important in their lives and even millennials are strongly influenced by religion today (YouGov-Mint Millennial Survey).

When it comes to religion, particularly Hinduism which is practiced by a sizeable section of the Indian population, the mother Goddess worship and her manifestations through time and space is an important facet and is of striking significance. No other modern civilisation has such a profound influence of the Goddess manifested in its culture, its social fabric and in its everyday mundane life.

Right from the pre-independence Indian cinema depicting a collective personification of the vastly heterogeneous land as a mother Goddess to the days of the righteous embodiment of motherhood depicted in *Aurat* and *Mother India,* to the present sensorial overload of modern Bollywood with its *Begum Jaan* or a subtle poignant saga in *Nil Battey Sannata*, heroines have been modelled on the various archetypes surrounding the myths of the Goddess which only proves what Mark & Pearson have said in their book, *The Hero and the Outlaw*: While the conscious power of a religious symbol is inordinately greater, the unconscious power of an archetype, even in an entirely secular context, is immense.

Which brings us to this book. While a lot of academic books have been written dissecting the Goddess in Hinduism, there seems to be a need for a book which could transcend the academic analysis of the mother Goddess, its various archetypes and the subsequent emergence of it in various subtle and overt forms in popular cinema, advertising and culture; something this book has successfully managed to capture and bring to the readers in a very lucid style, yet not forgoing the sharp insightful analysis and explanations which is so important and useful for handy researchers, academics and business professionals like me who are looking to further their knowledge about the Goddess in popular culture and its influences on the modern Indian consumer.

The influence of the Goddess goes deeper than we can easily fathom. Hence it is important for her various myths and archetypes to get a close looking-into, as they can have layers and layers of meaning and message coiled in them. They need to be revisited, examined, studied and scrutinised with the help of the many myths and lore surrounding them and in the context in which they are evoked so as to glean more information and arrive at a better understanding of them. Only when one is able to go through this rigour, can one be in a position to write a book such as this in which the manifestations are so explicitly brought out, leaving the readers with many'Aha' ' moments reflecting and smiling at their epiphanies and telling themselves, 'Now I realise why such an advertising campaign worked or why a film had this heroine trajectory'.

It is not an easy subject to tackle but Shyaonti Talwar has managed to execute it brilliantly, making this book not only insightful with in-depth analysis but also penetrable and easily fathomable for the generalist seeking to find answers for popular culture movements and trends. I am pretty sure that this book will become the conversation starter in the corridors of marketing and advertising institutions and become a recommended reading for academics, students and marketing, advertising and communication executives. At the same time this is one book that is bound to captivate the general reader who loves cinema and myth.

Saumya Chattopadhyay
Senior Vice President
Lowe Lintas

INTRODUCTION

HAVE YOU EVER wondered while watching a film or a web series that you might be actually witnessing an ancient myth unfolding? Or regarded the actors as gods and goddesses in the midst of epic action? Did Rani Mukherjee ever remind you of a serene and understated Saraswati or the chirpy, bubbly Preiti Zinta of a deep-in-love Radha? Would you believe me if I told you that Alia Bhatt in *Gully Boy* is a lot like Parvati or Vidya Balan in *Begum Jaan*, like Kali? That in *DDLJ*, Simran falling in love with a man of her choosing is a lot like Sati's love for Shiva?

And what would your response be if I told you that Rishi Kapoor and Shahrukh Khan actually in many ways embody Krishna? Or for that matter the marriage crises in *Thappad* or *Tanu weds Manu* could exactly be like the ones Shiva and Parvati's marriage may have gone through? And that much of our Hindi film song-and-dance sequences borrow from the tradition of the Radha-Krishna rasleela? Would you be able to imagine that *Sholay* could actually be a remake of the Ramayana and *Lagaan* might have the Mahabharata embedded in it? That most of what you watch on screen, whether it is a film or a web series or even the short narrative of an advertisement, is already a part of our epics and Puranas?

Mind you, I am not only talking of on-screen representation of stories from India. I know, it is not very easy to equate films with myths and even more difficult to see gods and goddesses in filmic characters but what if I told you, that is exactly what it is, at least most of the time? That is the secret of blockbusters and the timeless appeal of some actors who you would like to see playing the same kind of person over and over and over in film after film after film.

What I am referring to are essentially myths and archetypes that populate our 'collective unconscious', a term proposed by psychologist Carl Jung to describe a kind of collective memory shared by people, which may be repressed and projected or manifested in various ways. So, in order to be convinced that what we watch on screen most of the time is, in effect, that which is stored in our primal imagination, we first need to understand what exactly are myths and archetypes, how they come about to be a part of the whole psychic drama in us and why they acquire the form of cinematic plots and characters.

What is an Archetype?

Archetype is just a more difficult word to understand a less difficult idea. We all live with archetypes, embody them, identify with them, engage with them and are even drawn to, or repulsed by them. We just don't know that they are archetypes.

When we tend to label people or classify or categorise them or use a certain set of synonyms, words and phrases to describe them, we are actually talking about archetypes. For instance, when we predict about a person with comments like, 'I think she will understand. She is very empathetic' or, 'Oh! I'm sure she will turn this to her advantage. She is such an opportunist', or when you have to speak about yourself and say, 'I'm more of a recluse. I'd rather be at home with a book than be partying somewhere', or, 'I get bored too soon. I need to keep jumping from project to project, place to place', what we are actually describing is an archetype and archetypal traits people show.

We may have heard people saying things like, 'I am in my element when I am doing this…' or, 'This is me' or more commonly, 'It's in my blood', it mostly certainly is! We are actually hearing them express their archetype. As Caroline Myss, the author of *The Language of Archetypes* puts it, they are 'always charactersitics' – defined by characteristics that are consistent in a person when they are ten and when they are forty.

While tracing the history of archetypes, founder of analytical psychology Carl Jung describes them as, 'universal images that have existed since the remotest times'. Images can contain whole stories in them. And then what happens? Well, it is the stories, the messages, the ways of worlding that are encoded in images which are then stored in the unconscious and passed on. Archetypes, according to Jung, are contents of the 'collective unconscious' or what he even calls 'the transcendental imagination' that have found their way out of our collective repressed memory and are projected on people and situations that subsequently become packed with meaning. Archetypes then, are 'symbolic figures' that might be regarded as containing primitive worldviews and secrets, that may encode complex messages and truths and involve the 'transmission of collective contents originally derived from the unconscious'.

Identifying archetypes is a human need. It stems from a deep-rooted urge to be able to make sense of things, to see in them a hidden meaning, to look for a transcendental reality and to also appeal to a connectedness amongst people, to infer that all are but copies of the one.

Archetypes are a projection of our unconscious emotions and they are also stored in our unconscious. Though people normally tend to understand archetypes in terms of binary opposites like hero-villain, virgin-whore, master-slave, archetypes are complex, multi-layered and can present not-obvious nuances and dimensions when explored.

Archetypes and myths are closely related. Myss says that we engage with archetypes and speak archetypal language all the time. We associate with myths unconsciously and sometimes even enact them. The only thing is, we do not realise that this is a myth and this is an archetype because one seems to be too remote and primitive and the other sounds too theoretical.

What are Myths?

Myths are timeless tales remembered, retold, retained and replayed magically and almost effortlessly. Like archetypes, they too have an exalted psychic meaning. So how did myths come to be? According to Jung, pure physical phenomena happening outside and around the primitive human being needed to acquire a psychic dimension which enabled the process of meaning-making. The alien and the unfamiliar, the strange and the unpredictable, the arbitrary and the uncertain, deeply invested with mythic, spiritual and religious overtones, all began to make sense for the human being. Jung gives a very easy to understand example:

> It is not enough for the primitive to see the sun rise and set; this external observation must at the same time be a psychic happening: the sun in its course must represent the fate of a god or hero on a cosmic journey.

Thus, all the highly mythologised phenomena in nature or the cosmos, be it the changing of seasons, changing vegetation, the tidal occurrences, the solar, lunar and planetary movements need to be seen and understood through a subjective, psychic prism. We can then say that myths and archetypes surrounding these phenomena are manifestations or conscious projections of the psychic drama going on in the unconscious. There is a compulsion to establish a connection between the inner and the outer worlds which is a part of the meaning-making process.

Myths can be seen as an attempt to commune with nature, to seek out and identify with the oneness, to explain it and to control it.

Myths are also a means of reconciliation with that which is beyond human control and comprehension – aging, death, accident, calamity, illness, misfortune. They can be attributed to the action or the will of gods. Thus, if Indra is angry, he will not give rain, so he needs to be appeased. It not only means of resigning oneself to the unforeseen but also the inevitable and finding one's peace in doing so.

Myths are contagious. They are borrowed all the time. In fact, that is what makes a myth a myth.

In Michel de Montaigne's view, 'whatever time, place or circumstances, we merely annotate one another' whereas André Maurois refers to the myth as, 'mother fictions of all human thought' and Nicolas Malebranche regards it as the 'eternal model'.

So, what essentially is a myth? A simple way of looking at myth as Robert A Segal does is to regard it as a story with a certain argument or a point to make: the most common way of understanding gods, heroes, villains; in other words, archetypes. It is also a credo or something that embeds an archetypal situation like 'rags to riches', 'overpowering the monster', 'consecration of nature' and the like.

Myths and archetypes have a latent power to draw us to them, even as they appeal to that collective reservoir of memory in our unconscious. Myths of exile, the fight between good and evil, virgin births, foster parenting, trickery, abduction, annihilated pride, transgressive love resonate with us and transcend temporal, territorial, racial and cultural confines. Myths and archetypes are atemporal but at the same time they lend to temporal versions of themselves. They are universal, but at the same time they inspire cultural and territorial reconstructions of themselves.

Archetypes and Brands

Let us see how myths and archetypes lend themselves to a particular time, person, place or situation. Have we ever wondered why certain celebrities and brands are more enduring and more successful than others? It is because they have or essay an archetypal core. Pearson and Mark, in their book *The Hero and the Outlaw* trace the twelve main archetypes, part of the Western collective unconscious, observing their presence in certain brands. In fact, they offer case studies and success stories of brands that have an archetypal core and prove that brands that allow or enable themselves to be identified as an archetype and are consistent in their affinity to that archetype, are the ones that are able to send across a very strong message to the consumer and have a loyal consumer base and a strong and clear brand identity. So products with archetypal identities have a very strong likelihood of determining buying choices as they appeal to our core values and psyche through these archetypes.

When brands are built or evolve keeping an archetypal centre in mind, then they have a permanent imprint on the consumer's psyche. When actors, politicians and sportspersons build their brand image around an appropriate archetype or play the archetype that best reflects them or even choose the archetype that will best appeal to the consumer or the viewer or the audience, then they too are capable of leaving a lasting impression on the mind. Sometimes, their brand image might even have to undergo a change of archetype if it loses its appeal and they want to hold it up.

One instance of a celebrity who changed his archetypal appeal to last in an industry where things and people are in a constant state of flux would be the iconic Bollywood actor Amitabh Bachhan, who came to be associated with the Rebel archetype of the 'angry young man' in his youth. His films like *Deewar (1975), Kala Pathhar (1979), Coolie (1983),* starting with *Zanjeer (1973),* which cast him in this archetype, were hits, precisely because of this reason. In fact, there were storylines and characters that would be written to fit his archetype. They portrayed him as the underdog who rises despite all odds but with a seething, simmering anger that reflects the anger of the masses at an establishment that is both corrupt and indifferent.

With equal ease, Bachhan could play the Knight archetype who is not characterised by physical strength alone but also a certain level of mental resilience, someone who is set on a mission to save and rescue and may encounter a lot of dangers and threats in the path of his journey. The Knight has to win, he is chivalrous and a saviour and then he has to stick to his role of saviour even if it means self-destruction in certain cases.

Bachhan's films like *Sholay (1975), Muqaddar ka Sikander (1978), Silsila (1981) and Bemisal (1982)* show us glimpses of the Knight who needs to come to the rescue of the one he loves or cares for, even if that puts his personal life and well-being, his happiness at peril.

However, Bachhan's later films like *Jadoogar* and *Toofan* (1989), *Agneepath* (1990) and *Akayla* (1991) couldn't do that well in the box office despite *Agneepath* receiving huge critical acclaim and accolades following which the actor announced his temporary retirement. It was clear that perhaps in the light of the string of flops, with just the occasional hits like *Shahenshah* (1988) and *Hum* (1991), this was the best course of action and the interim period between 1992 and 2000 was not a very promising one for Bachhan who delivered forgettable films like *Insaniyat* (1992), *Mrityudaata* (1997) and *Major Saab* (1998).

Viewer and critic responses both seemed to indicate that perhaps the time had come for Bachhan to reinvent his archetypal brand image which happened and pronounced a definitive and commercially and critically successful comeback, starting with the film *Mohabbattein* (2000). The archetype he invoked was of the Grand Old Patriarch, who may be solitary and friendless but who is here to stay, which was also the actor's life's story at that point in time in the light of his box office failures and the bankruptcy of his production company. This archetype, unequivocally reflected in an image makeover (the salt and pepper hairdo and the beard) appealed to the audience and combined later with the Wise Old Man or Sage archetype which manifested in the *Kaun Banega Crorepati* series, establishing Bachhan firmly to play his second innings in the entertainment business.

A most enduring example of the success of this particular archetypal combination of Bachhan is the nationwide pulse polio ad campaign. A story featured in *India Today* emphasises the impact of the 'Do boond zindagi ki' punchline in a resounding baritone to appeal to a much wider population 'as Amitabh Bachhan was roped in by UNICEF as the brand ambassador for the Polio Eradication campaign in 2002.' The article further says, 'Soon after the advertisement was aired, mothers started thronging Pulse Polio camps in all of rural India. When asked what's making them come to the camps now, most of them said that they thought Amitabh ji had become angry, and they came because they didn't want to anger him further.'

Most of Bachhan's onscreen presence now sticks to the combination of these two archetypes; for instance, in movies like *Pink (2016)* where the whole debate on the issue of sexual consent and the reconfiguration of ways of perceiving the woman as a sexual being, acquire legitimacy because they have the voice of the Sage and the Grand Old Patriarch in the lawyer Deepak Sehgal played by Amitabh Bachhan – the ultimate voice of authority and wisdom that could possibly dominate the popular cultural imaginary in a patriarchal society.

Only occasionally has Bachhan veered from this formidable archetypal combination to the archetype of a Victim in the comic genre in movies like *Bhootnath (2008), Piku (2015), 102 Not Out (2018) and Gulabo Sitabo (2020)* but even in these films, the characters he plays are defined by the same

underlying wisdom and resilience underneath the superficial and capricious exterior of obstinacy and irrational actions. It is the wisdom that his archetypal silver screen identity reflects, that lies behind the huge commercial success of the several seasons of *Kaun Banega Crorepati,* better known as *KBC,* that is aired every year.[1]

In fact, the show did experiment with another anchor when it signed up with another Bollywood star, Shahrukh Khan (SRK) but its popularity dropped. Needless to say, this affirms the theory of the archetype even more strongly. SRK, despite being one of the most popular and enduring stars of Bollywood, simply does not mirror the Sage archetype. His on-screen role of the quiz master of *KBC* demanded the archetype of the Wise Old Man which couldn't come through his persona as he still embodies the archetype of the 'puer aeternus', Latin for 'Eternal Boy' and that of the 'Lover' combined into one which has been pivotal to the success of *his* films and in positioning his brand

1 https://www.indiatoday.in/lifestyle/health/story/amitabh-bachchan-world-polio-day-eradication-india-virus-pulse-polio-bill-gates-lifest-1070241-2017-10-24

image. Yes, he certainly has stepped into the Warrior archetype in movies like *Asoka* (2001) and *Chak de India* (2007) but he is far from being identified with the Sage and the Patriarch archetypes which a show like *KBC* hinges on. So, that is how archetypes can make or break brands and people and define the trajectory of commercial success and popularity.

Archetypal staging, thus, becomes something bigger than the individual, more than the person who embodies it. Archetypal identities are enduring and they are compelling. People or products that do not have a defining and a compelling archetype can very well have a limited shelf life and disappear from public memory. Additionally, it is also about an archetype and its appeal in a particular context and to a society that needs it.

The Lover Boy archetype has always had a special place in the Indian cultural imaginary, especially as a means of an escape into the realm of fantasy and an unreal world, probably because of the prominent presence of the archetype in the form of the popular and well-loved god, Krishna in Indian mythology, religion and music. The Lover Boy archetype successfully donned by actors like Rajesh Khanna, Kumar Gaurav and Rishi Kapoor reached its zenith in Shahrukh Khan whose boyish looks, dimples and irresistible charm enabled him to play the boy lover where he could assert his will against all the establishments, act the rebel and get or let go the girl he loves, in films like *Dilwale Dulhaniya Le Jayenge (1995), Kabhi Haan Kabhi Na (1994), Kabhi Khushi Kabhi Ghum (2001), Kal Ho Na Ho (2003)* and simultaneously also its shadow or negative, the pathological lover in *Baazigar (1993), Darr (1993)* and *Anjaam (1994)*. Both the archetype and its shadow were equally well-received at the box office.

Stories that are seemingly unheard of before, that appear new, that resonate with us, that seem to have a special appeal to us are always, invariably archetypal. Archetypes are prototypes, originals of characters, situations and encounters that then keep recurring to indicate a pattern. They have happened before, have been written about, and that is why they have such a strong resonance because they have been there already. They call out to something deep inside us that responds to them.

'Archetypal characters' and 'mythic plots' have an endless appeal. Why do the episodes in the Ramayana and the Mahabharata still dominate our imagination? Because they replay for us the archetypal situation of 'overcoming the monster', a situation that is replayed in all superhero movies, in fairy tales and even in children's classics like *The Jungle Book*. Why does Narendra Modi's appointment to the highest office of the land become such a national celebration and a rage? Because it is an enactment of the 'rags to riches' story that resonates so deeply with us because of its mythic relevance, 'rags to riches' over here implying Modi's rise from a nondescript party worker to becoming the most powerful leader of the country.

Why did the untimely and violent death of another Prime Minister, Rajiv Gandhi, plunge the nation in inconsolable doom equating in its intensity with a personal loss? Because it brings to mind the archetypal corollary of 'life… going out like a candle'. The inevitability and impartial treatment of everyone by the greatest leveller of all that is death, which took away the best, the most gifted and the noblest of warriors and leaders before their time, whether it is Othello in literature, Bhagat Singh in history, Rajiv Gandhi in politics or Anand or Jay in films like *Anand (1971)* and *Sholay (1975)*. The loss acquires mythic proportions and is deeply grieved and felt as an intense personal grief because it is a reproduction of the archetypal loss of the loyal Karna and Abhimanyu of the *Mahabharata* and the noble Hector of *Illiad*. An archetype of a good soul gone too soon fighting a battle, be it then a psychological, physical or a mental battle or for that matter a battle with an illness, apparently recalling the 'sacrifice of the most perfect man of his time'.

Myths and Archetypal Situations in Films

Just like some celebrities and brands are more successful and enduring than others because they have an archetypal core, some films too are more successful and are indelibly etched in our memory because of the timeless myths embedded in them that our unconscious immediately connects to. An example

would be the 1970s' blockbuster, Ramesh Sippy's multi-starrer *Sholay* and its continuing appeal even in contemporary times. *Sholay* embeds in its storyline the plot of the epic Ramayana. Jay and Veeru, two outlaws played by Amitabh Bachhan and Dharmendra, are, like Rama and Lakshman, in a kind of exile. They are hired by a retired police officer to destroy the deadly dacoit Gabbar Singh. Gabbar is the villain of the story just like Ravana is the antagonist of the epic *Ramayana*. Gabbar Singh even abducts Basanti, the girl Veeru loves and takes her to his lair just like Ravana took off with Sita. In the battle that ensues, Jay perishes at the hands of the dacoits just like Lakshman is incapacitated by Indrajit's deadly weapon *Vasavi Sakthi* in the Ramayana. Though Jay and Veeru are outlaws and small-time thugs who keep breaking the law and serving sentences, there is something noble and elevating about the two of them. They are men with a good conscience but men with their weaknesses too, which can be conveniently attributed to their circumstances as they may have been orphaned at an early age or may have been forced to resort to unlawful activities in adversity from their childhood itself. Their parents are conspicuously absent.

The two convicts, in the course of their mission, are brought from the margins and assimilated in the mainstream and this is repeatedly evident through the actions of the thakur. The thakur had two sons, both of whom are killed by Gabbar and his men. So he brings in two men who can take the place of his sons. He gives them quarters in the premises of his own property, which in itself is symbolic of his trust in them. This is how the project of mainstreaming the marginalised characters of Jay and Veeru is accomplished and new versions of Rama and Lakshmana are birthed. Jay and Veeru embody both, the Hero and the Outlaw archetypes and that is why they have such a universal appeal as they integrate seemingly antithetical archetypes.

Sholay, besides positioning and branding Amjad Khan as a villain par excellence with pathological and sadistic overtones unprecedented in Indian cinema till then, also celebrates the eternal bonding of two friends which is immortalised through the song: *yeh dosti hum nahi todenge*.[2] This celebration is yet another appeal to the collective unconscious by recalling the archetypal male-bonding and brotherly love so apparent in myths, whether it is in the epics Ramayana and Mahabharata, or even the kind of complementary relation seen in the holy trinity of Brahma, Vishnu and Mahesh.

A similar such mythological strain is identified in the highly successful 2001 Amir Khan starrer *Lagaan: Once Upon a Time in India*, a film set in colonial India. The entire film, as cultural critic Vinay Lal observes in his introduction to the book *Fingerprinting Popular Culture*, swivels around an impossible wager between the wronged natives represented by the villager Bhuvan (played by Amir Khan) and an oppressive, autocratic and arrogant British officer, Captain Andrew Russell (Paul Blackthorne). It draws from the epic Mahabharata and brings to mind the wager between the Pandavas and the Kauravas which led to the battle of Kurukshetra. *Lagaan*'s

2 https://www.youtube.com/watch?v=R2HQGNuIY-Y

wager is also followed by a battle, only on the cricket ground where eventually the morally upright side of the natives wins and the corrupt colonial power stands to lose. So, this film has two strong archetypal situations, that of the conflict between good and evil with good triumphing over evil in the end and also an impossible wager.

A renowned filmmaker, Manmohan Desai, who is credited with the birth of the Bollywood *masala* movie genre with the release of his on-screen epic *Amar Akbar Anthony* in 1977, when asked what his movies were about, simply stated that every single film he made was based on the Mahabharata. And true enough, if one were to watch his films closely, one does find too many themes of the Mahabharata manifesting themselves. In his blockbuster, which was a huge comeback for the singer Mohammad Rafi too, Amar (Vinod Khanna) is the archetypal Yudhishthira who stands for the law. Other archetypal situations like the mother separated from her children, foster parenting, male-bonding, brothers coming together to fight evil, all point to episodes from the Mahabharata.

Archetypes and their Potential in the World of Advertisements

Archetypes are needed not only to understand them beyond their unidimensional depictions but also to understand their valences and rediscover our deep ties with them and how they resonate with us. Archetypes have been known to be able to help writers write better and advertisers know the psyche of their consumers better. This is important not only for advertisers to understand what drives their consumer to buy or desire to procure a certain commodity or a product but can also lead to more positive and empowering projections of archetypes which the consumer can identify and associate with, as they are able to find the value of that archetype in the brand.

Archetypes are capable of stimulating emotional responses and project states of being like longing, desire, fear, rage, contentment, bliss, joy, peace, success, stability, etc. Columnist Justin Schamotta sees advertising as offering 'the chance for resolution of these feelings by buying a particular product or service. For example, a clothing manufacturer plays on the human need to be accepted by others; an insurance company causes people to worry about the future; a holiday company… the desire for new experiences; and a mortgage company focuses on the drive to provide stability for a family'.

Progressive, inspiring and positive projections through advertisements can go a long way in determining a sense of self-worth and self-esteem in the potential buyer which is good news for both the consumer and the product. Let us take as example the Tanishq range[3] of television advertisements for jewellery. Tanishq advertisements have always invested in 'out-of-the-box' forward-looking depictions and constructions of the personhood of the modern Indian woman. I will cite two such examples over here:

In one advertisement sporting the Mia range[4] of jewellery by Tanishq, a formally dressed woman in an attire appropriate for the corporate workplace, keeps on her pair of Tanishq earrings just before she enters the board room to make a presentation despite her female boss wanting her to remove them because she thinks they are too dressy and will distract the client.

In another Tanishq[5] advertisement, a man and a woman are getting married according to Hindu customs. As they do the rounds of the sacred fire or the saat-phere, the groom stops to pick up a little girl who has been watching the ceremony and wanting to join. The bride and the groom complete the rest of the circumambulations or pheras with the little girl in the groom's arms. Apparently, the girl belongs to the bride which implies that it is a child from an earlier marriage or from some kind of union with another man. The woman's bridal jewellery is of course Tanishq.

Both advertisements do two things: one, they position the brand on the bodies of two unconventional women and two, they situate the jewellery in an unconventional context and

---

3 Tanishq is a Tata Group entreprise. While their ads are avuncular, it is the very reason why it was targetted by fundamentalist groups intolerant of Hindu-Muslim coexistence.

4 https://www.youtube.com/watch?v=Qq3Kh-tHsyk

5 https://www.youtube.com/watch?v=P76E6b7SQs8

assign new value to it. In the first advertisement, the jewellery is not an ornamentation but is more of a subtle enhancer and confidence booster for the professional woman who finds Tanishq earrings just appropriate to perform this function, something that will not override her professional image.

In the second advertisement, Tanishq associates with a woman who would otherwise be beyond the conventional pale of matrimonial consideration. We are only left to imagine her ambiguous status. We could conjecture that she is a widow or a divorcee or an unwed mother (the third, of course, being the farthest stretch). But embedded in the advertisement is a strong social message saying that she too has a right to experience married life, her daughter is entitled to a father and through the groom's action of stopping midway and finishing the remaining pheras with his stepdaughter in his arms, comes the symbolic acceptance of single mothers and their children, and the Tanishq brand's embracing of them, and thus an attempt at mainstreaming them.

The advertisements are not merely about the brand or the range of jewellery. They are also about reconfiguring a woman's life and adding value to our perception of these personhoods who do not fit into conventional patterns or roles. The advertisements legitimise the women and the technologies of beings they project and eke out a space for them in the popular cultural imaginary of the consumer. Thus, they succeed in penetrating and rupturing the underlying scrupulous fabric of righteousness and morality which is the defining garb of the buying class, in other words the middle class and in their own way introduce a progressive discourse in this space.

Jewellery is mostly worn during religious ceremonies and festivals. Jewellery thus enjoys an auspicious position in the Indian cultural space. Jewellery, supposedly intended to serve the purpose of ornamentation or decoration, can also end up overwhelming the person who is wearing it, thus undermining the individual through its presence. The absence or presence of jewellery determines the material value of the woman too, in terms of how auspicious she is and also in terms of how materially well-off her parents, husband or in-laws are. Her body, in fact, is a prop to display the financial well-being and status of the family.

The Tanishq advertisements displace jewellery from the conventional space of marriage, ceremony and the utilitarian purpose of ornamentation of the female body and value assignment which they serve. In both advertisements, it is the story and the context and not the jewellery which is more important. The jewellery acknowledges the woman as an individual and does exactly what it ought to – complement and enhance her appearance and not the other way round. The Tanishq brand forges new alliances, announces new affiliations and in its inclusive projection, urges a more inclusive, assimilating and accommodating approach.

Nevertheless, jewellery has a referential and cultural significance and through this affiliation, brand Tanishq has been reaching out even to that highly-focused working woman who might not give a thought to associating herself with something as conventional as gold but all the same, does. Through this acknowledgement of the indispensable hint of gold in her appearance, somewhere she is also acknowledging her roots, her culture and her tradition. Not every successful working woman in the corporate space working with a multinational is irreparably divorced from her culture. Similarly, in the other advertisement, through the bride who is also a mother, the brand reconfigures the dynamics of matrimony and parenting in a modern India and also foregrounds a new kind of masculinity which is capable of nurturing and care-giving.

An undiscerning audience just absorbs these narratives and discourses through the semiotic field, without separating each narrative from the other. But the multiple narrative strands woven together create a tapestry that in most certain terms present a different picture for women of a particular class (the consumer class) in India. Archetypes can do the same thing. If they are studied and humanised, some of their aspects can be translated into empowering projections.

Archetypes and their Universality

Archetypes seem to explicitly reinforce certain qualities as more desirable than others. They also have something transcendental, timeless and trans-territorial about them that makes them seem original and also desire-worthy. Archetypes needn't always be the first but they are archetypes because they offer a full range and extent of all possible qualities we desire in them.

According to Jung, archetypes are that immense 'spiritual reservoir' from which we draw all our fantasies, imaginations, dreams, delusions, myths, literary images and symbols'. Jung claimed that one could unearth 'fundamental invariables' or commonalities across cultures once they set about the job of excavating archetypes. For instance, the 'third eye' which sees and absorbs all esoteric knowledge, or the invincible 'thunderbolt' (the weapon of both Zeus and Indra) and the 'phallus erectus' are some of the universal archetypal symbols that are manifestations of our own unconscious desire for immortality. This desire repeatedly and almost cyclically manifests, especially in the Puranic literature of India.

In the *Puranas* for instance, we have the demon Rambha, then Mahishasura and then Shumbha and Nishumbha, and Hiranyakashipu, all doing great *tapa* for thousands of years or more, to invite the grace of some or the other Vedic god, mostly Brahma, the 'Creator' of the universe, because finally what they all want is to be immortal and rule the three worlds.[6] So while some explicitly want immortality, others would like to have sons who are the mightiest of all and can rule the three worlds which again amounts to the desire to be immortal. The desire to live forever and to rule is thus primal and can be seen as an archetypal desire that manifests recurrently through myths.

How Archetypes get Created

Tracing Goddess Figures in Indian Mythology

Archetypes legitimise human will and resolve, and many times, desires and longings. They also personify the deepest of anxieties and tensions and act as ideograms. For instance, if

6 Heaven, Earth and the Netherworld are the three worlds referred to in the Puranas.

we had to consider the archetypal symbol of the serpent in the religious idiom or context, then we all might agree that the serpent over time has acquired the status of an unequivocal depiction of all that is evil in the world. But it is also true that the serpent acquires this archetypal status after the appearance of the Indo-Europeans in the Near East, shortly after 2000 BC. Merlin Stone discuss this at great length in her book *When God was a Woman.*

The advent of the Indo-Europeans on the scene leads to the rise of the Indo-European male deity which violently replaces the goddess religion. While the male deity comes to be representative of and congruous with light, the 'female deity is symbolised as a serpent or dragon, most often associated with darkness and evil'. The goddess cannot be entirely effaced but is made to acquire a symbolism in the new religious myths that lead to her 'eventual dispossession'. In this manner, the ideogram of snake formerly associated with the goddess, acquires a dark and negative valence, only *after* the Northern invasions. The emergence of this archetype stands for the projection of the anxiety of an invading race informed by patriarchal ideology, on another culture wanting to replace its existing female-centered order. As mythologist Sheila Collins rightly observes, 'All Theology is ultimately political'.

Religious motifs are powerfully encoded messages that reach us and strongly moor themselves in our minds. In the history of Indian mythology too, if one were to consider the Vedic texts, one would barely encounter a fully-formed goddess or a feminine power worth mentioning or worshipping. The *devi,* and her glorification and worship is a practice that is reflected in the later Puranic literature.

A common and not so inaccurate speculation, justifying this phenomenon, would be the possible and gradual assimilation and mainstreaming of the indigenous, female divinities or *gramadevatas* that were worshipped locally and restricted to a particular regional belt or even something as small as a hamlet. The devi, as described in the *Devi Bhagvatam*, drinking wine, with bloodshot eyes and a monstrous laugh, or even the goddess Kali could be regarded as a projection of this anxiety and also the predicament of a patriarchal theological practice on the way to acquiring a hegemonic status, which had to deliberate between assimilation and omission of female divinity and, therefore, perhaps experimented with various feminine depictions of the idea of *shakti* ranging from aggressive to domesticated to mild to seductive.

Many of the goddess manifestations of shakti and the matrkas in particular, which will be dealt with in detail, in the sections that analyse them, inspire mixed feelings that range from awe to terror and sometimes seem to even border on revulsion. This is symbolic of a project half-done, the conscious manifestation of an ambivalent 'unconscious' that Otherises the feminine. This anxiety subsequently leads to the manifestation of a certain combination of archetypes, the iconography and mythology of which make explicit the underlying tension and insecurity that speaks through a sometimes malevolent, feminine power embodying the darker and more sinister elements of nature and spirituality.

In her book *When the World Becomes Female*, which focuses

on the gramadevata, Gangamma of Tirumala and the myths, lore and rituals surrounding her, Joyce Burkhalter Flueckiger gives an account of the custom of worshipping the gramadevata and treating the gramadevata as a deity far more important than popular and iconic pan-India male gods of Hinduism like Krishna, Rama or Shiva. It is believed that the gramadevata was a presiding power, like a local guardian that looked after the village, tribe or community that worshipped it and ensured its well-being. These deities were female and had to be appeased because they were held to fly into a rage quickly if rituals were not observed properly. The gramadevata was believed to be capable of wreaking havoc and assuming her *ugra roopam* (aggressive and destructive form) if she felt slighted. This havoc could mean a natural calamity or the destruction of crops or some mysterious ailment or affliction.

In her ethnographic study, Flueckiger traces the local lore of Gangamma which is non-Brahmanical in nature. She also traces the reconfigured narratives by Purana Pandits appointed by the Government's (religious) Endowments Department to deliver discourses on Gangamma and the assimilation of the non-Brahmanical goddess in the Puranic myths, either as a version of the river Ganga or that of *adiparashakti*. Latest myths and discourses also try to situate Gangamma as the sister of Tirupati Balaji, worshipped as an earthly incarnation of Vishnu. Goddesses like Gangamma, Yellamma, Ghatandevi and Matangi are a few of the many gramadevatas which have probably retained their indigenous archetypal characteristics, the others having been assimilated in the ever-expanding and extremely elastic what we understand today to be the 'Hindu pantheon'.

Similarly, in his seminal book *Why I Am Not a Hindu*, Kancha Illaiah Shepherd mentions a pantheon of village and caste-specific deities, mostly female like Pochamma, Polimeramma, Kattamaisamma who are part of the Dalitbahujan pantheon and are not just looked upon negatively by upper caste communities but also fail to find a mention or a representation in their own right in texts and the 'Hindu' space of worship.

Why Archetypes need Revisiting

Archetypes are initiatory ideas which introduce a paradigm which subsequent creations and versions are based on. Regis Boyer describes archetype as a 'fundamental symbol that acts as a kind of matrix for repeated representations of itself.... Their images are like an inexhaustible ideogram that is infinitely suggestive and ever-renewable in ways that depend on the imagination and sensibilities of the individual'.

This implies that archetypes are discursive and subject to multiple interpretations too and it means that they need a close looking-into, as they can have layers and layers of meaning and message coiled in them. They need to be revisited, examined, studied and scrutinised with the help of the many myths and lore surrounding them and in the context in which they are evoked. Various texts bring out various aspects of these archetypes which make them open to subjective interpretation.

A simple example would be the various accounts of the same myth, like the *samudramanthan* or the churning of the ocean by the devas and the asuras. Certain Puranic texts glorify and establish the undisputed superiority of Vishnu, establishing him as the archetypal Hero who assumed the form of the tortoise, known as Kurmavataar, the second of his ten incarnations according to the *Dashavataar* (the ten incarnations of Vishnu). According to the myth, Vishnu took this avatar to support mount Mandhar on his back in order to enable the churning of the ocean and later, also assumed the form of the enticing Mohini, escaping with the ambrosia that resulted out of the churning so that the asuras wouldn't get to drink it and become immortal. However, there are certain other texts that establish Shiva in the supreme role as the consumer of the poison that was emitted during the churning and that could well have meant the end of both the devas and the asuras and the whole of Creation, if it hadn't been contained by Shiva. Shiva, in his characteristically unassuming manner, readily agreed to consume the poison to save all the others from its toxic and lethal impact. The poison was so concentrated that it charred his throat which turned blue and resulted in the creation of yet another epithet for him, 'Neelakantha' or the blue-throated one.

Similarly, the devi or the goddess, in her many manifestations and her earthly incarnations, needs to be studied closely and from different perspectives through alternative myths and lore that are perhaps not as popular today but may have come into existence and occupied the popular cultural imaginary in earlier times for a reason.

This means that the same god or goddess can be seen as a different archetype in the light of a particular myth which is different from the deity's popular myth. This also means that there exists within one god or goddess a range of archetypes that can become the focus in the light of a particular myth that brings out a particular aspect of the divine being, in other words a particular archetype.

Let us take another example: the depictions of Sita and the story of her origin in the popular versions of the epic Ramayana like the *Valmiki Ramayana* or the *Ramcharitamanas* by Goswami Tulsidas are vastly different from her depictions in the *Shakta* or the Kannada or the Oriya versions of the Ramayana. Every version can be seen as a crypt containing the practices, beliefs and ideologies prevalent in a particular community at a particular time, thus leading to multiple and more subjective interpretations/archetypes of the divine being.

An archetype, as Regis Boyer appropriately observes, is a 'symbol-producing animal'. To quote Boyer here when he likens the literary character of Robinson Crusoe to the archetype of the Divine Creator:

> Robinson Crusoe merely perpetuates the immemorial act of all discoverers and colonisers.... The difference is that he is at first alone, like all the divine creators in our various mythologies and religions, and that, unlike them, he is already rich with acquired knowledge, like all primitive giants. He is thus not absolutely archetypal in the first sense of the word. He does not create the world, he recreates it in the image of the one that he carries within him .... This also applies to the protagonists of all our futuristic novels and of some works of science fiction.

However, if one looked at Robinson Crusoe through a post-colonial lens, in other words through the eyes of (Man) Friday, the man he rescues and who comes to live with him and be his sole companion on the island, then the archetypal Divine Creator that Crusoe seems to epitomise is only according to the white supremacist gaze which sees the 'West' as 'self' and the 'East' as 'the Other' and this is bound to change when viewed from the perspective of the native or the colonised subject.

One could then say that Crusoe is the archetypal Coloniser, the shadow of the Explorer archetype who exploits everything around him to his advantage and claims all as his own. No doubt Crusoe saves (Man) Friday but he does not treat him as his equal. It is (Man) Friday who learns to speak Crusoe's tongue and not the other way round.Crusoe denies (Man) Friday agency and a subject status. The equation is clearly that of master and slave. Besides, Crusoe is on new and foreign territory but belongs to a world that is 'far more advanced', according to Crusoe, which is why he is able to save (Man) Friday with his gun.

So, then the question is which archetype to believe in? The answer is that both the Creator archetype and the Coloniser archetype are true and embodied by Robinson Crusoe. It is the responsibility of the researcher, the scribe or the critic to bring these archetypes to the fore in a single character. This means that the person who is analysing archetypes needs to embody the positive aspect of the archetype of the Shape-shifter who can make the reader see things differently and who can bring out different archetypes in the same character or different aspects of a single archetype.

In fact, it is the responsibility of the researcher, the scribe or the teacher to wear the Critic and the Shape-shifter archetypes so that they are able to invest the characters they come across with universal, human, multiple and even binary qualities; to consider all aspects of the truth which is what is required to analyse these characters in mythology and invest them with archetypal identities. Archetypes are elastic. We need to make them flexible, to ensure they bend all ways. There cannot be only one side to an archetype. There is the light and there is the shadow.

Neither can we afford a mere literal understanding of an archetype. For instance, if we consider the Mother archetype, out of the various aspects, we have the 'Nurturing Mother' and we have the 'Devouring Mother'. The devouring mother need not be someone who literally kills her children and feeds on them but someone who is wearing the metaphorical garb of the devouring mother, who perhaps exploits her children emotionally, is obsessively possessive about them, does not let them evolve or mature into adults and wants all the attention for herself. Perhaps Gertrude Morel in the novel *Sons and Lovers* by D H Lawrence could be seen as embodying aspects of the devouring mother archetype as she never really seems to let her sons, especially Paul, out of her grip. They are arrested and frozen for life in their Oedipal stage. This is the shadow side of the Mother archetype.

Equally, there could be a light side even of a shadow archetype. The devouring mother could actually be a positive force, a mother who stands up against the exploits and the misdoings of her children and punishes them for it. Radha (Nargis) in the iconic Indian film *Mother India* (1957), does exactly that. She shoots her own son because he is a threat to the entire community. Thus, the reason to look at all aspects of an archetype is because in the end, it is the projection of the human unconscious and to be human is to personify imperfection. Therefore, no archetype is perfect. It cannot be if it has to be real. And any archetype will have as many manifestations and as many expressions as there are people embodying it.

It is important that we do not jump to conclusions or try to go by our limited information and understanding of terms that signify archetypes. Myss gives us the example of the 'pirate' archetype. The pirate archetype does not have to only do with raiding ships and thieving or killing people for loot. It is also about getting away from the routine and mundane and embarking on a voyage. It is also about living with the belief that you are destined to find a hidden treasure and some day you are going to lay your hands on a treasure map that will lead you to it. Positive archetypes have a shadow and shadow archetypes have a light side to them. And considering both and all is the right way of approaching, identifying and understanding these archetypes whether they are in our culture, in us or in the people around us. Similarly, mythic figures, gods and goddesses can embody multiple archetypes out of which one stands out or is reinforced. It is therefore important that we humanise these archetypes.

Humanising Archetypes

Myss does exactly this in her book *The Language of Archetypes* when she familiarises us with the range of archetypes that pre-exist us and that we need to correctly identify, so as not to mix up archetypes and subsequently associate with the wrong kind of archetype. She posits that each individual is a cluster of archetypes or has a cloister of archetypes within him or her. Sometimes one is not aware of every archetype within that cloister. Sometimes the individual ends up identifying with the wrong kind of archetype and consequently experiences discord within.

Myss also says that any human being is a combination of archetypes and in time, one archetype overtakes the other or is more influential than the other. People, thus, are a combination of archetypes.

What is a little disconcerting, however, in the notion of the archetype, is the temptation to gravitate towards essentialism, to identify a core in one's identity or being and relate it to the original which is primal, transcendental and fixed. While this may be true and we might also be unwittingly walking into the trap of essentialising ourselves and others and fixing meaning, the redeeming thing about archetypes is that though they are commonly perceived as being fixed, they are subject to individual interpretation. They evolve and can be traced through anecdotal and episodic appearances of them in myth, lore, literature and culture. Archetypes help us realise the range and extent of possibilities. They are discursive and that is exactly why there are so many of them. And which is why the effort is to engage with them more fully through various discourses that shape and colour them.

Conclusion

Just as the comparative mythologist Joseph Campbell looks at the various stages, adventures and transformative experiences in the life of the Hero in his book *The Hero's Journey*, in her book *The Heroine's Journey*, Maureen Murdock charts the trajectory of the woman's journey and shows how archetypes play the hugely defining role of guiding the woman since they are already a part of the subconscious. She looks at the journey, the heroine who is an archetype in her own right (mythical and immediate at once, 'the original' and every woman) has to undertake, as she navigates the world, the goddesses she meets, the monsters she slays, the heroes she encounters and the complexities she resolves.

Though the archetypal journey of the heroine has a universal appeal about it, the route that Murdock traces is paved by Western myths and female archetypes of the Western world. Her book gives an account of the journeys and travails of the archetypal goddesses and characters from Greek mythology like Athena, Psyche, Iphigenia and their mythic associations with Aphrodite, Artemis, Persephone and many more. Through these journeys, the heroine's journey and the many archetypes she might encounter and embody become clear. The journey, however, is clearly informed by female archetypes from Greek mythology. Though some of the archetypes have a universal and contemporary ring and feel to them, there are many archetypes that are foreign to the Indian sensibility.

One instance is the myth of Iphigenia, the daughter of Agamemnon who decides to sacrifice her to get the winds to sail the battle ships towards Troy. For this end, he lies to his daughter, saying he is planning to marry her off to Achilles whereas what he is really planning is to have her killed. This story of horrifying deception, that too by a father of a daughter, fails to find an archetypal parallel in Indian myth, though the practice of female foeticide and infanticide resulting out of the preference for a male child is not uncommon in contemporary India.

This gives all the more reason to revisit female archetypal figures in Indian mythology, if we need to deliberate a course of the heroine's journey in the context of the Indian collective unconscious and want the Indian woman to go archetypal in her path to self-actualisation. Also, as discussed above, archetypal repertoire that is specific and unique to our culture is likely to do more towards more positive and empowering representations of women and constructions of femininities whether it is through films, television shows, advertisements or television and web series.

KALI: THE GODDESS OF EXCESS

EVEN WHEN SHE is reclining, she has eyes that simmer. Her lips curl into a smile that is difficult to fathom. Is it benevolence or malice? Her laugh – when it comes – is primitive and monstrous. Her wild tangled hair that shrouds most of her face, her posture exuding the power, magnificence and certainty of a tigress as she glares at you, the menace lacing the voice that emanates from some deep and dark recess inside her, her cleavage reminding you of ravines and secrets, her skin like liquid dark gold, and the invisible third eye taking in everything just above the point where her thick eyebrows meet like fast-gathering angry clouds, the whole of her bristling, forbidden self on forbidden ground create a sensation difficult to define. It could be called unreal, magical even but magic that is forbidden, magic that is frightening and alluring at once. With unparalleled force and swiftness, she reaches out and wrenches you out of your snug little hole, snaps your safety valve and shows you that which is raw and untamable in existence. She is predator and prey, hunter and hunted. She embodies the timeless myth of life feeding on itself in order to sustain. She protects and she devours. And she fights with strength, audacity and ferocity of mythic proportions unknown to lesser mortals. She is scathing in her anathemas, brutal in her actions. She is ready to attack with her army or even to wage a lone war and when she goes down, she does so with earth-shattering thunder that resonates for miles.

She is the indomitable and nerve-rackingly unconventional *Begum Jaan* of the 2017 Hindi Period Drama film by the same name, directed by National film award winning director Srijit Mukherjee and played by Vidya Balan. Begum Jaan's tenacity, rage and heroism, her outlaw and non-citizen status and the abiding philosophy of her life which makes her such an enduring yet perturbing presence, reflect in many ways, the terrible and fearful mother, the intoxicated and raving warrior, the goddess driven by bloodlust and rage who lies beyond the

pale of right and wrong, nothing like the normative nurturing goddesses of the Hindu pantheon – Kali.

Kali continues to be an enigma. Widely and extensively researched by scholars, adored by mysterious tribes, revered by devotees and invoked by followers of the *Tantra Shastra*, she and her terrifying manifestations have been variously interpreted, perceived and venerated. That she lies beyond the domain of the normative, the moral and the ethical is indisputable. It is, however, the reconciliation with this formidable goddess, that matters the most. Is she a projection of patriarchal anxiety towards unrestrained and overwhelming feminine power, energy and sexuality or is she Hinduism's way of making peace with that which dharma and its neatly laid out matrices can neither define nor dominate? Kali invokes images of blood, violence, gore, destruction and death, even lust, perversion and madness. In doing so she becomes unparalleled in mythology and a shadow to all existing goddesses. Perhaps revisiting her myths might reveal a miniscule portion of the colossal mystery she is.

The Myths of Kali

A goddess 'placed on the periphery of Hindu society and on the battlefield' in the words of David Kinsley, Professor of Religion and author of many scholarly works, Kali appears thrice in the *Devi Mahatmyam* (600 CE) – once to entice and twice to slay demons who are invincible. Mahakali assumes the form of Yoga Nidra, who emerges from the inert body of Vishnu to wake him up so that he can save Brahma the Creator and the whole of Creation from the assailing demons Madhu and Kaitabha. Vishnu wakes up and fights a valiant battle with the two mighty demons which goes on for thousands of years without either side winning or losing. The demons take turns to fight while Vishnu wards off their attacks singlehandedly. After a considerable period, Vishnu is exhausted. At this point Mahakali assumes the form of Mahamaya and steps in as an enchantress to distract the two demons. Predictably enough, the ploy works as Madhu and Kaitabha, enthralled by the divine woman, lose concentration and are killed by Vishnu.

The narrative structure of the *Devi Mahatmyam* is cyclic in nature and the two slain demons reappear as Chanda and Munda who attack the goddess Durga, who is a manifestation of Shakti. So infuriated is she by the appearance of the demons and their audacity that her golden face turns black like thunder and a dark form emerges out of her forehead to slay the two demons. This is Kali who becomes Chamunda after killing Chanda and Munda.

Kali is subsequently summoned again when Durga and her assisting Matrkas, after fighting on the battlefield for a long time, realise that the situation is worsening, particularly because of a demon by the name of Raktabeeja. The more wounds they inflict on him, the more blood he spurts. Every drop of his blood that touches the ground creates a clone of his and very soon the battlefield is swarming with clones of the demon. Shakti then splits herself into two, the many-armed Chandi who dashes into the battlefield mounted on a tiger followed by the dark, emaciated and gaunt Kali, with protruding tongue and a bowl in her hand. While Chandi deftly swings her sword and slays each clone of Raktabeeja, Kali stretches out her bowl to collect its blood and drinks it up before it has spilled and touched the ground. She also throws the limp bodies of the clones into her wide open mouth. Thus Chandi and Kali together neutralise the demons in this fierce battle.

In the *Linga Purana*, Shiva approaches Parvati and beseeches her to destroy the demon Daruka. Parvati enters Shiva's body and assumes a new dark form which is nourished by the concentrated poison Halahala in Shiva's throat which he consumed during the samudramanthan. Out emerges Kali of terrifying appearance, from the body of Shiva, who charges at Daruka along with a host of *pisacha*s or flesh-eating spirits and defeats the demon. Likewise, Kali is also part of Shiva's army when he sets out to conquer Tripurasura's three cities. The *Vamana Purana* describes an episode when Shiva addresses Parvati as Kali or the dark one and earns her wrath. An offended Parvati performs austerities to rid herself of her dark complexion and returns as Gauri or the fair one. The dark skin that she sheds off however assumes the form of the angry goddess Kaushiki, who then creates Kali as a manifestation of her wrath and fury.

In the *Skanda Purana*, Kali makes an appearance and plays a significant role in the myth of Sati, when the latter, to avenge her husband Shiva's humiliation, immolates herself in the *yajna kund* or the sacrificial pit of the yajna organised by her father Daksha Prajapati. Shiva is mad with fury and grief when he hears of Sati's immolation. In his rage he tears a lock of his hair and flings it on the ground out of which emerge Veerabhadra, a dark and angry form of Shiva and Bhadrakali, the vengeful form of the devi. Both storm into Daksha's yajna and destroy it completely. While Veerabhadra is attacked by Vishnu who has come to attend the yajna, Bhadrakali manifests as Mahakali, Kattyayani, Chamunda, Ishani and Mundamalini and wreaks havoc on the battlefield with the ganas of Shiva. A fierce battle ensues, both on the field and at the site of the yajna, with Veerabhadra finally striking Vishnu numb and emerging victorious with Bhadrakali. Another myth describes Sati rubbing her nose in anger when Daksha badmouths Shiva, resulting in the appearance of Kali. In still another version of the myth, an inflamed Sati is supposed to have transformed herself into ten vengeful warrior-like goddesses or the Dasamahavidyas as an expression of her wrath, the first among them being Kali.

In Valmiki's *Adbhuta Ramayana*, the story continues even after the ten-headed or Dasanana Ravana has been killed by Rama. Once in the court of Ayodhya, when everyone present is singing praises of Rama for having defeated Ravana, Sita is described as breaking into uncontrollable laughter. Realising that all the appreciation and flattery is inflating her husband's ego, making him lose his humility, Sita describes the dead Dasanana Ravana's elder brother, Sahasranana Ravana or the Ravana with the thousand heads living unvanquished in Pushkar and waxes eloquent about his might and power. Reeling under personal humiliation, Rama decides to launch an organised attack on Sahasranana Ravana.

The thousand-headed Ravana, who did not want to get involved in the battle of Lanka, is perplexed by this sudden attack. Nonetheless, he wards off Rama's formidable army almost single-handedly and is even able to resist the Brahmastra which Rama had used to kill Dasanana Ravana. He then strikes a blow, knocking Rama unconscious. A flustered Lakshmana and the vanaras are still gathering their wits when they hear Sita's loud laughter getting louder and louder. Lakshmana is surprised and angered that instead of worrying about Rama's well-being, Sita has chosen to laugh. He turns around and a most frightening sight awaits him. Looming over the decimated and defeated army is Bhadrakali, one of the most fearful aspects of Shakti.

Bhadrakali charges at Sahasranana Ravana and begins to slash his many heads with her scimitar. She goes on with her frenzied attack till Ravana is dead, lying in a bloody pool. But still she doesn't stop. From her daunting being erupt the terrible Matrkas who start playing with the decapitated heads. Bhadrakali herself is unstoppable in her dance of death and destruction and is described as 'mad with grief and fury' as her husband is lying unconscious on the battlefield. The myth then describes Brahma descending from Satyalok and reviving Rama to calm an impassioned Kali. Once Rama is revived, Kali goes back to being Sita, leaving Rama humbled by this aspect of the mighty feminine.

The Kalikula sect of Shaktism adores Chinnamastika, also worshipped as a Tantric goddess. According to a legend in the *Narada Pancharatra*, Parvati, while having a bath in the river gets into a state of excitement and turns black. Her two attendant maids, Dakini and Varnini, are hungry and express their urge for food. Though Parvati promises to feed them on returning home, she is known to have decapitated her own head and offered her blood to her maids to satiate their hunger.

One of the names the *Shakta Pramoda* mentions to address Chinnamastika is Prachanda Chandika, a form of Kali. Oral legend has it that after a prolonged battle between the devas and the asuras, Prachanda Chandika celebrated the victory by decapitating her own head and drinking her own blood. She is known to hold her severed head in her own hand while blood spurts out of her open neck. A third legend describes Chinnamastika drinking up the asura's portion of the elixir or ambrosia procured from the samudramanthan and then beheading herself so that they are unable to consume it.

The *Jaiminya Brahmana* (800 CE) has an episode on Dirghajivhi or the one with the long tongue. This divine woman with her long, outstretched tongue, drinks up all the *soma* or elixir generated during the yajna leaving the devas deprived and longing for it. A frustrated Indra identifies a handsome young man, Sumitra, to seduce Dirghajivhi and kill her. When Sumitra approaches Dirghajivhi, she scorns him and his ability to satisfy her sexually, as he has just one manhood and she, many female organs. Sumitra returns and Indra blesses him to possess many manhoods. Thus equipped, he approaches Dirghajivhi again. This time, she takes him. While the two are locked in a sexual embrace, Sumitra catches her unawares, gets over her and pins her down, and in her moment of vulnerability, kills her, thus neutralising the threat to the devas.

Dirghajivhi and Chinnamastika can be regarded as versions

of Kali the same way the Vedic goddesses Nirrti and Ratri can be regarded as proto-Kali. Descriptions of Nirrti project her as inauspicious and corresponding to images of death, decay, ill-health, destruction, old age and cowardice. She is depicted as a malevolent, dark divinity, wearing dark clothes but with golden hair. She is a female power who has to be kept at bay and appeased by giving her a share of the yajna. All prayers beseech her to depart from auspicious places and go away to far off places, away from human settlement. She is known to be vindictive and temperamental.

Ratri is the other Vedic goddess, the twin sister of Ushas who might be said to have qualities of Kali. The two symbolise night and day respectively. She is supposed to keep people secure in the dark hours of the night with its many mysteries till Ushas returns. She resembles Kali because there is an air of mystery surrounding her and she is capable enough to keep dangers lurking around at bay.

Analysing Kali in the Light of her Myths

While earliest references and descriptions of naked, bejewelled women date back to before 2000 BC, the term 'Kali' first appears in the *Atharva Veda.* It surfaces as a name for the first time in the *Kathaka Grhya Sutra*. The *Mundaka Upanishad* describes Kali as a dark blue flame of Agni, the fire god. She appears in the epic Mahabharata in the battle of Kurukshetra as Kalaratri or the queen of the night and the goddess of death, a destructive form of the goddess with a blood-smeared face and a noose in her hand when Guru Dronacharya's son Ashwatthama deceitfully, kills the sons of the Pandavas in the dead of the night. It is at this time that Kaalratri or Kalaratri supposedly makes her appearance seeming to personify the horrors of the war and the mindless destruction and massacre it has resulted in.

Kali is a very complex deity to understand though her various manifestations as Kaalratri, Kaushiki, Raudri, Chamundi, Chinnamastika, Bhadrakali and Mahakali have one thing in common. They all depict her along the same lines and more or less have a similar iconography. If nature is the feminine then Kali is the dark, unknown side of the feminine symbolising untamed, unharnessed supremely powerful female energy. Tantric cults seek to confront her to get into the darkest recesses of the human mind to imagine the unimaginable. She embodies our deepest, darkest, most terrifying and most repressed fears and perhaps that is why the iconography is so terrifying.

Kali is black, sometimes blue, naked with loose dishevelled hair and a fierce expression on her face. Her eyes are bloodshot due to rage and intoxication. In many cases, she has a third eye too as she is the raw incarnation of adiparashakti, the ultimate divine feminine in Hinduism. Some of her manifestations like Chamundi and Kaushiki are gaunt and emaciated unlike the other Puranic goddesses who are voluptuous and maternal. She is generally four-armed, equipped with slaying weapons and an upturned human skull serving as a bowl to collect blood. She usually holds the decapitated head of an asura by her fist. Kali wears a skirt made of human arms and a garland of skulls around her neck. Sometimes she may have fangs protruding from her mouth. She has a long, lolling tongue. She is generally shown as having stopped in her tracks with one leg in the air and the other on Shiva's chest who lies passively under her, almost like a corpse. Sometimes as Bhairavi, she is depicted as sitting on top of Shiva suggestive of her role as initiator of sexual action. She usually rides a tiger and is surrounded by hungry jackals, dogs and hyenas.

There have been various speculations and interpretations of her postures and stances. For instance, it is a popular belief that when Kali has her right foot on Shiva and her left foot in the air, she is the terrible yet protective and loving mother who safeguards her children against unforeseen danger. In this form, she is worshipped as Dakshinkali denoted by the dakshinmarga or the right-handed acceptable path of devotion and love for the goddess. On the other hand, when she has her left foot forward and her right foot in the air, it is considered to be a formidable and a forbidden aspect of Kali indicating the vamamarga or the more sinister left-handed path of *Tantra Shastra* or the occult. In this form, she is worshipped as Shmashan Kali or the Goddess of the crematorium. There are actual temples of Shmashan Kali built in the premises of crematoriums, where the goddess is worshipped by tantrics and rituals that might seem to be repulsive and non-normative to regular mainstream devotees are followed.

Kali symbolises raw female power and unbridled sexual appetite which is not only indicated through her position as Bhairavi with Shiva but also in the myth of Dirghajivhi, with many vulvas who it was hard to sexually satisfy. Unlike Parvati who keeps Shiva's destructive power in check, Kali unleashes it and complements it with her presence. The two together participate in the dance of destruction. As Mahakali she has not four but ten arms, suggesting the ultimate feminine power which controls and monitors the entire universe. There are various myths surrounding her iconography, and especially her lolling tongue. While the lolling tongue could be an extension of the depiction of Dirghajivhi, upper-caste, middle-class sensibility, while assimilating Kali in the pantheon probably found this disturbing, which necessitated a new myth, especially in eastern India where Shakta worship dominated the religious landscape.

Devotees of Kali in Bengal, Bihar, Assam and Odisha believe that Kali was unstoppable on the battlefield and continued on her rampage long after everyone was either dead or had fled. She killed and slayed whosoever came in her way and soon the worried devas approached Shiva for a solution. It is believed that with the intention of stopping her and calming her, Shiva decided to prostrate himself in her path. As Kali comes along dancing in frenzy, she steps on Shiva's chest, looks down and is embarrassed to see, it is her husband. The awkwardness of the situation and her embarrassment of having stepped on her husband, which no devout Hindu wife is supposed to do, prompts her involuntarily to stick out her tongue in shame. A fierce and unrestrained goddess is thus domesticated through the power of myth.

Left-handed Tantric schools use a different myth to explain the reason why Shiva is prostrate and lying under Kali. In the Tantric version, Shiva is mesmerised by Kali's glorious victory on the battlefield. He has never ever witnessed such heroism and unfettered power. He wants to express his veneration for the supreme feminine and wants a small portion of her power to transpire and pass into him, which is why as a mark of respect, he lays himself in her path and when she steps on him, presses her foot close to his heart in sheer admiration and reverence.

Kali symbolises nature in its most primal form. She stands for nature, red in tooth and claw and represents both the nourishing and devouring aspects of nature. The dynamics of the predator and prey, the credo of nature feeding on itself and its own is nowhere brought about as strongly as in the legend of Chinnamastika who beheads herself to nourish herself and those she has the responsibility to feed. The imagery is violent and repulsive but loaded with meaning. Nature is about survival. It is one thing to eulogise the tender and the beautiful aspects of nature, quite another to confront and accept its predatory and menacing side. This is probably the reason why the Tantric school, through the ritual of *Panchatattva*, demands of the follower and the devotee of Kali to attain her by embracing that which is forbidden. The *sadhaka*, according to the ritual, has to embrace five things – wine, fish, meat, drug and illicit sexual intercourse – all of which are not only forbidden but taboo. It can get even more difficult and challenging when the sadhaka has to go to the extent of consuming excrement or charred bits of human flesh from corpses burning on funeral pyres. By embracing these perverse elements, the sadhaka transcends the binary of pure and impure, good and bad, moral and immoral which are but artificial and superficially imposed cultural restrictions that are meaningless and irrelevant on the road to spiritual realisation with the goddess. Kali, in fact, is that aspect of the divine power that is neither good nor bad, neither cruel nor kind, that is beyond linguistically and culturally conceptualised binaries of the human world.

A less ferocious and aggressive aspect of the goddess is depicted in the *Karpuradi Stotra* which decontextualises Kali from the battlefield and positions her as ruler and queen who, along with her husband Shiva, is the ultimate governing power in the universe. It also depicts her as less gory and perverse. Kali and Gauri are two extremes, binary opposites even as the names suggest, both in appearance and qualities. While Gauri balances Shiva's ascetic and destructive heat, Kali brings out his destructive tendencies. Gauri is the domesticated woman – the wife and companion ideal for any man – while Kali is the allure of the unknown, situated beyond the limits of the normative. Durga could be plotted somewhere in the middle of the continuum, her loose hair indicating untamed intense female energy and bridal markers like her vermillion and nose ring suggesting domesticity. Kali's bloodlust, especially the blood of men, can be only symbolic of her primal revenge for keeping her repressed and suppressed for so long, for making her bear everything for so long.

Kali not only means dark but also *kala* or time and its devouring and levelling ability. In this context, she is the consort of Mahakaal or Shiva, the ultimate destroyer of Creation. This suggests an expropriation of the qualities and powers of the Great Goddess and passing them on to male gods to establish their supremacy. Equally, Kali symbolises triumph over death. The only way to overcome the fear of death and finitude is by surrendering to her who rules over death. This could account for the literary depictions of Kali as the presiding deity of thugs and bandits, especially in colonial literature which demonised Kali, so terrified were they of the iconography surrounding her. The demonisation of the goddess and the furthering of her understanding as hideous and frightening also justified the so called 'white man's burden' of civilising the natives as much as it enabled to exoticize and Otherise the 'Orient'. But despite the Occidental politics of an exaggerated and demonised representation of the goddess, Kali is known to have been venerated by bandits. A temple by the name of Dakait Kali in South Kolkata draws thousands of devotees even today, and legend has it that bandits used to worship the goddess before setting off to loot villages.

Kali enters the popular imaginary as a mother goddess in colonial Bengal through the poems of Ramprasad Sen and then gains unprecedented popularity through Ramakrishna Paramahamsa, the non-traditionalist sadhaka who became a mystic and a seer and was believed to have visions of the goddess. In this tradition she is regarded as a mother goddess and the ultimate protector and the only way to approach her is as a child, with unconditional love and a self, absolved of all ego. Thus, for the tantric and the devotee, the paths to the goddess may be different but the underlying pattern and intent are the same. Both surrender to her, acknowledging her as the supreme power. The tantric transcends the laws of the world by embracing that which is taboo whereas the devotee returns to an infantile state of being where one is ignorant of the rules of the world.

Kali and her Archetypes

Kali has a presence and a prominence unparalleled in any mythology or religion of contemporary times. In present times, it is hard to find an Occidental equivalent to the goddess with her intensity and the range of powers she embodies. She is the archetypal Great Goddess who was worshipped before the Northern invasions and before the Great Goddess was effaced and her powers distributed into minor goddesses, who had limited autonomy and reflected qualities that were relatively more acceptable in an order that believed in the Father God.

Elizabeth U Harding, in her book, *Kali - The Black Goddess of Dakshineshwar* traces the various manifestations of the Great Goddess in ancient cultures and civilisations across the world. Ancient images of deities dating back to the Neolithic age are often of women and black in colour. Kali's Aztec equivalent in Mexico would be the Great Goddess Coatliciu who embodies the dual creative and destructive forces of the Earth Goddess. The likeness to Chinnamastika and the iconographic resemblance with Kali is uncanny, as this goddess too holds her severed head in her hand and out of her open neck flow two streams of blood in the shape of two serpents. She wears a skirt of serpents and a garland of human hearts. She holds a human skull in one of her hands. Her other manifestations are Rhea in ancient Crete and the goddess Rha in Russia, clothed in bloodied garment symbolising Mother Time who ate up all her offspring. In Ireland, she is Caillech the Mother Goddess in the Destroyer archetype, who inflicted smallpox and the Celtic Goddess Rhiannon who was also known for consuming her children.

The archetypes Kali embodies are, thus, quite unconventional and can sometimes prove to be unpalatable too, harkening back to an age and a time before patriarchy took over. The most prominent and glaring archetype she embodies is that of the Outlaw, which is evidenced through her complete disregard for anything and everything to do with culture. Neither does she don conventional clothing nor conventional jewellery. She is naked and for jewels, she has corpses or human body parts that embellish her terrifying persona. Loose, tangled hair which is yet another symbol of unrestrained power and boundless freedom is one of her defining features. She does not hide her raw energy nor her bloodlust and this manifests through her intoxicated red eyes. Notions like modesty, shame and honour which are normatively associated with the feminine form and the female body do not apply to Kali.

In her actions as sexual initiator and inflictor of unrestrained violence, she defies all standards and stands to epitomise the Outlaw and the Rebel who goes against societal dictates of culturally appropriate ways of behaving for the man and the woman.

If fair skin is a prerequisite and determiner of beauty in a woman, then Kali certainly does not qualify as she is not merely dark but dark as the night. If, for a woman to be desirable, she needs to be broad-hipped and large-breasted, Kali is gaunt and emaciated. If a woman has to reflect humility and naturally get into the role of a subordinate, Kali is fearless and likes to lead. If it is desirable for a woman to be decked in gold or flowers depending on whether she identifies with regalia or asceticism, Kali conforms to neither and has her own ensemble of decimated human body parts. She even wears embryos as earrings. If the naturally acceptable goddess position is the stationary standing or sitting posture reflecting benevolence, Kali is running with one leg in the air and all that her posture conveys is terror and lack of restraint. If the other goddesses convey a kind of composure and poise, Kali conveys the undoing of anything like it.

The other goddesses have animals around them that are beautiful, innocent, wise or majestic; Kali, on the other hand, has raw-boned, ever-hungry, bloodthirsty canines that keep her company. Other goddesses are worshipped in temples, she on the cremation ground. Other goddesses usually sit on their mounts or on a lotus or on the laps of their husbands; Kali sits on a mound of corpses or is standing on the inert body of her spouse. If the faces of the other goddesses radiate a serene expression and a blissful smile, Kali has her tongue sticking out absurdly, complemented by a wild, ferocious look in her eyes. If the other goddesses have flowers or musical instruments or pots in their hands, Kali has a decapitated head and a bowl to collect blood.

Kali is the archetypal Rebel defying every human rule in bold letters and is unabashed about it. Her dance is not the graceful and feminine *lasya* but the dance of death. She is also the archetypal Victor as there isn't a single battle she loses. She challenges Shiva to a *tandav* (dance of destruction) and beats him at it. She is the goddess of the battlefield and, therefore, embodies the Warrior archetype very prominently. She plunges into violence without fearing consequences. Driven by bloodlust and the desire to slay, she is difficult to stop or satisfy, just like she is difficult to be satisfied when it comes to her erotic urge. She is a goddess of excess. Her anger, her love, her sexual appetite, her indulgence in violence, her inebriation, her bloodlust, her desire to vanquish and overpower, her actions and her movements – everything about her conveys excess. Even when fighting on behalf of the gods, she 'tends to get out of control'.

Kali is a difficult goddess to contain and appease. She assumes different forms and diffuses her power into the Matrkas. She can manifest through Sita and emerge out of Vishnu's body as Yoga Nidra. She can also assume the terrifying form of Mahakali. In all these myths, she expresses the archetype of the Magician and the Shape-shifter, suddenly manifesting out of nowhere in her terrifying form. Equally, she is also worshipped as Raksha Kali or the Divine Protectress, which is one of her archetypes as she time and again comes to the rescue of the devas and even the devi.

She embodies the archetypal Devouring Mother in contrast to other goddesses who mostly stand for the nurturing mother. Kali's depictions as Chinnamastika and as Bhairavi – where she takes turns to hold Brahma's decapitated head – or her depiction as Kaalratri where she drags away bodies of dead soldiers and elephants from the battlefield, are symbolic of the devouring and the terrifying aspect of existence and nature. She revels with the dead. She indulges in violence. A simple act of feeding can involve something as gory as decapitating her own head and giving her own blood to the famished. She is that mother who, through her devouring aspect, nurtures and nourishes.

Kali is the paradox that defines nature which is both nurturing and ruthless. The weak in nature will always have to die so that the strong can survive. That is the way of the food chain. We all need to first kill and destroy in order to eat and survive. Kali symbolises this unwavering universal law of nature which has remained unchanged since the dawn of existence, a law which cultural interventions constantly try to undermine. The mother cannot be just the nurturer; she also has to perform the act of devouring in order to maintain cosmic balance and stability in the ecosystem. Kali's iconography and myths bring home this truth in its most brutal form. Though the devas and the asuras are both, the children of the universal mother, one lot has to perish at her hands for the other lot to flourish.

Tracing Kali in Popular Culture

The character of Begum Jaan is a convincing portrayal of the Outlaw archetype in Kali. Begum Jaan is the madam of a brothel which becomes disputed territory during the partition of British India as the Radcliffe line passes right through her *kotha,* cleaving it into two. In every verbal encounter with the government officials, Begum Jaan shows the spirit of a Warrior, always highlighting her Outlaw status. Like Kali, Begum Jaan symbolically occupies a property outside social jurisprudence. It is as off-limits as a cremation ground and probably more taboo. Thus, when the women in the brothel start celebrating the nation's independence, she lashes out fiercely reminding them of their Outlaw and non-citizen status once again. The women who work in the brothel are either destitute or victims who have been given shelter by Begum Jaan and then initiated into the flesh trade. Thus, she is the devouring mother who saves helpless girls and then offers them to men to run her brothel. She is ruthless in her profession, fearless in her stand and yet she has a kind side to her which she rarely reveals as she does not want to give people a soft, vulnerable impression of herself. Neither does she want her girls to display or acquire any vulnerable or delicate traits, as they need to be survivors and play the game shrewdly and carefully, if they want to live in a man's world.

In the face of imminent encounter with the authorities, Begum Jaan begins to train her girls intensively in the use of weapons. Her gang of women warriors is reminiscent of the Matrkas who accompany Kali on the battlefield and fight bravely alongside her. Just like mythic battles, Begum Jaan's brothel too turns into a veritable battleground as it is attacked and set ablaze. Like a martyr, without bothering about consequences, Begum Jaan fights to save her house and finally dies a heroic death when she knows that things have gone beyond her control. Here she embodies the Protectress archetype of the Great Goddess and the Divine Mother Raksha Kali. Her insistence on sticking to her place conveys her deep sense of belonging and an ownership of where she lives, because, there is absolutely no space within the conceptual framework of the nation state where she will be accepted or assimilated.

Begum Jaan lives and dies like a victor as she is beyond the pale of cultural norms and social mores. Her unbridled fury, her fierce obstinacy, her unapologetic demeanor and her raw sexuality inspire both awe and fear and make her almost venerable like the goddess she embodies. It is easy to overcome attachments compared to overcoming aversions. The actual place of Kali's worship is the cremation ground, but our denial of death and the unknown makes us seek her in safe spaces like temples and shrines. Begum Jaan's character, just like Kali's persona, compels us to question our aversions and the rituals associated with Kali's, demands a transcending of them.

The protective yet uncompromising nature of the divine mother, which is essayed through Begum Jaan, is a manifestation of Kali. Kali could be a woman who is fiercely protective of her female and male subordinates but quite uncompromising when it comes to their performance. She is someone who goes to any extent to protect them from coming in harm's way, but at the same time displays ruthlessness towards the ones she protects so that her very behaviour appears ambiguous.

The character of Annalise Keating in the legal thriller television and web series (2014-2020) *How to Get Away with Murder* streaming on Netflix, is predominantly the Kali archetype, who is constantly on the watch and protecting her students from being prosecuted by the Law for inadvertent crimes they have committed. At the same time, Annalise is quite pitiless and authoritarian, a really hard taskmaster demanding results from her trainees. She embodies both the devouring and nurturing mother archetypes in her character.

Kali mostly enters the filmic space as a vamp, since a collective unconscious, informed by patriarchal myths, finds it difficult to accept the absolute power of the primordial goddess and perceives her powers as a threat to the patriarchal status-quo. The anxiety-ridden projections are obvious in on-screen feminine constructs who live on the edge, engage in extremely erotic, sometimes perverse and mostly dangerous and illicit sex, are drawn to convicts, criminals or outlaws, live in the underbelly of a city, entertain thoughts of violence, engage in unlawful acts of violence, use unsuspecting people as pawns in an elaborate plan of destruction and who do not flinch from death, destruction and gore. These women characters often inspire ambivalent viewer responses which clearly reflects the patriarchal dilemma around Kali.

The character of constable Bhumika Pardeshi (Aaditi Pohankar) in the Indian crime drama web television series *She* on Netflix is not merely ambiguously conceptualised, but is non-conformist in the most startling and unexpected ways. While the camera captures frames of an average looking, nervous and complying Bhumika in the domestic space and at the workplace, it reveals her raw sexuality and her intense

sexual urge in the private space of a hotel room, the bathroom, a dark alley and the passage of a rundown restaurant. Several times during the first few episodes, the narrative keeps going into flashback mode, pinning Bhumika in a highly aroused state, with a drug dealer Sasya (Vijay Verma) who she has gone to nab undercover, disguised as a prostitute. Bhumika keeps transitioning and shape-shifting between a prostitute's attire and a police uniform, thus symbolically switching roles between an Outlaw and a Protector of the Law.

Ironically, it is not the police constable's uniform which is empowering for her. It is in dressing up and performing as a prostitute that Bhumika experiences a different person in her. Someone who is braver, more outspoken, more assertive and more combative. It is in her outrageous performance as a prostitute that she seems to unleash her true powers and what she is capable of attaining. As a constable in her uniform, she is average; as a constable in a prostitute's getup, she is outstanding at her job.

This blatant display of raw sexuality on the part of women which is taboo in a society, informed by prescriptive patriarchal dictates that regiment women's sexual agency and behaviour, finds its way out through the ruptures enabled by the law enforcement system and the undercover operations it wants Bhumika to be a part of. Not only does she develop a more assertive sexuality like the goddess, but finds this reclaimed and newly actualised sexuality, emboldening and profoundly liberating. She takes an initiative to eke out this place for herself, perhaps because somewhere deep down, she realises that her road to self-determination is through embodying this aspect of the goddess.

The viewer response to such a character is ambiguous. On the one hand, our moral rootedness prompts us to be judgmental and critical about her, on the other we empathise with her condition and celebrate her right over her body and her resolve to develop an intimate relationship with her sexual self and through it, to attain self-actualisation.

In Indian films, a popular manifestation of Kali that directly borrows from her iconography is the bloodthirsty avenging woman who is on a rampage, a killing spree. She is an onscreen incarnation of the avenging goddess. What links these femininities to Kali than with other manifestations of Shakti – like Durga or Parvati – is the revelry in violence and killing. The villain and the wrongdoer is not just neutralised. The destruction is gory and intense. In *Zakhmi Aurat* (1988), the women go about castrating the men who have raped them while in *Chingaari* (2006), Basanti (Sushmita Sen), the village prostitute, slays the village priest, Bhuvan Panda (Mithun Chakraborty), who sabotages her one chance to happiness by killing the man she loves. It is a reversal of roles as the prostitute assumes the form of the terrifying goddess while the priest, who serves the idol of goddess Kali and abuses power in her name, is the demon who needs to be destroyed.

The Shekhar Kapur directed Indian biopic *Bandit Queen* (1994) on the life of the infamous dacoit Phulandevi is yet another revenge story, where the lead character Phulan (Seema Biswas) in her cinematic presence comes very close to Kali. Phulan embodies the archetype of the Outlaw, who is doubly marginalised and cannot be absorbed in society – one because she has been raped, the burden of shame falling on her as in any patriarchal society and two, because she chooses the life of a bandit. She has to be on the fringes of society to exact her revenge.

In the action thriller *Khoon Bhari Maang* (1988), a wealthy widow Arti Verma (Rekha), who is duped by Sanjay (Kabir Bedi) who professes his love for her has her revenge by feeding him to crocodiles and letting the water monsters tear him limb for limb. All these films have one thing in common. They indicate that a woman resorts to extreme and violent measures only when she has been unscrupulously, violently, and ruthlessly violated and traumatised, leading to an irreversible loss for her. In many cases it is the death of a near one or a violation of her body and her dignity which she cannot reconcile with.

Similarly, in the 2014 erotic thriller *Hate Story 2*, Sonika (Surveen Chawla), an apparently helpless and tortured mistress of a high-profile and powerful politician embarks on a killing spree after she escapes, eliminating several men, including officers of the law who are on her trail. She becomes a most-dreaded criminal and is at large for her macabre crimes. The character of Shivani Chopra (Madhuri Dikshit) in *Anjaam* (1994) also takes a similar turn, after she is wrongly framed and convicted for a crime she did not commit. While in prison, she has a miscarriage because of the tortures she is subjected to. As revenge, she kills the prison guard in a most horrifying manner but does not get convicted since there is no evidence. After serving her sentence, Shivani comes out and sets off on a killing spree avenging her sister, her husband and her daughter's deaths. The archetype of the Outlaw who kills on the sly, and that of the Warrior, manifest unmistakeably through her. So does the devouring mother archetype. Shivani is an angered mother who has turned into an unforgiving killer because her children have been killed.

The character of Shraddha (Rakhee) in the film *Shraddhanjali* (1981) follows a similar Kali construct of the solitary woman, with the Warrior and shades of the Outlaw archetypes, who avenges the death of her family members by resorting to such extreme forms of torture and violence that drives her adversary to desperation, who finally begs her to kill him. The Devouring Mother archetype, likewise, manifests in the character of the widowed Shraddha when she decides to abort her unborn child to look after her very young and orphaned brother-in-law. She, thus, kills her own child to give her undivided love to her husband's brother and win his absolute trust.

A particularly chilling portrayal is that of Sarika (Urmila Matondkar) in the 2004 neo-noir thriller film *Ek Haseena Thi*, where she goes on from an unsuspecting and gullible woman to metamorphose into a supremely-smart avenger, who lays out an elaborate plan to destroy the man who got her wrongly convicted and serve a prison term. The transformation is complete and deep. Sarika has not merely changed her appearance but also overcome her deepest and darkest dread of rats. In a blood-curdling climax, she leaves her boyfriend – the man who betrays her – chained in a rat-infested cavern where the rats come out of the dark recesses to gnaw at him and devour him alive, bit by bit.

Other than revenge, films where women resort to gory means, violently killing and decimating the adversary in self-defence or to resist or destroy evil are also imagined along the lines of the archetype of the mythical Great Goddess. One such film is the 2015 thriller *NH 10*, starring Anushka Sharma who plays the character of a carefree urban woman Meera, who gets inadvertently mixed up in an honour-killing along with her boyfriend on a weekend getaway. In their bid to save the girl who the family members are determined to kill, her boyfriend Arjun (Rajkumar Rao) pays with his life. Meera finds herself on alien territory, literally outside the pale of civilisation and the law as she desperately looks for help.

Then the killings start. Initially she kills for self-defence but later she kills with a compulsion to destroy evil. As the last scene of the film pans out, Meera is seen to be leaving the village and probably heading citywards, after having killed the entire gang of men who were involved in the honour-killing and the brutal killing of her boyfriend. She is, thus, seen to be leaving the alternate other-worldly universe where she was forced to take up the form of Kali and destroy evil-doers with her own bare hands because someone had to do it.

Kali is believed to undermine and negate the darkest and most sinister forces at work. Devotees commonly believe that she is dark because she absorbs all that is vicious and evil in the universe. Her presence arrests dark energy and prevents it from causing harm to her devotees. Seen thus, in the archetype of the Protectress, the mythical goddess manifests in women characters who have the mental resilience and the toughness of spirit to confront the unknown, the supernatural and vanquish it even if it means putting themselves in harm's way. Jhilmil (Sushmita Sen) in *Vaastushastra* (2004), Sanjana (Bipasha Basu) in *Raaz* (2002), Sanjana (Tabu) in *Hawaa* (2003), Sarita (Rekha) in *Bhoot* (2003) are some such characters who personify this aspect of Kali in the genre of horror movies.

Bipasha Basu can be considered in many ways to personify several aspects of the archetypal Great Goddess, which are attributed a deliberately negative connotation. The steamy and seductive Basu makes an appearance as the conniving vamp Neeta, under the identity of Sonia Bajaj in the 2001 thriller *Ajnabee*. The film foregrounds two 'immoral' themes – that of couple swapping and murder, both of which are planned and neatly executed by Neeta alias Sonia and her paramour Vikram (Akshay Kumar). Naturally, poetic justice prevails and both die in the end. The film, however, marks the commencement of Basu's onscreen journey as the archetypal Kali or the Outlaw, who often engages in perverse acts and likes playing with fire.

Certain scenes in the 2003 Indian erotic thriller film *Jism*

capture Bipasha Basu in a way that evoke images of Kali and her unbridled sexuality. Since a blatant expression of sexuality is unbecoming in a woman, such a woman can obviously be up to no good and spawns evil. In the film, Basu plays Sonia Khanna who wants her husband dead and, therefore, uses Kabir (John Abraham) as a scapegoat to carry out her plan. The archetype of the Outlaw manifests through Sonia in the steamy extra-marital affair she has with Kabir. The intimate scenes in the film foreground her role as the sexual initiator and the woman-on-top which is of symbolic relevance from the perspective of the plot, quite an unconventional depiction unless one goes back to Bhairavi mounted on a passive Shiva. Sonia is not merely riding the man but also riding his fate and controlling his mind. The depiction also brings to mind one of Kali's lesser known archetypes – that of the shape-shifting seductress – which she assumes as Yoga Nidra when she enchants Madhu and Kaitabha.

A more convoluted and distorted version of Kali manifests as the avenging spirit of a dead woman, usually wronged and unfairly killed who has come back from the dead to exact her revenge by killing the person who has caused her death. The spirit is not just frightening, she is all powerful and, especially uncontrollable by men. She personifies excess. This depiction is again symbolic of patriarchal anxiety as a woman capable of excesses and unimaginable power has to be removed from the realm of the human and relegated to the spirit world. Once situated in the other world, the patriarchal dilemma disappears and her spirit is shown as unrestrained and of malicious intent. Her spirit status gives legitimacy to her bloodlust, her unstoppable ferocity and her destructive tendencies. The spirit projections in films like *Raaz* (2002), *Raat* (1992), *Alone* (2015), *Bhoot* (2003) and *Raagini MMS* (2011) fall in this category of films where the overwhelming presence of an embittered and raging spirit of a wronged woman driven by bloodlust and revenge steers the plot.

Of particular interest is Kali's archetypal manifestation in the plot of the 2015 horror film *Alone*, which is a story of conjoined twins, Sanjana and Anjana, both roles played by Bipasha Basu. Sanjana is happily married to Kabir (Karan Singh Grover) while a jealous Anjana's malevolent spirit lurks around. Sanjana and Anjana are literally crude adaptations of Gauri and her alter ego Kali, who has to be kept off limits as her destructive tendencies can be ruinous to the well-being of the household.

In *Raat, Bhoot* and *Raagini MMS*, the spirit does not assume a human form but the excesses, the wrath and the bloodlust is more than evident. In the 2002 Vikram Bhatt directed horror film *Raaz*, which also got Basu the Filmfare Best Actress award, and led to the making of the *Raaz* series, the avenging female spirit makes her bloodlust and her wrath evident by exhibiting her superhuman destructive power and threatening to turn the couple's life upside down. Though she makes very few appearances in the form of a spirit, the terror and fear she can create in the hearts of her victims is projected on Sanjana's (Basu) petrified and panic-stricken character throughout the film.

Basu makes a comeback in the third film of the *Raaz* series in 2012, *Raaz 3: The Third Dimension*. This film, like *Alone*, again plays on the psychological theme of the ego and the alter ego, and its mythological manifestations in Gauri and Kali, depicted through the characters of Sanjana (Esha Gupta) and Shanaya (Bipasha Basu) respectively. The Outlaw, the Black Magician and the shadow of the Warrior express themselves through the various machinations Shanaya resorts to in order to undermine her rival, the rising star Sanjana. Shanaya is also shown to engage in a lot of indiscriminate and opportunistic sexual liaisons to further her sinister designs.

The myth of Dirghajivhi has a very strong and recurring presence in thrillers around the world. Dirghajivhi stands for any powerful woman who operates independently and whose ambition overrides her. At times, she bites off more than she can chew and ventures into areas procuring and obtaining things that are either not rightfully hers or that, if procured, could be to the disadvantage of others. She is someone who makes a lot of enemies because of her ambitious and unrelenting nature. An elaborate trap is usually laid out to destroy her for good. She is usually caught off-guard in a moment of vulnerability and has to pay with her life. Her destroyer could either be someone who she has become a threat to, or a killer hired by the person who stands to benefit from her death. Sumitra, the young man who lures Dirghajivhi, is nothing but a hired killer while Indra is the one who wants her gone because she is posing a serious problem for him by drinking all the soma from the yajnas. In other words, Dirghajivhi is reaping the benefits of entitlement which the devas see as exclusively belonging to them.

Zoe Barnes (Kate Mara) is an upcoming reporter at the *Herald* in the political thriller *House of Cards* (2013-2018) streaming on Netflix. Ambitious and eager to rise up the ladder, Zoe enters into a shady deal with Congressman Frank Underwood (Kevin Spacey) who leaks sensitive bits of information to her from time to time, which then become raging news stories and serve to advance his political career. Zoe soon overtakes her other colleagues at the *Herald* and is in the limelight for being the first to report on several sensitive issues concerning the White House.

Zoe and Frank are into a clandestine relationship till Zoe accidentally chances upon information that can bring Frank down and wants to keep investigating. In other words, the metaphorical tongue of Dirghajivhi lusts for more. After a couple of guarded and circumlocutory warnings, under the pretext of meeting her, Frank himself throws Zoe under a running train, thus repeating the role of the mythological Indra who has Dirghajivhi neutralised as he fears that her presence will compromise his power and throne. Frank realises that if the

sensitive information Zoe is after, gets out, it would mar all his chances of becoming the President of the United States.

There are innumerable thrillers that play this myth even more graphically than symbolically. The 2012 erotic thriller *Hate Story* has a similar plot. Kavya Krishnan (Paoli Dam) pulls off a sting operation on business tycoon Siddharth Dhanrajgir (Gulshan Devaiah). Plotting his revenge, Dhanrajgir offers the ambitious journalist a job with a 300 per cent raise which she accepts immediately. On a business trip abroad, he succeeds in seducing her and making her believe that he loves her. On their return, Krishnan, however, finds her access to the company denied and that is when Dhanrajgir reveals to her his true intentions behind hiring her. In a chilling adaptation of the Indra-Dirghajivhi myth, when Krishnan threatens him with a DNA testing of her unborn child which will prove his paternity, he invites her over and traps her when her defences are down. She is knocked unconscious and the threat neutralised. Siddharth kills the foetus and has Krishnan's ovaries removed. The gutsy Dirghajivhi is, thus, taught a lesson.

The myth of Yoga Nidra, likewise, is repeatedly embedded in many filmic plots. Yoga Nidra emerges from the body of a sleeping Vishnu, to wake him up and alert him about the impending danger in the form of the demons Madhu and Kaitabha. She then acts as a decoy to distract the demons. Films like *Hero – The Love Story of a Spy* (2000), *Naam Shabana* (2017) and *Raazi* (2018) use this myth. In *Hero – The Love Story of a Spy*, the local Kashmiri girl Reshma (Preiti Zinta) is the metaphorical Yoga Nidra, who is an informer for the Indian Secret Service (RAW), personified by Major Arun Sharma (Sunny Deol). She is trained and planted in the house of a high-ranking Pakistani official believed to be linked with terrorist outfits to get sensitive information on imminent attacks on the Indian state. The girl thus serves as a decoy.

In *Naam Shabana*, Shabana's (Tapsee Pannu) simmering rage is constructively channelled into working as a field agent for secret services, just as the goddess did for the devas. At one particular juncture in the film, Shabana actually becomes the archetypal Yoga Nidra even as she lures a Pakistani middleman (who runs a travel agency as cover), to a hotel room where he is nabbed jointly by her and Ajay Singh Rajput (Akshay Kumar), the agent she is working with. *Raazi* is yet another instance of Sehmat (Alia Bhatt), an apparently innocent, newly-married girl, who serves as an undercover agent. Her marriage into a high-profile Pakistani family is just a ploy to get access to their defence secrets. She manages to keep her husband enticed just like Yoga Nidra, while establishing communication channels with her handlers back in India. It is her role as a spy that is eventually instrumental in the sinking of the Pakistani submarine INS Ghazi by the Indian INS Rajput. The devas yet again vanquish the asuras with the help of Mahamaya, who is adept at taking on different guises and beguiling the enemy.

Contemporarising and Humanising Kali

Myth and literature reimagine Kali by borrowing certain aspects of her and making them manifest through characters like Draupadi and Radha, who embody the Outlaw archetype but are not entirely non-normative. Draupadi's bloodlust and Radha's transgressive love reflect Kali-like qualities. Shades of the wild, untameable Kali are also to be found in significantly smaller proportions in the Greek goddess Artemis, who is also known as the goddess of the wild and considered to be one of the three virgin goddesses. Virgin over here does not imply sexual purity. It connotes female autonomy and independence, a woman whose sensibility is not penetrated by man or patriarchy in any way. However, Jungian psychologist Jean Shinoda Bolen in her book *Goddesses in Every Woman* observes that when the Great Goddess, which lives on in Kali in the subcontinent, was obliterated in the Western world, she was replaced by minor goddesses who collectively became the repositories of the full range of qualities and archetypes and powers of the Great Goddess. Positive and empowering projections of Kali, therefore, have to be traced in women in parts as no woman can express or experience the full extent of the Great Goddess archetype.

Kali may manifest Artemis-like in women who have a love for wilderness and seclusion where they can be in harmony with nature. These are women who are independent and free-spirited by nature and do not care much for societal norms. They might be indifferent to their appearance too, and may not fit the template of being conventionally beautiful or even trying or aspiring to be so or fit into any sort of standardised format of acceptable and compliant femininity. In fact, they might subvert standard notions of beauty and femininity. They are women who normally lead life with a devil-may-care attitude and have high risk-taking abilities.

Kali women are smart, adventurous and fearless with an underlying ferocity. They do not give up easily and can sometimes be seen as a threat to the status-quo. In the Nobel Prize winner Toni Morrison's novel *Paradise*, the women in the Convent on the outskirts of the village of Ruby are embodiments of the Kali archetype. Each woman is running away from her past and in that sense an Outlaw, who starts over in the Convent which is diametrically opposite what a real convent is. So completely liberating is the experience of these women where they are beyond the bounds of patriarchal dictates that, very soon, a myth materialises like gathering mist around them. Word goes round in the village that these women with their unholy and rebellious habits are actually witches and need to be terminated. This could be a general patriarchal reaction to Kali's manifestation.

Women with the Kali archetype do not believe in gender stereotypes and predefined roles. For them, their liberated existence and their autonomy is of the highest worth and they are not willing to compromise their independence on any count. They can go to great lengths to live the life they want. They are not domesticated identities who will look for material comforts. They can make a home for themselves in the wild or in the middle of nowhere. Sometimes they may not even need a home as all of nature is their home. If they have children, they will raise them like lionesses raise their cubs, in the wild and without much fuss, egging them on to be independent and self-reliant early in life.

They are mostly women who exercise their full sexual autonomy and who may not believe in settling down for the rest of their lives with one man. Women with a strong Kali archetype will gravitate towards other women who have a similar strain of recklessness and wild abandon in them, and play out their adventures together. The film *Dedh Ishqiya* (2014) loosely based on *Lihaaf*, the most infamous and controversial work of the Indian Urdu writer Ismat Chugtai, is the story of two such women who, like Chandi and Kali, are in it together almost as one organic entity – so well do they complement each other and in the end prove to be better than all the men put together. Kali women may resort to outlandish behaviour and display outlaw-type tendencies and earn flak and criticism but that is only because they dare to be non-conformists.

A woman can be said to have an activated Kali archetype when her partner looks up to her for support and regards her as a guide and navigator, and mostly as a protectress. Where s/he depends on her to pull them out of a mess and acknowledges her superior capacities. Kali is any woman who shows and has above average wisdom and physical prowess, libidinal energy and a combative and resilient nature. She is usually an attacker, not a defender. Such a woman like Begum Jaan will not mince her words or try to sound pleasant and complying. She will be openly rebellious in action and spirit. A woman with the Kali archetype may be fiercely protective of the ones she is responsible for and willing to go to any extent for their safety. She is also someone who inspires fearlessness in her loved ones and teaches them to fight their own battles, just as Kali inspires fearlessness in her devotees. She can be the backbone of social agitations and the voice of revolutions, impossible to contain or curb.

One will certainly not want her as an adversary because she can be dangerous. She has the ability to destroy her opponent thoroughly and with ruthless and clinical precision. If she is in the forces, her military strategy will reflect an extraordinary level of adeptness and competence. Kali-type women are also very often the last resort for some people and may demand complete surrender. When someone approaches this woman for help or guidance, they have to be in a really terrible spot, having fought at least half the battle themselves and seeking her out only because they know it is impossible to win it without her. Surrender from the mightiest and even the most dreaded is what Kali expects just like Bhumika in the series, *She*, who has the most dreaded drug lord Nayak (Kishore Kumar G) surrendering to her in the final episode of the first season.

The Kali Archetype in Brands

Brands and film narratives, when using the Kali archetype, might want to follow the strategy of the Bhakti poets who conceived Radha as a woman defying all norms in an increasingly conservative society. As Indian mythologist Devdutt Pattanaik rightly observes, 'Radha is Kali in thought', Radha's transgressive love needs a symbolic treatment. An advertisement projecting Kali can depict the woman as someone who wants more and does not flinch from saying so.

She can be projected as someone prone to taking risks like a mountain-climber, someone connected with canines and wild animals like a dog trainer, an investigative journalist pulling off a dangerous sting operation, a secret agent in an undercover operation, a fighter pilot or an army officer as part of a daring mission. Her construct should reflect her voluntary engagement with something that is dangerous, life-threatening and out of the ordinary which will inspire fear and awe in the viewers.

The television series *Khatron ke Khiladi*, which showcases celebrities accepting challenges and dares, brings out the Kali archetype in women who come to participate in it. She may be shown completely at ease in odd, unconventional settings like hitchhiking across the land, or sleeping under the stars or spending the night at a rundown inn. Someone who really likes it rough, not just pretends to. She can be situated in physically tough and demanding situations. The focus could be on her invincibility and her formidable personality through a brand of denims or even a watch with messages like: *wearing this makes her invincible, she controls time.*

The Kali archetype can be projected through the Explorer archetype too, of the woman who is on her own, travelling the length and breadth of the world. It could be used in combination with the Sage archetype to construct a travel writer or a travel photographer whose work is a combination of her creative force and her adventurous spirit. Someone who can live out of bags and in makeshift accommodations to explore the wilderness or untrodden territories or even someone like a war reporter. This construct can be used for products like a camera or a phone which aids her documentation process and keeps her connected with civilisation. Likewise, the construct would be suitable even for products like a protein bar, undergarments, sanitary pads that make it easier for her in the wild.

Brands could work on the theme of 'Woman in the Wild'. As avenger women, advertisements could actually situate the woman in the wild, or depict her as wild and as someone who brings out the wild and free side of her partner, maybe by introducing them to a kind of drink or shoes meant for long treks or sports lingerie or a condom suggesting wild, unconventional and innovative sexuality.

The idea of one woman splitting into two for the successful outcome of a task expressed through the myth of the complementary personas of Chandi and Kali can be used to depict women who are partners in a physically and mentally demanding project and complete it with precision. This will also foreground the narrative of competence and efficiency in women. Advertisements can also work around the theme of women embodying the Kali archetype and reclaiming public spaces at night which are deserted and thus asserting their fearlessness. The product for this context can be a brand of biscuits or chips and the women can be shown munching on them with an air of nonchalance, even as they set out to take ownership and reclaim forbidden spaces, especially at night.

A face from the world of film celebrities that reflects the devil-may-care attitude and is capable of wearing the Kali archetype with confidence is Swara Bhaskar. She has been a part of protest movements in real life and is known for her fearless and unabashed criticism. Likewise, she has an attacking spirit and can be belligerent if need be. She has played positive and negative characters with great ease and has been equally accepted perhaps because of the prominent presence of the Outlaw archetype in her. Swara Bhaskar could be the ideal combination of Kali and Saraswati, with her intellectual bent and her outspoken nature.

Alia Bhatt, likewise, could be another celebrity who could pull off the Kali archetype. The characters she plays in films like *Udta Punjab* (2016), *Highway* (2014), *Raazi* and *Kapoor & Sons* (2016), all have shades of the wild goddess in them. The third face would be that of Surveen Chawla whose portrayals in *Hate Story 2*, Netflix web series *Sacred Games* (2018) and *Parched* (2015) put her in the league of archetypes associated with Kali.

Though Kali seems like a goddess who embodies forbidding and forbidden traits, her manifestations and positive projections are more frequent than we would like to believe. With more women coming out in the open to talk about issues like sexual harassment, rape, molestation and domestic abuse and reclaiming public spaces for political agitation and social equity, Kali is certainly picking up. Slut walks, reclaiming one's body, asserting one's sexual autonomy along with financial independence and contesting conventionally perceived notions of femininity are instances of Kali at work. Women will certainly want to identify with such empowering constructs which can also bring about intersections of social and political issues which are of increasing relevance today. Likewise, feminine constructs situated in unconventional settings in advertisements and films, women taking up unconventional roles gives legitimacy to women in real life wanting to venture into domains traditionally off-limits and thus, opening up newer possibilities of transcendence for them.

DURGA: THE GODDESS WHO WON

SHE HAS A look of resilience on her face. Her eyes move from one to another in the room. She is irritated when answers don't come her way. She doesn't understand minds that do not work as fast as hers. But she is quick to suggest another road, quick to change the course of her action and follow suit. Tirelessly, unrelentingly, she keeps going at it, inspiring mixed reactions from the men in the room. Some think she is on a wild goose chase, some conjecture she must have lost it, some want to believe her but find it hard to. She knows she is being judged, evaluated, assessed. Outwardly, she feigns exasperation and impatience, inwardly she smiles her secret smile. For she has a plan. She knows exactly how to go about it, what to say, when and who to confuse and befuddle. With her wide-eyed look she can make herself seem naïve, vulnerable, even desirable so that no one gets to see her resolve of steel. She deceives everyone as she enacts her part flawlessly. Despite being heavy and voluptuous, she is nimble on her feet and discreet in her moves. She knows – every act, every scene is going to bring her closer to her prey. And at the opportune moment, when her adversary is expecting it the least, she strikes – vehemently and unflinchingly, finishing him beyond a doubt. Sometimes, the fight gets tough. She bears battle scars but they don't deter her. And then, as effortlessly as she had materialised out of nowhere, she takes care to disappear without a trace. As if she never existed, leaving those who spent time with her dumbstruck and scratching their heads. Back in her space, her interaction with an elderly man tells us that she has done what she was expected to do; in fact, done better than expected. The flames which blazed inside her have now turned into smoldering cinders. They will take a long time to calm down. Yet calm down they must, because that can't be her perpetual state, she tells herself with a faraway look in her eyes. Radiant in her beauty, emanating an indefinable power, elusive and clever, brave and indefatigable, she is Vidya Bagchi of *Kahaani* (2012), the film that went on to win three National Awards and five Filmfare Awards, including the Best Actress Award that went to Vidya Balan for portraying the Durga-like woman who uses both strength and cunning to fight and win a lone battle against a formidable and elusive enemy.

One of the most popular, most widely worshipped and most venerated goddesses of the Hindu pantheon across India, Nepal and Bangladesh, the primary deity of the Shakta school of Hinduism, invoked by many names, Durga or 'the unassailable one' has victory embedded in her persona. Invoked by epic heroes, imperative to conquests, the presiding goddess of weapons and warfare, the divine feminine principle coursing through all of creation and the most significant symbol of fertility myths, Durga stands for a different world order in different communities. In agricultural communities she is venerated as the fertility goddess, in warrior and tribal clans, she is the ultimate protector and in feudal society she is the benefactress. Durga symbolises that woman who can assert herself without subverting hegemonic institutions. People look up to her as the benevolent and gracious mother and also the warrior who kills so as to usher in a better world.

The Myths of Durga

In the *Devi Bhagvatam*, Durga comes to the rescue of her devotee, the prince Sudarshana, the rightful heir to the throne of the kingdom of Kosala, not once but twice when he faces imminent death at the hands of Yudhajita, the grandfather of his stepbrother Shatrujita. Their persecution have led him and his mother Manorama – the first queen of King Dhruvasandhi of Kosala of the Ikshavaku dynasty – to flee the land. Manorama seeks refuge in the ashrama of rishi Bharadwaj and raises her son there. Sudarshana becomes a fierce devi-bhakta after the goddess materialises before him one day and blesses him with a bow and arrows. She frequently visits him in dreams and visions, guiding his path.

Sudarshana turns into a formidable archer. Durga materialises next to him again, riding her beast when Yudhajita and Shatrujita attack Sudarshana and his father-in-law, king Subahu, with their army to slay them. Durga is even known to multiply and her many selves vanquish their vast army. When she wants Subahu to ask for a boon, the overwhelmed king merely expresses his desire to be her devotee all his life. Sudarshana follows suit and pleased, Durga asks him to celebrate the *Navratri* in autumn as an oblation to her. She thus proves to be *Durgatinashini* from which comes her name Durga or the destroyer of evil intent. Durga's power and the tale of her divinity spreads across the land from Kashi where she appears before Sudarshana to Kosala, where Sudarshana starts the tradition of worshipping her.

In another myth, unable to vanquish the asuras Sumbha and Nisumbha, who have laid siege to Indra's kingdom Amravati, the devas approach the goddess Parvati for help. The goddess flies into a rage and her whole body begins to tremble and shake violently. Two forms come out of her – a white Ambika and a dark Kali, the former often associated with Durga. Both the forms proceed to the immortal garden Nandana which is now asura territory, where Ambika starts singing in a soft and melodious voice. Very soon, they are spotted by the asuras Chanda and Munda who beseech Ambika to accompany them to their lords Sumbha and Nisumbha. When the devi refuses, they go back to report to their lords. Sumbha and Nisumbha, bewitched by the description of the fair goddess, send messenger after messenger to the garden to convince her to come to them. Ambika lays down her condition to Sugriva, the asura messenger, that she would like Sumbha to come and defeat her in battle as that is a prerequisite for anyone wanting to marry her.

It is said that when Sumbha is conveyed this message, he considers it an affront and decides to use force to imprison Ambika and get her to his court. He delegates this responsibility to one of his most powerful asuras, Dhumralochan, promising him that he could have Ambika as his wife. Not for a moment do any of the asuras believe that the devi actually wants to fight them. They presume that she is using metaphors of war, the battlefield, violence and victory to imply sexual union with the asura and his prowess in bed. So, Dhumralochana, with sixty thousand *daityas*, goes to the garden and tells the devi what they think. At this, Kali bursts into a terrifying laughter.

An incensed Dhumralochana attacks the devis. While Ambika razes the soldiers, Kali reduces Dhumralochana to ashes with a deafening roar. Ambika blows the conch so hard to announce their victory that Sumbha hears it from where he is seated on his throne. Subsequently, Chanda and Munda who are sent next, meet with the same fate at the hands of the devis. Again the conch shell is heard by Sumbha. The bloodied and maimed asuras who have survived, rush back to Sumbha describing the devi to be a combination of Gayatri, Sandhya, Saumya and Bhadrakali. Shaking with anger and humiliation, this time, Sumbha deputes Raktabija to kill the devis who have gone to a mountain top now and are still singing sweetly since the Nandana is reeking with the stench of rotten flesh and drying blood of wounded and dead asuras.

This time, there are three devis instead of two, Chandika

being the most recent to have emerged. Ambika, along with Kali, Chandika and the Matrkas who descend from all sides, is able to vanquish Raktabija's army while Ambika and Chamunda are able to decimate all of Raktabija's clones. In the last leg of the battle, Kali and Chamunda are struck by Sumbha but Ambika comes in raging to their rescue, laughing her intoxicated laugh even as a bewildered Sumbha sees her for the first time.

At that moment she is attacked by Nisumbha, in which Ambika is brutally wounded but holds her ground and then with her gigantic axe, chops of Nisumbha's head which goes rolling, and then his limbs and arms, since his headless body needs to be stopped from inflicting further violence. Despite the destruction and the death all around, Sumbha, in an aroused and passionate state, is still enamoured of Ambika and pleads with her to stop fighting and take him instead. A laughing Ambika instructs Kali and Chamunda to kill Sumbha, which they do.

In yet another myth, Durga, it is said, comes to Sachi's rescue when the latter is in great distress since her husband Indra has fled Amravati after killing Vrtra, and Nahusha rules over Amravati now. Nahusha wants Sachi to be his wife which she resents. Durga appears before Sachi one night and gives her a messenger who takes Indra's queen to Kailasa Manasarovar where Indra is hiding as a serpent in the hollow stalk of a lotus. Sachi and Indra then decide on how to overthrow Nahusha. This brings to mind the popular cognomen where Durga has been described as the devi of buddhi in *Devi Mahatmyam*. Durga is supposed to be difficult to attain but her grace can ensure absolute removal and erasure of all obstacles and problems.

There is a myth surrounding the origin of Durga's name. Once, an asura named Durgama decided to observe the severest of penance and austerities to please Brahma. His objective was to procure the Vedas since he realised that it was knowledge of the Vedas that made the rishis and the munis powerful and the devas were powerful because of the chanting g of the Vedas and the yajnas that were performed. It is said that he underwent rigours and performed tapa for thousands of years till finally appeased, Brahma appeared before Durgama.

Durgama asked to be blessed exclusively, with the sole possession and knowledge of the Vedas. Brahma could not deny him and granted him the boon. Soon, the Vedas disappeared from earth, the rishis lost the ability to chant the hymns and failed to perform rituals, the devas lost their power and hid in thickets and caves and disaster struck the earth. Everywhere, there were droughts and famines as plants, animals and human beings began to die and the earth gradually became empty and barren like an arid desert.

Duragama now ruled over Amravati and was resplendent like a thousand suns because he possessed the Vedas. The devas, at their wit's end, started praying to devi Bhagawati to come to their rescue and save the earth. The devi appeared and when she saw their plight and that of the earth, tears flowed from her eyes and became streams and rivers on earth. She strewed seeds on the earth from above and soon life returned on earth. Meanwhile, Durgama, hearing this flew into a rage and set off to attack devi

Bhagawati and the devas. The devas trembled and Bhagawati drew a circle around them, which would protect them.

In the fierce battle that ensued, devi Bhagawati let off fifteen arrows in the direction of the asura which dismembered him, killed his horses and blew his chariot to smithereens. The asura's heart exploded and a ray of light emerged from his body and merged with the devi's body. The rishis, munis, brahmanas and devas fell at the devi's feet. A luminous light shone in her hands. It was the Vedas which she returned to the rishis. From here on, she was hailed by the name of Durga, the slayer of the terrible Durgama.

The most famous myth of Durga is around the asura king Mahishasura, who performed *tapasya* for ten thousand years to please the Creator of the universe, the four-faced Brahma. Pleased with his tapasya, when Brahma finally appeared before the asura, Mahishasura asked Brahma to make him immortal. Brahma explains to him about the destructible and mutable nature of all things in the universe. So Mahishasura modifies his request, demanding invincibility against men of all three worlds. He is more than certain that there is no woman who can ever kill him.

Mahishasura is born of the union of the asura Rambha and a buffalo, Mahishi, on the funeral pyre of his father and his buffalo mother who immolates herself on her husband's pyre. Rambha has the blessing of Agni or the fire god that his son will be the most powerful being in all three worlds and coupled with this blessing, is Brahma's boon which makes Mahishasura a most formidable power in all three worlds. He becomes the 'undisputed sovereign' who no one dared to challenge. Soon the half-buffalo, half-human asura, his eye on Amravati, challenges Indra to fight him. A cornered Indra, along with Brahma and the other devas, reaches Kailasa for Shiva's advice. All the gods along with Shiva go to Vaikunth where, with Vishnu's counsel, they decide to face the asura and his legions.

Mahishasura is also a gifted shape-shifter and a sorcerer and he uses his gift and cunning, along with his might to create illusions on the battlefield, which leave the devas confused and panic-stricken. In an unusual turn of events, Mahishasura manages to strike a mighty blow to Vishnu who falls unconscious. Shiva attacks the asura but in vain. This leaves the devas in a state of frenzy. Soon the trinity Brahma, Vishnu and Mahesh flee the battlefield, though the other devas hold their ground. The fierce battle lasts a hundred years, at the end of which, the devas have exhausted all their weapons and soldiers and are driven out of Amravati by the victorious Mahishasura.

The perplexed devas again collect at Kailasa to discuss a strategy. They are aware of the boon the asura is blessed with, and know equally well that none of the goddesses, whether it is Shiva's wife Uma, or Indra's wife Sachi or for that matter the serene Saraswati have the capability to kill the asura. On Vishnu's suggestion, the trinity emit a fierce light or their 'shaktis' from their beings and each of the devas present there follows suit.

Soon all the flames emitted by the devas converge into one gigantic, mountainous flame that burns brilliantly and that slowly begins to take shape. A goddess appears from the flames, it is said sometimes with eighteen arms and sometimes in her cosmic form, with a thousand arms. Her beauty and brilliance are unparalleled, nothing like what the devas have seen so far, her form beautiful yet fierce. She is bedecked and armed by the devas, Vishnu giving his lethal Sudarshan Chakra and the mace Kaumodaki and Shiva his trident, among others. It is said that Surya even gives her his light, Himavan the mountain god his mount, and Indra, his thunderbolt.

There is a hint of sarcasm as the Goddess marvels at the presence of Brahma, Vishnu, Mahesh, the king of gods, Indra and all the other devas, the greatest and loftiest of beings who have invoked her and want her help to kill a *danava*. She lets out a monstrous laugh that reverberates through all three worlds like a deafening roar and it reaches even Mahishasura, who is inflamed by this impudence. He immediately sends his asuras to find out who has dared to commit such an act of insolence. The danavas come to the mountain top and see the devi in her terrifying and splendid iridescent form, drinking from the cup of wine that dribbled down her lips and flee the place in terror, so blinded are they by her radiant persona.

When Mahishasura is given this news, he is certain that she is a woman fit to be his queen and so sends various emissaries with his proposal. Durga tells the asura commander of her plan to sacrifice his master for he is a buffalo, and restore the devas' kingdom. While Virupaksha assures Mahishasura that this is nothing but an empty threat, Durdhara reads it as a metaphor indirectly expressing the devi's love for the asura and her desire to be with him. Tamra expresses his paranoia and the ominous indications he has been receiving since morning, spelling impending doom, reminding him of the loophole in the boon Brahma has conferred upon Mahishasura.

When Tamra is sent to the devi, she tells him she is already married to Shiva and scoffs at the idea of being with Mahishasura. When this news is brought back, some deterministic and visionary asuras like Vidalaka, Asiloma and Durmukha sagely state that probably Mahishasura's time had come and commit themselves to fighting till their last breath for the asura as they served him while some like Vaskala in their arrogance and ignorance, pledge to drag the 'woman' to Mahishasura's court.

This time when the asuras repeat their message to Durga, she humiliates them by referring to Mahishasura's ugliness and repulsive appearance, which is half-buffalo and half-demon. The battle breaks between the fierce asuras with their death-defying and terrifying legions and the goddess, all alone. But they are no match for her. Each asura from Mahishasura's court comes to the battleground with his army and is dreadfully defeated and sent back maimed and mangled. Many are slain.

Finally, Mahishasura assumes the form of a resplendent youth and arrives on the battlefield to confront the goddess who he fears will recoil and abhor his beast-like appearance. He tries an argumentative approach to convince Durga but the latter challenges him to a fight. Aided by more asuras like Trinetra, Andhaka and Durdhara, Mahishasura launches a full-blown attack on Durga. He uses his gifts of a shape-shifter and assumes many forms from a bull-elephant to a terrible bird and back to a buffalo-demon. In a bloody battle, Durga is repeatedly injured by the hooves of the asura, stung by his arrows and drenched in her own blood. She strikes him on the chest with her trident and immediately releases the Sudarshan Chakra which beheads the mighty demon king, thus ending this bloody spectacle. Amravati is restored to the devas, peace prevails in all three worlds and it will be many *manavantara*s before Sumbha and Nisumbha conquer Amravati and Durga has to be invoked again.

In the Ramayana, there is an episode in which the goddess Durga features. During the battle with Ravana, Rama gets an indication that he can defeat Ravana only if he has Durga's blessings and grace. So he decides to invoke the goddess. Rama performs a puja with hundred and eight lotus flowers. As he utters the holy chants and offers the flowers one after another, the goddess decides to test him. So, she makes one flower disappear. When Rama comes to the end of the puja he suddenly realises there are only hundred and seven lotuses and not hundred and eight. A resolute Rama decides that he will make up for the missing lotus by offering one of his eyes to the goddess, because didn't his mother always address him as the lotus-eyed boy?

As Rama is about to remove his eye, Durga, pleased with him, appears before him and stops him in the nick of time. She assures him of his victory in the battle. It is believed that Rama invokes Durga in autumn long before the springtime harvest season when she is normally worshipped as he is heading for Lanka. After Rama wins the battle of Lanka and defeats Ravana, he decides to observe Durga Puja in autumn when he had invoked the goddess. This is why the Durga Puja celebrated in autumn is also known as *akal bodhan* or untimely invocation. The last day of the autumn Durga Puja also witnesses the burning of the effigy of Ravana in the northern parts of India, which is symbolic of and syncretic with the goddess' primary concern in the myths – which is destruction of evil forces that tend to wreak havoc on earth.

Analysing Durga in the Light of the Myths

Scholars of religion and theology often see the incarnations of Shakti, the Mother Goddess – and those of Vishnu (*Dashavataar* and the minor incarnations), as serving the same purpose – that of restoring equilibrium and balance on earth and ensuring cosmic stability by neutralising demonic and destructive forces. The reincarnations can also be read in the light of the increasing prominence of the Shakta and the Vaishnava schools of worship in the Brahmanical religious economy of medieval India.

In his speculation about the historical origin of the goddess, David Kinsley makes an interesting observation. In all likelihood, Durga is a non-Aryan, indigenous goddess who is assimilated in the Hindu pantheon. The mythologist Joseph Campbell and the scholar Marija Gimbutas in several of their works have suggested the strong possibility of appropriation of local, tribal or regional goddesses by the usurping Indo-Europeans who had started coming to India right from the 4th millenia BC but who only gained ground and stabilised as a community around 1800-1600 BC. This was an exclusively warrior race informed by a male-oriented religion and one that believed in a father godhead. However, the presence of a goddess culture too strong to be negated or effaced may have demanded a confluence of the two religious traditions.

Thus, despite a paucity of well-formed goddess figures in Vedic texts, in Puranic texts there is a surge of manifestations of the divine feminine or Shakti and their marital associations with the gods. Thus Parvati, Uma, Durga, Kali – all versions of the same feminine are believed to be married to Shiva whereas Lakshmi is Vishnu's consort and Saraswati is normally associated with Brahma. Images of a Durga-like goddess slaying a buffalo begin to surface around the 4th century of the Common Era and Durga becomes a pan-India goddess between 5th and 6th century AD.

If one were to consider the hegemonic myth of the goddess Durga, the assimilation is more than clear. All of Durga's powers can be attributed to the pantheon of male Hindu gods who have lent their weapons to her. She is the result of their cumulative efforts and spiritual energy. She embodies the *sattva* of Brahma, the *rajas* of Vishnu and the *tamas* of Shiva. When she mentions in one of her exchanges with an asura, that she is married to Shiva, the assimilation is sealed. Thus, armed and equipped with the grace of the male gods, Durga vanquishes Mahishasura. Interestingly, Durga's idols show her as fair-skinned unlike Kali, whereas Mahishasura is dark-skinned and half-beast. Mahishasura's description can be regarded metaphorically as representing the supposedly uncivilised ways of the dark, indigenous people of the land who need to be overthrown and conquered. Their goddess, who has been assimilated, in all likelihood has been given an Aryan appearance to distance her from the local tradition.

In recent times, several regions in Uttar Pradesh, Madhya Pradesh, Jharkhand, Chattisgarh, Odisha, Bengal and Karnataka have witnessed a surge of the commemoration of the 'Mahishasur Martyrdom Day' by tribal people, especially the 'Asur' tribe and Dalitbahujan communities who look up to the iconic asur as their ancestor and leader. Scholars of subaltern studies like Rajendra Prasad Singh and Badri Narayan have also observed that the term 'asur' has undergone linguistic pejoration from standing for 'life-giver' to symbolising 'demon' just like the term 'mahish', which initially meant 'great' (Mahishmati, as in the film *Bahubali),* then 'king' and finally 'buffalo'. Subaltern narratives and ethnographic studies claim that animalising and demonising an indigenous leader and attributing him qualities of a beast through myth is a classic example of brahminising descriptions of longstanding conflicts between the 'outsider' Aryans and the indigenous tribes.

The assimilation and semi-transformation of a non-Aryan goddess Durga and turning her against her own also serves two purposes – one that she bridges the gap between the indigenous people and the invading/incoming people and two, she establishes the superiority of the outsiders over the indigenous population by attacking and subjugating them. In doing this, Durga is not merely validating the incoming Aryans as a superior race but also establishing their patriarchal ideology by allowing herself to be equipped with their powers. In the other myth, where Durga frees the Vedas from the possession of Durgama, she is ensuring retention and circulation of knowledge only within one community, that of the devas.

This is almost parallel to the Greek myth of the warrior goddess Athena who is called upon to cast her vote for Orestes who has murdered his mother Clytemnestra to avenge the death of his father Agamemnon, who has sacrificed his daughter and Orestes' sister Iphigenia for victory in the war. It is a hung jury till Athena casts her vote in favour of Orestes, thus siding with patriarchy. Just like Durga owes her origin to the collective spiritual energy of the male gods and emerges as a full-grown adult, Athena also does not have a mother because she has sprung out of Zeus' head as a full-grown adult and owes her origin to the most prominent male god of Greek mythology.

Symbolically, goddesses like Durga and Athena are the recalibrated versions of the old goddesses from the female-oriented culture, now born out of patriarchy and who will strive to protect the interests of patriarchy. Durga's disdain for Mahishasura with respect to his appearance and the latter's decision to confront her as a handsome youth, reflect the Indo-European community's superior racist gaze and condescending attitude towards the indigenous people.

Despite her complete Sanskritisation, there are aspects of Durga's description that rupture the forced discourse of domesticity and matrimony around her which try to undermine her autonomy. Durga is unorthodox as she drinks wine from a cup and the liquor keeps dribbling from her mouth, suggesting her inebriated state and an economy of excess. Durga's strong association with the mountains, especially the Vindhyas, her iconography which has the mountain in the backdrop and her mount which is a mountain lion as also her real form, which is Uma or Parvati, the daughter of Himavan the mountain god, all indicate that she is an indigenous goddess of the mountains.

Scholars believe her to be a goddess worshipped by indigenous communities and forest-dwellers in the mountainous regions of the Vindhya. Like Kali, Durga too is a goddess bordering on the wilder, untameable side of nature but her makeover is to a greater degree than Kali's. She is the goddess of the battlefield, a goddess who is invoked primarily to kill and destroy evil and fight on behalf of the weak who are unable to hold their ground.

Durga is also the goddess of fertility who had to be once pleased with animal sacrifice. Animal sacrifice has been common to plantation and pastoral cultures which thrive around the principle of death and rebirth of life. For new life to be born, sacrifices are imperative and that is why the plantation cultures which primed fertility myths saw more animal sacrifices than hunting cultures where there was already so much of bloodshed that their myths focused on atonement and penance for the deaths caused. This is probably the reason why in several parts of India, when Durga and Kali are worshipped, animals like the buffalo, the goat and the sheep were and still are sacrificed at the altar of the goddess.

Durga's military prowess, her fierce power combined with her radiant and seductive beauty, are attempts to position her somewhere between the wild and the domesticated on the continuum. In Bengal where Durga is worshipped extensively, she is with her family – her children Lakshmi, Saraswati, Kartika and Ganesha, and her body is inscribed with markers that are used on a married Hindu woman. She wears the prominent vermillion or *sindoor* in the parting of her hair and her hands and feet have *alta*, a red liquid, again a mark of a married woman on them. The last day of the Durga Puja, which is called the *Vijaya Dashami* after Ram's victory over Ravana, is celebrated by married women where they play with vermillion and smear the goddess' face with vermillion bidding her adieu till she returns the next year.

Durga is the daughter of the village who comes home with her children every year for four days and returns to Kailasa after this short visit. In other parts of India, seeds are sown in an earthen pot (*ghata*) and the pot worshipped as a symbol of the goddess for nine days, which is called navaratri. In the course of these nine days, the seeds sprout and germinate. This ritual positions Durga as a fertility goddess whereas the earlier one domesticates her and presents her as Shiva's consort. There is also a ritual to collect the first lump of clay for the goddess' idol from the homes of prostitutes and earth that has been dug up by different animals, again alluding to her persona as *prakriti* or nature in which all is regarded through an objective lens.

Traced etymologically, Durga could also have evolved from the word '*durg*' meaning impenetrable or impregnable, which is why fortresses are called durg in Hindi. The goddess Durga too is an invincible force as she never fails her devotees. Durga appears as a central goddess in the Shakta tradition, with her myths featuring in the *Devi Mahatyam* believed to have been composed between 400 and 600 CE. She is a predominant presiding deity in the eastern belt of India. She is also a prominent deity in Tantric and Japanese Buddhist traditions.

While Durga, as a goddess, emerges only around the 5th century, the word Durga occurs in the *Rigveda* and the *Atharvaveda*. A goddess by the name of Durgi also appears in the *Taittiriya Aranyaka*. Durga even appears as a goddess to grace the heroes in the epics Ramayana and Mahabharata at the start of the common era. Likewise, she is projected as a goddess in *Harivamsa* by Vishnu who sings her adulations and through King Pradyumna who invokes her. Besides the *Devi Mahatyam* which is the canonical text of the Shaktas or the worshippers of Shakti, the major Puranic literature which focuses on Durga are the *Devi Bhagavat Purana* and the *Markandeya Purana*. Durga was conflated with the construction of Mother India by Bankim Chandra Chatterjee, especially through the song *Vande Mataram* in colonial Bengal.

Durga and her Archetypes

Durga undoubtedly is primarily a warrior goddess. She is invoked only in times of crisis to fight and win a war. In that sense she is a temporary incarnation and has no life story and no childhood and adolescence like Parvati or Sita. She cannot be viewed in different contexts like Lakshmi or Saraswati other than those pertaining to impending or ongoing battles. She is venerated as a warrior goddess who it is impossible to vanquish. Durga fights lone battles and when she needs help, she manifests further into shaktis like Kali, Katyayani and the like or calls upon the Matrkas, the warrior goddesses to her aid. Though armed with the weapons of the devas, she never has devas fighting by her side. Even as a solitary presence, she is formidable and can win battles single-handedly. According to the argument presented in her myths, her primary objective as a warrior is to ensure the conquest of good over evil.

Durga is a war-strategist and approaches her adversaries with planning as is evident from the accounts of most of the battles she fights and even the counsel she offers. During both the battles with Mahishasura, and later with Sumbha and Nisumbha, there are several exchanges of words between Durga and the emissaries of the ruling asuras before an actual confrontation. She chooses her words carefully, anticipating the next move of the adversary and accordingly deploys her resources to win. In the battle with Mahishasura, she saves the Sudarshan Chakra and the trident till the very end, since she knows the power of these weapons.

In her, one sees not a hot-headed, wild warrior like Kali who is on a killing spree, but a careful and sophisticated strategist who plans each move with deliberation. She systematically decimates the entire army of the asuras and their commanders before killing the ruler. Being in the possession of the key weapons of all the devas is evidence of their faith in her superior capacities and her intelligent deployment of the arms she has at her disposal to inflict maximum destruction. She is not just out to finish the asura king but the entire race of asuras. When she appears in front of Sachi, she proposes a plan of action to the latter which will eventually ensure restoring Indra to his throne and the fall of Nahusha.

Durga, with her irresistible beauty, also has a strong Seductress archetype which she exploits to her best advantage. She is a goddess who is not merely beautiful but is keenly aware of the power of her beauty and charm, especially when they join the strategist in her. She knows how her words to the messengers are going to be variously interpreted and what military decisions they will prompt. She is a spell-caster too, as she mesmerises the asuras with her voice in Nandana and later with her aura when they see her. She is proud and confident of her abilities and makes a public proclamation of her victory over the milling army of the asuras by blowing her conch time and again. This is symbolic of her extraverted, assertive and fearless spirit. This is perhaps why she is widely worshipped as a warrior goddess by the kshatriya or the warrior clans of India, especially in Rajasthan and the Deccan where she is believed to live in the swords of the Rajputs and the Marathas.

Durga is a shape-shifter as she can beguile her adversaries effortlessly. She is so also because this is not her original form. She is originally Parvati who has transformed into Durga. Anthropologically speaking, she has crossed over and metamorphosed to acquire a different identity which makes her a shape-shifting goddess. Durga has not two but eighteen arms and sometimes even a thousand. In front of Sachi she appears as a serene and demure goddess whereas on the battlefield, she wears red. She can waylay and confuse her enemies with her words. She is patient as she keeps sitting on the mountain top waiting for her enemy to come to her. In doing so, she establishes the Ruler archetype in her which demands the other person to bow down to her and come to her rather than she going to them.

Aspects of Durga bring out the Queen and Mother archetypes in her just as they ensure her domestication. Durga displays queenlike concerns for the devas and ensures their safety. This is especially evident in the myth of Durgama where she actually draws a circle of protection around the devas before confronting Durgama. She is queenly in her bearing and attire and queenly in her stature and posturing as she engages in dialogue with the asura emissaries. She displays a keen awareness of her superior status and it is her condescending, supremacist gaze that is the cause of Mahishasura and Sumbha's ire. She is venerated as a Mother Goddess by her devotees. To reinforce her mother archetype, Shakta worshippers often include her 'so called' children around her. The narrative is that, every year Durga comes to her natal house on earth for a period of four days along with her children where she is pampered and tended to. This myth is prevalent in the eastern parts of India.

Though Durga in her manifestation as a warrior goddess epitomises the transgressive potential of the more domesticated and conventionally feminine Parvati or Uma, she is not a rebel. Durga is a traditionalist as she upholds the law of patriarchy and the supremacy of the devas. Rarely does she act on her own accord. She acts only when invoked. She uses her power but her sensibility is informed by the overarching ideology. Unlike Kali, she is clearly more a goddess of culture. This is especially clear through the myth of Sudarshana who is aided by Durga. In her Protector archetype, Durga helps the weaker of the two brothers because she is pleased with his devotion.

Clearly in Durga's scheme of things, it is not always the most powerful or the strongest who is the fittest, which is the governing law of nature. Her intervention especially as a result of her invocation suggests a cultural intervention. Thus Durga is an upholder of culture and tradition. This is reinforced in her act of returning the Vedas to the rishis. This is also reinforced through her assistance to Rama in his victory against Ravana since Rama is an upholder of tradition and cultural norms. Her rebelliousness as a non-Aryan mountain goddess of one of the little traditions, is turned into traditionalism which is explicit in her appearance as a married woman in all finery and in her introduction of herself as the wife of Shiva.

The myths that celebrate Durga say that she is a goddess difficult to appease. Her name too means someone who is impregnable or inaccessible. This could be a reference to her valour and could also refer to her grace. These contexts brings out the Assessor or Evaluator archetype in Durga. The numerous myths surrounding her devotees, all point to the extent to which she tests their devotion and sincerity. Sudarshana has been her devotee for years. She arrives only in the nick of time to save the prince. Similarly in case of Sachi, when the latter has exhausted all her options, Durga appears in front of her, in a vision, after innumerable prayers. In Rama's case too, she appears only when Rama is about to strike himself in the eye and make an offering of his eye to her.

Tracing Durga in Popular Culture

The mother, shape-shifter and warrior archetypes of Durga come together very convincingly in the character of Vidya Bagchi (Vidya Balan) in the 2012 mystery-thriller film *Kahaani*. In the film, a very pregnant Vidya Bagchi is in reality someone who has been deployed to work undercover to dig up the real people behind the poison-gas attack on Kolkata's metro rail which has led to numerous casualties, her husband an IB agent being one of them. Vidya uses her pregnant state to convince people and the audience that she is a desperate and helpless wife who has come to India looking for her missing husband Arnab Bagchi (Indraneil Sengupta).

The fact that she shows a photograph of a suspect in the terror attack, Milan Damji (Indraneil Sengupta), a rogue turned IB agent claiming him to be her missing husband alludes to the undercurrent of sexual tension between Durga and her adversaries, whether it is Mahishasura or Sumbha. Vidya's methodical tracking down of the elusive shape-shifting Milan Damji is akin to Durga's chase of Mahishasura in the mountainous terrain as he assumes different forms and tries to mislead her.

Just like Durga, Vidya works out a strategy to bring her adversary to her. She arrives from London to Kolkata as the fair Ambika arrives at the garden Nandana in the proximity of her target Sumbha and then devises a plan, laying out an elaborate trap to get him. The whole narrative of the film unfolds in the backdrop of the *Sharodiya Durga Puja* celebrations, the goddess serving as a recurring motif. Like Durga who fights in the interest of the devas, Vidya Bagchi works for the patriarchal state represented in the film by a retired IB (Intelligence Bureau) official and she is equipped by the state with a false identity, the guise of pregnancy and classified information on the terror attack suspects.

In the final face-off with Milan Damji, Vidya uses her Sudarshan Chakra. She throws him off guard by casting off her prosthetic belly and sticks her hairpin in Damji's neck killing him instantly even as the deafening music of Durga Puja celebrations is heard in the background against a blurred backdrop of the immersion procession of the goddess. Her job done, Vidya Bagchi disappears into being the nondescript entity she was just as the idol of the goddess Durga is immersed in the waters. In the end the audience comes to know that Vidya Bagchi is her pseudonym and, in fact, she is the widow of an IB agent Arup Basu who was killed in the poison-gas attack which caused her a miscarriage. Before leaving, Vidya hands over retrieved data which may have possible intel that can implicate more people to Inspector Rana (Parambrata Chatterjee) of Kolkata Police who has been helping her from the very start. This echoes the mythic situation of the battle

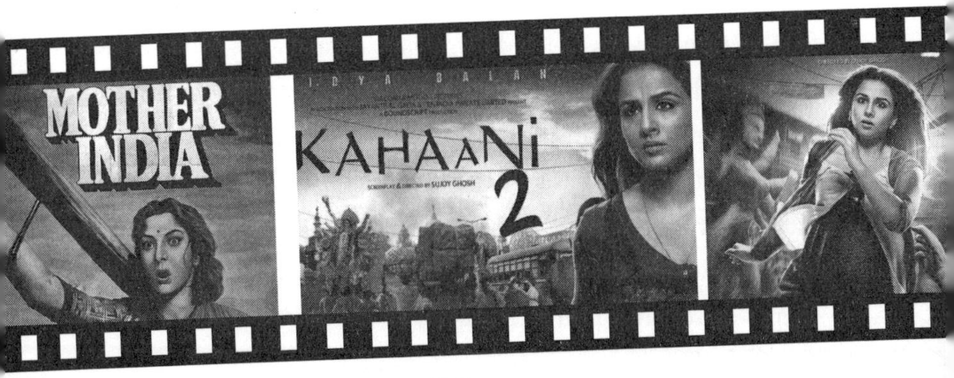

with Durgama, after which the goddess hands over the Vedas to the rishis for safekeeping.

In the 2016 mystery-thriller *Kahaani 2* different myths and archetypes of the goddess Durga are foregrounded through the female protagonist Durga Rani Singh (Vidya Balan). Just as in the myths, in the film too, Durga is fighting grave injustice and putting her life at peril to save a girl from a sexual predator who happens to be the little girl's own uncle. The film brings out the warrior, mother and shape-shifting aspects of the goddess through Durga. A foster mother to Minnie (Tunisha Sharma), Durga assumes an alias Vidya Sinha to protect the girl and lives under a different identity till she is tracked down by her adversary. She is aided in her clandestine fight by her former husband Inderjeet Singh (Arjun Rampal) who is a police inspector. With the law enforcement on her side, albeit surreptitiously, Durga manages to save Minnie from her abuser. It is a bloody fight and Durga bears war wounds just like the goddess.

An unforgettable and legendary on-screen Durga deeply entrenched in the popular cultural imagination is the character of Radha (Nargis) in the 1957 epic drama film *Mother India*. In the film Radha, in a Durga-like incarnation, shoots her own son Birju (Sunil Dutt) who has become wayward and now threatens to compromise the stability and peace of the village. Though he has a personal score to settle with Sukhilala (Kanhaiya Lal), a conniving moneylender who has given much grief to Radha when she was younger, Radha refuses to see Birju's act of murdering Sukhilala as retribution. She kills her son and in the process also rescues Sukhilala's daughter who Birju has kidnapped. Thus, Radha, through this difficult sacrifice, transcends the material and the personal to ensure cosmic stability in her universe which is also the goddess' responsibility.

The act of rescuing a younger and weaker woman is also reminiscent of Durga coming to Sachi's aid when the latter is distressed over Nahusha. Like in the myth, the underlying sexual tension between Radha and her adversary, her son Birju is apparent in its Oedipal manifestation in the character of Birju and his obsessive love for his mother, whose suffering has led him to become belligerent and vindictive. And also, in the extra mise en scen(ic) space where Sunil Dutt saves the life of Nargis on the sets of the film and goes on to marry her. In the film, Radha, as a mother has to transform into Durga the protector and destroyer of evil and slays her son to uphold the sanctity of the power and the position the village has conferred upon her.

Durga as a goddess is appealing, precisely because she does not violate the patriarchal status quo and instead fights to preserve the hegemonic order. A Durga-like character would be the lead female protagonist Poornima Amre (Priya Bapat) in the crime thriller web series, The *City of Dreams* (Season 1), streaming on Hotstar. Born to a politician who is the founder of his party, Poornima has always aspired to take after her father Amey Rao Gaikwad (Atul Kulkarni) and deserves to be his successor in every way but her father, who is a conservative and a traditionalist believes that women do not have what it takes to be a good politician. They do not have the nerve, the grit and the streak of ruthlessness and unscrupulousness which are qualities imperative for becoming a politician and retaining power.

Gaikwad says this to his daughter in so many words that though she is more deserving than her younger brother, it is only because of her inability to kill and safeguard her interests that she cannot be in politics. Poornima, who has been an obedient daughter and who has taken care to conceal her spark from her father and has always maintained a low profile, now assumes the persona of Durga and slays her own brother, the Mahishasura of the family, whose callous and reckless ways can not only jeopardise the goodwill the party enjoys but whose crimes if exposed can destroy the empire her father has built so painstakingly over the years.

Poornima thus proves her mettle on the basis of the patriarchal parameters and expectations articulated by her father, the highest patriarchal authority in her life. In her transition to Durga, Purnima is aided by men who either have a score to settle with her brother or who sincerely think that she will make a better leader. Her last exchange with

her father in the final episode of season one is evidence of the sophisticated strategist she is and clearly reflective of the fully formed goddess who has internalised patriarchal dictates and is ready to play by the rules of the game.

In the Tigmanshu Dhulia directed 2019 web series *Criminal Justice* (Season 1) streaming on Hotstar, glimpses of Durga can be found in the celebrated Supreme Court lawyer Mandira Mathur (Mita Vashisht) who takes up the case of a man Aditya Sharma (Vikrant Massey) accused of rape and murder, to represent the cab company he works for. Aditya is innocent but Mathur is not interested in the truth. She wants a narrative that stands the test of the court. Mathur is celebrated, highly acclaimed and respected because she plays by the rules of the game. She knows there is no point in having a humanitarian interest since cases cannot be won in that manner. In her very sorted out mind, she knows very clearly that law and justice are two entirely different things.

Fully armed with a formidable arsenal of counterarguments and minute details which the prosecution may have missed, Mathur is a strategist whose objective is to collapse every argument made by the public prosecutor. While she aims for a minimum sentence, Aditya wants to plead not guilty. Their interests clash as she realises that he is not playing the game as per the rules. Mathur leaves the case and this proves that she will not collaborate or empathise with someone who does not understand rules and procedures and moreover does not have regard for her superior wisdom and understanding of how the law works. She is an implementer of rules and does not go by her gut or instinct.

Mathur makes it very clear to Aditya when she is prepping him that the law is not interested in the truth. The defence will have a story and the prosecution will have another story and it is all about whose story sounds more convincing and is legally fool-proof. She believes in fighting a case as per prescriptive rules of the law and when she finds out that her junior assistant Nikhat Hussain (Anupriya Goenka) has subverted the law and influenced her client to plead not guilty, she leaves the case. Thus, we see over here a woman who is uncompromisingly loyal to the patriarchal institution of law that she represents and will wage a full-blown war only on the basis of rules espoused by that particular institution and who demands the same uncompromising loyalty to her ways from her subordinate and her client.

Films which show women police officers committed to the cause of destroying evil-mongers and criminals have female protagonists characterised on the lines of the goddess Durga. Examples would be the characters of Tejaswini (Vijayashanti) in the film by the same name, loosely based on real life Indian super-cop Kiran Bedi and Namrata (Rekha) in *Phool Bane Angaarey* (1991) or more recently Gunjan (Jahnvi Kapoor) in *Gunjan Saxena* (2020). These are extremely committed and valiant officers who are sometimes physically, sometimes mentally assaulted, and time and again put their lives on the line for the sake of duty but do not budge from their commitment to the job. They are honest representatives of the state. In *Phool Bane Angaarey*, Namrata actually transforms from a Parvati into a Durga after she loses her husband who is also a police officer.

The Mother, Strategist and Warrior archetypes of the goddess converge in the character of DCP Vartika Chaturvedi (Shefali Shah) in the 2019 Emmy award winning crime drama web series *Delhi Crime* streaming on Netflix, based on the true incident of the 2012 Delhi gang rape case. As a mother of a young woman, Vartika is biased and has a personal vendetta against the rapists but suppresses her personal rage to guarantee utmost safety to them when they are caught since she represents the police force. Here she represents the goddess who acts when invoked and only destroys who she is supposed to.

In the myth, Durga even says in so many words to both Mahishasura and Sumbha that she will destroy them since Amravati needs to go back to Indra. CO Saloni Bhatt (Gul Panag) of the Indian Army stationed in Kashmir and in charge of a special unit monitoring the activities of a Kashmiri militant in the action drama web series *The Family Man* (2019) streaming on Prime is another example of a Durga who goes by rules to neutralise the enemy. Despite being a Kashmiri, Bhatt is on the side of the Indian state which resonates with the goddess Durga's non-Aryan indigenous origin and her representation of the devas.

The 2016 social thriller film *Pink* has her lead female protagonist imagined on the lines of the goddess. Minal (Taapsee Pannu) escapes sexual assault and rape by attacking and seriously wounding her assaulter Rajveer Singh (Angad Bedi) who belongs to a prominent family of politicians. She displays the Warrior archetype of the goddess in resisting the threats that follow and even in taking a decision to file an FIR

(First Information Report) with the police. The plot makes it very clear, however, that if she wants a win, she cannot fight it alone. She is aided in this fight of hers by senior lawyer Deepak Sehgal (Amitabh Bachhan) who offers to help her. The case and the fight suddenly seem less futile and the whole debate of sexual consent acquires legitimacy in the idiom of the grand old patriarch and the veteran lawyer Deepak Sehgal. Minal, like the goddess, puts up a valiant front in the court of law and withstands the repeated attempts of her character assassination. But it is evident without the shadow of a doubt that her biggest weapon, her Sudarshan Chakra in this fight against her assaulter is her lawyer, the ultimate voice of patriarchal authority who commands the absolute respect of the court.

A similar delineation of a Durga-like character can be claimed in the 2016 Indian sports-drama biopic *Dangal,* loosely based on the Phogat sisters. Geeta Phogat (Fatima Sana Shaikh) is moulded into a formidable wrestler by her ambitious father Mahavir Singh Phogat (Aamir Khan) who wants to live his dream of becoming a world-class wrestler through his daughter. The war metaphors are transferred to the world of sports with the wrestling arena becoming the battlefield for Geeta. Geeta gets to the nationals with her father's training but then decides to follow her own mind and allows herself to be mentored by her coach. She begins to lose as her father apparently understands her strengths the best and the coach is just trying to distract her as he may have a personal vendetta against Geeta. Finally she starts following her father again and is able to win the world title. This narrative is clearly indicative of the coming into being of Durga as a powerful goddess who can overpower her adversary because she is the personification of the spiritual energy of the devas who are male powers and also carries weapons given by them. This also demonstrates Durga consistently upholding the superiority of patriarchy.

Geeta's subjectivity and agency is denied as she is solely controlled by her father and is the personification of her father's unbridled ambition. True, as a woman Geeta seems to be a model of transgressive femininity just like Durga because she engages in acts that are appropriate for men. But her action is validated and goes uncensored because it has the backing of the highest patriarchal authority in society for a single woman – her father. The anxiety over the physical appearance and behaviour of the transgressive feminine manifests in *Dangal* too just as it does in the myth. While the devi's wild side is revealed through her intoxication and loose hair, Geeta's rebellion against her father is symbolised by her act of growing her hair and watching Hindi movies at the academy. She refuses to go on accepting her father as her mentor as she finds his ways too prescriptive. However when she starts losing, she decides to give up her agency and autonomy and starts to identify once more as her father's daughter which will get her the medal just like Durga who introduces herself as Shiva's wife and champions the cause of the devas.

Panga (2020) in which a former female kabaddi player strives to revive her game and go back into the player mode and compete with others with the help and support of her husband and son and the biopic *Mary Kom* (2014) which shows Mary

Com's arduous journey and rise to fame as a boxer with the help of her coach (symbolic father), and her comeback into the game with the support of her husband and films like the ones mentioned above, reinforce the critical role of patriarchal support and sanction that validates the existence and actions of Durga-like women, their comeback and even their creation in the first place.

The warrior, strategist and shape-shifting aspects of Durga manifest through Rani Lakshmi Bai (Kangana Ranaut) in the 2019 period drama film *Manikarnika,* based on the legendary queen of Jhansi. From a grieving woman who has lost both her husband and her son to a horrible political conspiracy, Lakshmibai transforms into a strategist and a warrior transgressing norms of conventional femininity and normative widowhood. She plunges into a bloody battle with the British to save Jhansi, which is essentially her dead husband's legacy. She forges alliances and develops strategies so as to figure out the best possible way of vanquishing her adversaries. As queen of her subjects, she takes responsibility and, just like the goddess, does everything in her power to protect them. Her valour, her vision, her loyalty to the state and her selfless commitment to a cause much bigger than herself make her Durga-like.

An aspiring Durga can be seen in the character of Captain Shikha Sharma (Nimrat Kaur), in the Nagesh Kukunoor directed web series *The Test Case* (2020) streaming on AltBalaji, who has the resolve of a rock to weather all conditions and is determined at all costs to set the unprecedented record of being the first female combat officer of the Indian Army. Her assiduous journey is mostly about changing mindsets and preconceived notions of femininity and suppositions of what women can or cannot do. Her aim is to meet all expectations and parameters set by the training standards and qualify as a combat officer. In making the forces her career choice and wanting to be a combat officer, Shikha is very clearly spelling her action of embracing the highly-patriarchal ideology of war and the decree of the institution.

Unlike in the myth, this contemporary Durga's adversaries are in her own team – some highly misogynistic army officers who consider the army as an exclusively male space and whose speculations about women range from treating them as sexual objects to undermining their strength and resolve, based on an attitude that is informed by biological determinism and hence renders women as the weaker sex. Shikha even goes to the extent of denying her own sexuality when she chooses not to officially report that she was raped and brutally assaulted by a fellow officer during a very difficult phase of the training. While in the myth, neither Mahishasura nor Sumbha can even as much as touch Durga despite desiring her, in the series, Durga in the form of Shikha is humanised and the sexual tension and misogyny reach a culmination point in her rape. But Shikha is seen to transcend her humanness and acquire a strength and resolve of mythic proportions. Despite missing out critically on the training, she beats all her male competitors and even settles her scores with her rapist by overpowering him.

The shadow side of Durga is visible in characters who are anti-establishment and work against the interests of the state following the dictates and ideological stand of an organisation which functions like an alternate dark state. Veerender 'Veeran' (Tabu) in *Maachis,* the 1996 period political thriller directed by Gulzar, toes her fiancé Kripal's (Chandrachud Singh) line to join separatist groups and becomes a missile shooter. A disillusioned and distressed Kripal who has witnessed the brutal and reckless atrocities his friend and Veeran's brother Jaswant (Raj Zutshi) was subjected to at the hands of the Punjab police, crosses over to the other side to join militants. The men keep referring to some missile shooter who has been designated the important task of shooting a politician. It turns out to be Veerender. Like Durga, Veerender is specially endowed with an ability none of the men possess. She has been specially chosen for this mission and it is she and she alone who can neutralise the enemy.

In the 2003 action-thriller film *Jaal , The Trap*, the seductress and shape-shifting archetype of Durga is incorporated along with the Warrior and Strategist archetypes of the goddess in Neha Pandit (Tabu) who is actually Nusrat Rabbani, an undercover Kashmiri militant. Nusrat as Neha seduces an army officer's son Ajay Kaul (Sunny Deol) and gets married to him only to get leverage and use him as a pawn in the larger fight against the Indian nation state. She has no personal agenda but is one of the Kashmiri militants fighting against the state. Yet another example of the shadow Durga is Kaya (Kangana Ranaut), in the 2013 superhero film *Krish 3* ,who is a shape-shifting female mutant, the creation of Kaal (Vivek Oberoi) and serves as a hench(wo) man for him. She wages wars on his behalf and destroys people who can pose a threat to Kaal and his dark empire.

Teresa Lisbon (Robin Tunney) in the television series 2008-2015, *The Mentalist,* is a police officer who believes in following the legal route to nab a criminal. She is aided in her pursuit and in the journey of unravelling the crime by Patrick Jane (Simon Baker) or 'The Mentalist', a psychic who is the power behind her power. In the crime-comedy-drama series *Castle*, similarly, Inspector Kate Beckett (Stana Katic) of New York Police Department is aided sometimes with and sometimes without her knowledge by the speculative genius of her boyfriend/husband/ally Richard Castle (Nathan Fillion) who is a crime fiction writer and spends time with Beckett, observing her closely since the lead female protagonist of his novels is based on Beckett. Thus he is not only offering his power to Kate who is an astute follower of the law and does not encourage unlawful means of attaining information or getting to criminals, but he is also recreating and literally 'rewriting' her in the realm of fiction and in the process, immortalising and mythicising her through his fictionalised representation of her.

Humanising and Contemporarising Durga

Durga is someone who does not leave a job half finished. She is good at taking and executing orders on behalf of an institution. She will always have the best of all resources at her disposal and will also know the best means of using these resources. She is a sound planner and a meticulous execution of the job assigned to her is her strong point. She is also a competent delegator of tasks and responsibilities and knows exactly when to use what kind of human resource and how. She identifies the strengths of her aids, assistants or subordinates and allots and assigns duties accordingly. She is a multitasker and that rare woman who believes in accomplishing a task on her own but also invests in team work when required.

Durga is a woman who is loyal to the institution. She is rule-abiding and her actions are always in the best interests of the institution. Her flawless execution may be time-consuming at times but in the end her patience reaps rich results. She is usually always the last resort who can come to one's rescue. She is approached when all other roads are closed or inoperable since she has that special acumen of carving a way and coming up with a solution even when there seems to be apparently none.

Durga is usually a woman who appears rebellious but is extremely loyal. She might choose to be in a space and in a profession which is conventionally dominated by men. This is because, like the goddess Athena, she enjoys masculine pursuits. She does not get romantically or erotically involved. Outwardly she may seem reckless and ultramodern but deep inside she is a traditionalist, with unwavering faith in the world of norms and in institutions and their sovereignty. She usually enjoys high risk challenges that demand a show of intelligent planning and valiant combat. Therefore, it is very common to find women with the Durga archetype in the defence services, in politics, in the police force and in the legal arena.

If she is an IT professional, she will prefer to work in Intelligence or Secret Service. If she is a journalist she will prefer a field job to a desk or studio job. If she is a sportswoman, she will show an inclination for sports that are combative in nature. She might also excel at martial arts. If she is a professional, she will start with a dialogue with the explicit objective of negotiating but will not flinch when her confronter chooses a competitive and combative approach. She is a woman who is normally deployed by her institution to strongarm a negotiation. She is known for her impromptu tough calls.

A woman with the Durga archetype is fiercely competitive and fiercely protective too. She considers her subordinates and her colleagues to be her responsibility and often takes risks to safeguard their interests. She generally lets people be deceived by her traditionally feminine ways allowing herself to be undermined either as a temptress or a conservative. She waits for the right opportunity to confront her adversary or rival when she knows that she is bound to have the upper hand. She uses her strength strategically, not recklessly or unmindfully.

A Durga-like woman would like to project herself as a conventional figure even if she has a certain transgressive charge in her. She would like to announce her wins and is eager for more. She is also someone who bonds with her family when she is off duty and believes in quality family time. The woman with Durga in her, will have females as her confidantes and allies in a crisis. At the same time, the cause for which she is fighting may be gender-neutral. Men find the Durga woman highly dependable. In government organisations, she generally enjoys a high authoritative position and commands unanimous respect regardless of her gender.

A woman like Durga may be very difficult to approach and when approached, difficult to convince. But once she is convinced, there is no stopping her. She generally has a protective shell around her and people do not know the real person she is behind the shell. She hides her vulnerabilities well. She can appear feminine without appearing weak or submissive. She enjoys the grace and goodwill of her colleagues, her superiors and her seniors who are ready to bet their last buck on her loyalty and competence. This is because they know that even they can't accomplish what she can. Even if they begrudge her externally, inside they admire her deeply and even try to emulate her.

A Durga woman can be a hard taskmaster if she takes to training and mentoring juniors. She can put them through trying tests and observe them calmly battling extreme situations. She is someone who will take her trainees to the extreme to make them realise what it takes to win. She has tremendous integrity, and she believes in organisational ethics. She is a traditionalist and an 'innocent' who believes that a fair world can and must prevail and is someone who submits to grand narratives and institutional ethics. She is different with those she mentors and those she protects. She is stern towards her mentees but motherly towards her proteges or those who are under her care.

The Durga Archetype in Brands

The Durga archetype can be used to depict women with social capital, both on the personal and the professional fronts. She can be positioned in a traditional male role and a male space like a sports coach or a martial arts trainer, a fighter pilot or an officer of the law. The product can be a health drink, vitamin supplements, a cough syrup, an immunity booster, a brand of honey or tea and the narrative contextualised around the theme of invincibility and changing perceptions.

Durga can be brought out in a context that foregrounds her productive and goal-oriented attitude, or her strategist side in a firm. A brand of cosmetic, a planner or a handbag can be the products for this context. She can be even projected as a woman who loves and venerates her uniform or the office where she sits and which has given her power and respect. The focus can be on the sanctity of the institution, its permanence and the tradition it upholds. This context can be for products or brands that have been around for a long time and that are legendary names in themselves, bringing out their dependability.

A Durga woman can be shown leading a team of women after identifying their core competencies. Likewise she can be shown helping out male colleagues or a particular male colleague or her boss. She can be projected as involved in important decision-making. She can also be projected as a job applicant facing an all-male interview panel and getting selected for the job over male candidates because she has the best qualifications and on-field experiencc. The product can be some instant food or soup which gives her the time required to devote to these pursuits.

On the home front, she can be projected as a strong woman, who steps in to help her husband and his colleagues whenever they are in trouble. She could be shown as an IT professional or a freelancer working from home, who is an invaluable asset to her husband's colleagues when it comes to retrieving sensitive data or devising some sort of strategy. This could also mean displacing her from the kitchen, a traditional domestic space and reinstating her in a professional space within the household, thus acknowledging her other qualities and attributes that go beyond her homemaker identity.

Durga can also be projected as a more powerful woman helping out a less powerful woman especially if the latter is facing a threat of domestic, physical or sexual abuse. Here the Durga woman could be an activist, a social worker or a journalist. In these roles, she will be different from the woman with the Saraswati archetype and a predominant sage-like quality about her as the Durga woman believes more in hands-on experience and action on the field whereas the Saraswati woman is more likely to approach her problem intellectually. The product could be a detergent, a whitener, a fabric conditioner or even a toothpaste which foregrounds the immaculate and idealistic intent of the Durga woman.

Durga can also be projected as a former professional trying

to make a comeback with the help of her husband, son, father or mentor. The product could be something like a washing machine which is part of the support system at home which she needs in order to be able to dedicate time to her passion and her vocation. The simple machine can be operated by her husband. Other products following the same theme could be spices, a pressure cooker, a fridge, ready-to-cook, ready-to-eat packs, etc.

The Durga woman can also be constructed in a context where she is receiving a badge of honour, an award or a medal for outstanding achievement from superiors or the institution she is attached to. Here again the product can be a health drink, a sanitary napkin, a cosmetic product, or a brand of jewellery. While the latter two can be made to work around the theme of subtle embellishment or an accentuation of the personality, the former two can be on the lines of the woman's journey made easier with the help of the product. The Durga woman can be shown as disappearing and resurfacing after considerable lapses in time at times of crisis, keeping in synch with the shape-shifting aspect of the goddess in the myths surrounding her. This can be a metaphor for an emergency service, an insurance policy, a data card or a mobile phone.

Durga personifies a feminine principle which regards society and culture over the natural order and serves her best to ensure stability and peace in society. Her crusade is against those out to disrupt the social order. Endowed with liminal qualities that situate her on the peripheries of civilisation, she is gradually mainstreamed, emblematising the heroine's journey to self-actualisation and veneration. At one level, she can be seen as the cumulative power of the male gods. At another level, Durga symbolises the return of that primary feminine divinity which was forcibly effaced by subsequent theological orders. Durga transgresses many social dictates representative of the Aryan way of life and at the same time she also symbolises true feminine potential and power which can both create and destroy in order to stabilise.

SATI: THE GODDESS WHO REBELLED

THERE IS SOMETHING feline about her. Her hair raises to an end when she senses something amiss. And she has the uncanny knack of sensing very clearly when things *are* amiss, except when she has let down her defences. She is quick on her feet and fast as the wind. Her mind races at a speed inconceivable for lesser mortals. There are things she does and things she says that are frowned upon by others – people older than her, superior to her. It leaves them worried, sometimes displeased. And yet she holds on to her ideas and her beliefs sullenly, like a stubborn child. Her faith in herself is unshakeable. And she has good reason to trust her gut more than anything else in her life for it has never let her down. Her gut is what has saved her, not once, not twice but multiple times in life-and-death situations. When she knows, she just knows. And yet, apparently she goes wrong. Or at least others seem to believe so and tell her so, berating her that makes her cringe and cry. And that breaks her. Something snaps inside her leading her to doubt every move, every step, every call she has made. Till she has to let it all out in an agonised scream, 'I was never so sure and never so wrong'. Only to later realise that she had been right, bang on, all along. She hadn't missed it. She had merely succumbed to the pressure she was under, to admit she was wrong. And now she glows. Knowing she was right. Her gut was right. *They* had been wrong. *They* had not seen what *she* had.

It isn't easy for her. The right-wrong business. Trying to tell others, bring them up to speed with all that her mind seems to be able to figure out and fathom in no time. Yet, she is painstakingly patient and slow and keeps waiting for the laggards to catch up with her. Anyone bossing over her all the time and trying to keep her under vigil makes her uncomfortable and implies she is wrong or even if she isn't, implies something is not right and is bound to go wrong. Till it does and the cycle repeats. And yet again she is up for a fight. Yet again, they try to break her. Yet again, she finds herself all alone fighting a solitary battle. Yet again, it is *she* versus the rest.

She is Carrie Mathison (Claire Danes), the protagonist of the American thriller series *Homeland* which bagged the Primetime Emmy Award for Outstanding Lead Actress in a Drama Series and Golden Globe Award for Best Actress – Television Series Drama among many others. Mathison, every bit of the bristling protagonist embodying the predicament and the rage of the mythological Sati, always called forth by the people she loves the most, to defend and justify her decisions,

up against the invincible authority of the patriarchal state, undermined for her uncommon insight and humiliated for that which is laudable in her till she snaps and decides to leave a trail of death and destruction in her wake.

The Myths of Sati

The *Devi Bhagavatam* gives an interesting account of the origin of Sati. It is said that once Shiva and Vishnu engaged in a terrible battle with the danavas which lasted thousands of years. Finally, they were able to vanquish the danavas and returned jubilant. The two were full of the pride of the military conquest. Seeing them thus bloated with pride, Gauri and Lakshmi started laughing softly, for it was actually their shakti infused in their husbands' beings that had enabled Hari and Hara to win. The gods however, in denial or feigning ignorance of this contribution, berated their wives and were abusive towards them. At this, the parashaktis Gauri and Lakshmi, sensitive to this insult, left their husbands. The moment their shaktis left them, the gods became dull and lacklustre. They felt drained of power and might.

With the shaktis having left, disaster struck the earth and sent everyone in a quandary. Brahma, already overburdened with the task of Creation, now had the additional responsibilities of Shiva and Vishnu. He called his sons and asked them to organise a yajna and observe rituals to appease parashakti. Daksha, who was one of Brahma's sons born out of his right toe, took to religiously uttering the bija mantra of the goddess for thousands of years till finally the devi Bhagavati appeared before him and blessed him. At Daksha's request she agreed to be born to him and his wife Aksini as their daughter Sati who would grow up to marry Rudra or Shiva.

In due course, Sati was born in the house of the illustrious and prosperous king Daksha Prajapati. Right from an early age, it was evident that she was emotionally and spiritually invested in Shiva and that she would grow up to marry him. When the time came, Sati and Shiva were reunited but with certain forebodings. Different myths have different versions to offer. According to some versions, Daksha who is extremely fond of his daughter is reluctant to marry her off to the hermit Shiva whose lifestyle he is not particularly pleased with. In other versions, Daksha has a change of heart and goes from being a devotee of Shiva to hating Shiva after the latter beheads the fifth head of his father Brahma. In still other versions, it is said that Daksha marries off Sati to Shiva but without proper observation of rituals and failing to worship and appease the required planets. The marriage is solemnised in a haste leaving Daksha unsatisfied with the way things have gone and so he becomes belligerent towards Shiva for taking his beloved daughter from him.

It is said that Daksha is particularly incensed when once he goes to attend a yajna, and Shiva and Sati who are also attending the same yajna do not pay their respects to him. This is because they have come to attend the yajna as divine beings and not as Daksha's daughter and son-in-law. However, an arrogant Daksha insults Shiva to his face, calling him an aberration and regretting the day he married off his daughter to an outlaw like him. He makes especially incisive comments on Shiva's uncivilised appearance, the bad company he keeps and his wild lifestyle. Daksha is brought to book by Nandishwara but seething with humiliation, Daksha decides to hold a yajna of his own and in order to avenge his insult, he invites everyone who are part of the Vedic Brahminical political economy – the devas, the rishis, the munis, the gandharvas, the brahmanas, the siddhas, all except for Shiva and Sati. It is a glorious affair and Sati, all too curious and a little offended, decides to attend the yajna intending to get her father to explain his action of not inviting Shiva.

Sati arrives at the yajna and on asking Daksha, is appalled, as Daksha, in a full hall, starts hurling insult after insult at Shiva accusing him of perverse behaviour, an outlandish and scary appearance and loathsome company. Infuriated beyond words, Sati lashes out at her father and at all the people present attending a yajna which is not graced by Shiva. Promising to destroy the yajna, Sati uses her yogic powers and immolates herself in front of her father's very eyes. Everyone present is distressed at this tragic turn of events but the worst is yet to come. When news of Sati's immolation reaches Shiva, he turns mad and violent with grief and begins his tandava nritya or dance of destruction, wreaking havoc in all three worlds. He breaks a lock of his hair and thrashes it on the ground out of which erupt Virbhadra, a dark form of Shiva and Bhadrakali, a dark form of Shakti. The two reach Daksha's yajna and destroy it beyond reparation. Everyone present is killed and Daksha himself beheaded.

Shiva arrives at the spot and picks up Sati's charred body. In his grief and rage he takes off with her body roaming wildly across the length and breadth of the land. The *Devi Bhagavatam* says that Shiva collects Sati's ashes and wears a garland of her bones and wanders deliriously. Wherever Sati's ashes fall, it becomes a holy place. In another myth, in order to stop Shiva's dance of destruction, Vishnu uses his Sudarshan Chakra to decimate Sati's body parts, which fall at different locations as Shiva is on the rampage, each becoming a holy site or a shakti-pitha. With Sati's body gone, Shiva finally calms down, restores everyone to life and even brings back Daksha to life by giving him a goat's head. Shiva will now immerse himself in a deep trance to allay his grief and will remain in that meditative state for several thousand years till Sati is reborn to the mountain king Himavat and Mena as Parvati, and is married to Shiva.

It is said that Sati is so angry at her father when he starts making humiliating remarks about Shiva that her wrath and fury take the form of Kali. In another myth, she splits herself into the dreadful Mahavidyas who then destroy Daksha's yajna.

Just before she immolates herself, Sati vows to come back and expresses her desire to be born of a father who she can love, who will respect her wishes and who will bow down to Shiva.

Analysing Sati in the Light of the Myth

According to the *Vishnu Purana* and the *Padma Purana*, Daksha has 24 daughters while the *Matsya Purana* says that he has 62 daughters of which one is Sati. The *Brihat Samhita* gives an account of the shakti-pithas, each corresponding to a fallen body part of the goddess. The episode of Sati features very prominently in the *Devi Bhagavatam*. What is interesting is Daksha's initial acquiescence to marry his daughter off to Shiva followed by his gradually increasing disdain for the latter. Sati's myth is symbolic of a father and a daughter's mutual rejection of each other. This rejection has larger symbolic and ideological implications. In choosing Shiva as her husband against her father's wishes, Sati is rejecting the worldview and the practising ideology of Daksha. In rejecting Shiva as a son-in-law, Daksha likewise is making his oppositional stand very clear. Interestingly, Shiva's initial reaction to Daksha's attempts to humiliate him is indifference followed by wrath and then forgiveness.

Sati can be conflated with the Indian sub-continent since her body parts are strewn across the continent. The number of body parts and consequently the shakti-pithas range between four and 110 as per accounts and descriptions in different Puranas. Studied observations by scholars suggest that the myth of Sati enables entire regions of the Indian sub-continent to be sacralised and Hinduised. The expanse the myth covers, not only comprises the length and the breadth of the present-day Indian nation state but also Pakistan, Nepal, Bangladesh, parts of China, Tibet and Sri Lanka. Understandably, there is a concentration of pithas in the Eastern part of India which also emerged as a hub of the Shakta line of worship in medieval times.

The shakti-pithas, which are today woven in the myth of Sati, could very well have been indigenous and regional places of worship of feminine power which were subsequently assimilated in the Hindu Brahmanical pantheon through the myth of Sati. For instance, the yoni of Sati as per the myth, is believed to have fallen in Kamarupa in Assam. David Kinsley points out that although the worship of the feminine principle or Shakti in this part of India is an ancient phenomenon, the worship of the divine feminine as the yoni or the genitals of Sati is not older than sixteenth century. In fact, in the seventeenth century, the ruling Ahom dynasty of Assam encouraged the worship of Kamakhya or Kamarupa as a shakti-pitha, which gave this religious place a pan-India popularity.

The Sati myth is also symbolic of a lot of other religious transitions that may have been taking place historically. Daksha and his yajna stand for the old Vedic way of life and a theological practice that propounded rituals and sacrifice and that was premised on an economy and logic of exchange. The host of the yajna made sacrificial offerings and in return was blessed with material prosperity and power. With the growing popularity of heterodoxic faiths like Buddhism and Jainism, however, that were premised on a theology of detachment, non-violence and truth, Vedic ritualistic Brahmanism gave way to Puranic devotion. Shiva's agency and role in destroying Daksha's yajna is thus symbolic of the displacement of one kind of religious economy and its replacement by another.

While Daksha is a king, Shiva is a hermit. Daksha symbolises attachment, Shiva detachment. Daksha is rooted in materiality, Shiva has transcended materiality and is rooted in spirituality and asceticism. To add to this is the episode of Brahma's beheading by Shiva because of the former's incestuous advances towards Saraswati or Shatarupa, varying in different versions of the Puranas. Brahma is the iconic god of Vedic ritual and sacrifice, and Shiva's act of beheading him and then Veerbhadra's act of beheading Daksha seem to reinforce the same message – the old Vedic way and its patron deities and practitioners need to go and be replaced by a new theology.

Also implicit in the myth is the corrupt mindset of both Brahma and his son Daksha, pointing to the self-fulfilling Vedic economy. However, the Vedic way cannot be effaced completely and therefore Brahma loses only one head and as penitence is known to incessantly chant the four Vedas from the four mouths of his remaining four heads. Whenever an unpleasant act of obliterating a canonical deity or figure needs to be carried out, Shiva and Vishnu need to transform into another entity. Hence we have Shiva as Bhairava decapitating Brahma's head and Shiva as Veerbhadra decapitating Daksha's head. Shiva is also not completely absolved of the act he has committed and therefore as Bhairava, is stuck with Brahma's severed head in his hand. As Veerbhadra, he kills Daksha and as Shiva he brings Daksha back to life by fitting the sacrificial goat's head on the body of Daksha. The sacrificed and the sacrificer thus become one. Daksha's penance following the destruction of the Daksha yajna and his devotion towards Shiva are also symbolic of the acceptance of the superiority of this new philosophy and the path of devotion rather than the path of ritual.

All of this is orchestrated or brought about by Sati, the personification of adiparashakti or the ultimate feminine power. This, read historically and symbolically, means that the Puranic devotional philosophy has the approval of Shakti or the feminine power. At the same time, it also retains its patriarchal ideology by having the personification of Shakti advocate and champion the new tradition symbolised by Shiva and acknowledge Shiva as the supreme deity. This is an interesting transition as Puranic myths repeatedly reinforce and reiterate the superiority of Shiva and Vishnu over the Vedic gods Indra, Agni, Varun and the like. The Sati myth besides, also brings together the sometimes conflicting traditions of Shaktism and Shaivism.

While some myths say that Sati's body parts fell on their own since they were badly charred when Shiva was carrying her corpse flung over his shoulders, other myths say that Vishnu himself either entered Sati's corpse through yogic powers and sliced it from inside or decimated her with his Sudarshan Chakra to stop Shiva from destroying Creation. The Bible has an episode that is somewhat similar to the episode of Sati's decimation. In the Biblical narrative, there is an episode in which a Levite (a man from a priestly class in Israel) is bringing back his concubine from her father's house. On the way they halt at the Benjaminite city of Gibeah in the house of an old man who is kind enough to give them food and shelter for the night. The men of the city, however, want to sodomise the Levite. At this, his host proposes to hand over his daughter and the Levite's concubine to the unruly mob that is threatening to break down the door of his house. The mob, however, does not relent and the Levite hands over his concubine to the violent mob who rape her all night till she dies. In the morning, when the mob has left, the Levite opens the door to find the badly mutilated body of his concubine. He then dismembers her body parts and hands over each part to each tribe of Israel and all the tribes collectively promise to wage a war against the Benjaminites and to never give their daughters in marriage to the sons of Benjamin.

While in the Puranic narratives, the woman is elevated to the status of a goddess and exercises her own agency to destroy herself, in the Biblical narrative, the woman is denied a subject status and agency (in fact even her name remains unknown) and is handed over as commodity by the Levite to a barbaric crowd that pounces on her like scavenging beasts. In both cases, however, it is the woman who perishes and is the locus centre of a bloody massacre. It is her body which is the site of violence and mutilation. She is at the centre of clashing ideologies and warring clans. It is her mutilated and mangled body that makes a statement and becomes the pretext to trigger further violence between two factions or communities that have perhaps been bristling and waiting for a pretext to go to war. And it is her body that is rendered vulnerable and easily violable to groups with antithetical or competing beliefs and intentions.

Sati and Her Archetypes

Sati symbolises the strong, committed married woman who is by her husband's side no matter what. She essays independence of spirit in choosing an outlaw for a husband and great courage and resolve in marrying him against her father's wishes. In this she is the archetypal Rebel and in marrying Shiv and displacing herself from the palace and beginning her cohabitation with him, she becomes the archetypal Outlaw herself.

Sati depicts strong aspects of the Princess archetype which is evident when she anticipates that she will receive the same attention in her father's house despite marrying against his wishes as she did, before she was married. In this sense, she is also a traditionalist with visible traits of the archetype of the Innocent who presumes the world to come clean with them. She chooses to attend her father's yajna more out of a need to question him about not inviting her husband than out of a desire to be a part of a divine ceremony. This act of hers suggests that she believes she has a right in her father's house and a right over her father, contrary to orthodox Hindu belief in which the daughter is always regarded as parkiya or belonging to another and a guest in her natal home, who will eventually leave and therefore has no lawful right or say over matters as such, either over the house or over its inmates. It perhaps also suggests the liberal upbringing she may have had. It is as a result of her upbringing that Sati not only makes a decision but also carries it through without any qualms or apprehensions.

Sati epitomises tenacity, resolve and will and her unwavering love for her husband. She gives up her life to safeguard his name.

This is a discomforting thought and it will find manifestations time and again throughout history where women will be indoctrinated with the myth of Sati, her sacrifice and how she privileged her husband's name and honour over her own life and sacrificed herself to prove her point. Sati, through this act of hers, wears the Martyr archetype. A martyr is willing to die for a cause which they consider much bigger, much greater than them.

Sati also has the archetype of the shape-shifter even as she proclaims to be reborn to a father she can love and respect. In this, she reminds one of Vedavati in several versions of the Ramayana, who just before she offers herself to the fire god, promises to be back for her revenge and is believed to be reborn as Sita. Sati is vocal and does not believe in keeping her views to herself. She castigates the people present at the yajna for attending it, knowing fully well that Shiva has not been invited. If Shiva symbolises an ideology and a theological tradition looking for acceptance, then Sati and her incandescent rhetoric can be seen in the light of her Advocate and Activist archetypes which stand fully activated in making a very strong case of this tradition.

In many ways Sati has many of the characteristics of the archetypal wife but those that are markedly different from a Sita. Sati is more Hera-like than Sita-like as a wife. Like the Greek goddess of marriage and conjugality, Sati is belligerent and fierce in her defence when it comes to her husband. She is rebellious and incisive in her verbal attack. She reacts to a crisis with rage rather than depression like Demeter or silent fortitude like Sita. She is tempestuous and simply cannot tolerate an assault on her husband. For her, marriage is the most important institution of all and she primes this relation over all others. So, though she is a non-conformist in many ways, she is perfectly traditional when it comes to her marriage and accepts her complementary role as a wife to a powerful god. At a more symbolic level, Sati is a woman who believes entirely in the sacredness of her marriage. Even if it is the entire world against her, she does not waver, she does not flinch, she never has any second thoughts about her marriage and she is ready to assail anyone who attacks her.

She is also a daughter deeply disappointed in her father who has let her down. It is perhaps this disappointment that leads her to take such an extreme step to make a point, making it clear that she may have been a 'father's daughter'. More than her sacrifice is also her final rejection of her father and her desire to be born to a father who will see *her* point of view. This could probably be a woman's appeal to patriarchy to see her point of view. It could be read as an act of rebellion resulting out of a father's refusal to grant autonomy to his daughter, to let her make decisions or to see reason in her actions. It could also be read as a father's tendency to infantilise the daughter and presume that she is incapable of taking the right decision.

In a society permeated by patriarchy, it can be seen as the tendency of patriarchal institutions to often dismiss decisions taken or opinions and observations given by women. This is manifested in the episode of the infamous debate between Yajnavalka and Gargi in the court of Janaka, the king of Mithila, where Gargi had to withdraw from the debate as she was threatened that if she went on, she could be beheaded. In Victorian times, it was standard to imply that women were animalistic and emotional beings incapable of logical and rational thought and therefore could not be taken seriously. In contemporary times, it would mean implying that women think not with their heads but their hearts and actually establishing a hierarchy of head over heart. This discourse is very common in the armed forces, in law enforcement agencies, where women are usually not seen as capable for combative positions and in the field of teaching, manifesting as a positive bias where it is implied that women make better teachers because they have a high emotional quotient. In Western hegemonic discourses, women have always been associated with feeling and men with logic and reason.

Sati's disappointment in her father has echoes of Iphigenia's disappointment in her father Agamemnon in Greek mythology when the latter conspires to sacrifice his daughter to please the gods so that his ships can set off for Troy. Though Daksha does not conspire to kill Sati, his actions eventually lead to Sati taking her own life.

Tracing Sati in Popular Culture

There are many works in popular culture that reflect a replication of several of the archetypal situations and crises in the myth of Sati. The love of Sati, the daughter of a king, for a hermit and a recluse like Shiva has manifestations in the rich-girl-poor-boy love story and the love story of the girl falling for the outlaw with a good heart. The former is the theme of films like *Phir Wohi Dil Laya Hoon* (1963), *Kala Patthar* (1979), *Coolie* (1983), *Betaab* (1983), *Chameli ki Shaadi* (1986), *Mr. India* (1987), *Saajan* (1991), *Andaz Apna Apna* (1994), *Lagaan: Once Upon a Time in India* (2001), *3 Idiots* (2009), *Mirzya* (2016) and *Gully Boy* (2019) to name just a few.

In *Lagaan*, it is the rich English woman falling in love with the poor villager, in *Gully Boy*, both women who fall in love with Murad (Ranveer Singh), the underdog, belong to a socially superior class. A feisty representation of a Sati-like character with a dominant Princess archetype is that of Chameli (Amrita Singh) in *Chamel ki Shaadi* who exercises her agency very strongly in making advances towards the man she loves and then puts up a fight to marry him, much against her parent's wishes. The class anxiety underlying the rich-girl-poor-boy love story is brought out in a lighter vein in the Hrishikesh Mukherjee film *Chupke Chupke* (1975) where a married Sulekha (Sharmila Tagore) pretends to be in love with her driver much to the consternation of her family members. All ends well as it is a prank she is playing along with her husband who is impersonating as a driver.

A film that plays out the archetypal clash of Shiva and Daksha's opposing ideologies with Sati caught in between, is the enormously popular 1.33 billion grosser *Gadar Ek Prem Katha* (2001), a project in muscle-flexing and jingoistic nationalism set in the context of the partition of India. A fanatic, headstrong, bloodthirsty Pakistani father-in-law Ashraf Ali (Amrish Puri) who also is inadvertently representative of the state of Paksitan as Daksha, is completely discredited, demonised and pathologised. He resorts to immature and absurd ploys which turns his well-meaning Sikh trucker son-in-law Tara Singh's (Sunny Deol) Shiva-like benign indifference to wrath.

In classic Shiva style, Tara begins his dance of destruction depicting superhuman strength by uprooting a hand pump and single-handedly overthrowing whoever comes his way as he escapes with a live Sati, his Muslim wife and the daughter of Ashraf Ali, Sakeena (Amisha Patel) and his son. Sakeena, who was saved by Tara during the Hindu-Muslim riots of the Partition, has been married to him for several years and visits her parents in Pakistan for a reunion, only to find out that they are conspiring never to send her back to India, in other words to her husband. Most of the agency is given to the onscreen Tara-Shiva and his masculine prowess as Sati's powers are undermined and reduced to a feeble verbal protest unlike her titanic rage in the myth. Just like in the myth, in the film too, the father-in-law finally has to bow down and acknowledge the greatness and magnitude of heart of the son-in-law. In literature, the ideological clash and hostile exchange between the culturally and racially 'superior' father-in-law

and the 'inferior' son-in-law where the former feels betrayed by his daughter resonates very deeply in the Shakespearean tragedy Othello.

The girl falling in love with the outlaw against parental wishes, or the will of patriarchal institutions and authorities that define and govern her life, is visible in the narratives of films like *Pyaasa* (1957), *Kaagaz Ke Phool* (1959), *Mujhe Jeene Do* (1963), *Zanjeer* (1973), *Deewar* (1975), *Kalia* (1981), *Satte pe Satta* (1982), *Hero* (1983), *Arjun* (1985), *Agneepath* (1990), *Highway* (2014), and *Kalank* (2019). While in most of the films, the hero is an outlaw in the eyes of society, either because he is on the wrong side of the law or because he is an illegitimate child, in *Pyaasa* and *Kaagaz ke Phool*, the hero embodies the Struggling Artist archetype whose ideological beliefs place him outside normative society. Most of these films focus more on the Outlaw archetype and the transgressive nature of the love that blossoms or the outlaw love story embedded as a sub-plot in a larger plot, thus disabling the agency of the Sati archetype.

The spy thriller television series *Homeland* streaming on Hotstar resonates the archetypal qualities of Sati through the character of the lead female protagonist. *Homeland* centres around a CIA agent Carrie Mathison who plays more than a key role in tracking down and neutralising most dreaded and wanted terrorists and terror outfits or rival spies that are a threat to national security. Despite her unparalleled work in the organisation, she is always under the radar and her own colleagues find it difficult to believe her 'hunches'. It is her intuitive abilities and her uncanny knack of reading between lines that finally get her to her adversaries or even have her initial suspicion (Seasons 1&2) on a war hero Nicholas Brody (Damien Lewis) who she suspects has been turned during his captivity and is working for an al-Qaeeda commander Abu Nazir (Navid Negahban). But the organisation has little patience for intuitions and unorthodox means of arriving at the truth.

There is also a systematic and a categorical undermining of agents like Saul Berenson (Mandy Patinkin) and Carrie Mathison who are more human than others and refrain from objectifying 'terrorists'. They are termed as 'soft' and unfit for the CIA, with various charges brought against them because they fail to show the objectivity and ruthlessness supposedly needed of agents. In other words, the implication is that they use their hearts and not their heads. And yet, it is these agents with their definitive feminine qualities like their deep intuitive abilities, their empathetic approach and their tendency to humanise 'the other', that are able to strike a dialogue with the other side and get valuable intelligence and even pre-empt and thwart attacks on the United States.

Carrie is wedded to her job as an intelligence agent but the agency, a highly patriarchal institution, is more like a hostile father-figure who undermines his daughter's competence and judgement. Time and again she falls out of favour. She is kept on a tight leash and her expertise and intel is used whenever required. The research on Abu Nazir which she painstakingly undertakes is undermined and she hardly ever gets full credit for busting plans of terrorist attacks on American soil. She is labelled as emotionally unstable and thus highly unreliable.

She serves a utilitarian function at the agency. She is repeatedly used and discarded. Interestingly she is the only significant woman agent in an all-male space. Like Sati however, Carrie is absolutely sure of her hunches and the moves she makes accordingly, which earns her not just the wrath of the director of the CIA but also costs her, her job. Even after being solely instrumental in neutralising Abu Nazir, she is uncertain whether she will get her job back at the agency.

Carrie displays yet another quality of Sati by falling in love with Sergeant-turned-Congressman Nicholas Brody who is technically an outlaw. Brody is a war hero who was held in captivity for eight years by Abu Nazir till freed by American soldiers in Iraq. What no one knows however is that Brody is working for Abu Nazir. In fact it is only Carrie who believes that and is able to track down his movements and then turn him from working for Abu Nazir to working for the CIA. She falls in love with this deeply wounded man who carries emotional and physical scars but in the end Brody is someone who has worked against the interests of the nation state and is therefore an outlaw. He stands for an alternative ethics which questions the legitimacy of the violence of war and the strong-arm tactics of America in the Middle East which cannot be in the best interest of the nation and loving him also means, for Carrie, accepting this alternative ethics and ideology.

Since popular culture stands mostly informed by patriarchal sensibility, most of the films that replicate or reflect the Sati myth focus on Shiva more than Sati. An interesting echo of Shiva's revenge following Sati's death is to be found in the action thriller film *Ghajini* (2008) which has a man suffering from anterograde amnesia laying a meticulous and elaborate assassination plot to avenge the brutal murder of the woman he loved. Another replication of the myth would be the plot of *Hostages* (Season 1) streaming on Hotstar which has shades of the revenge story of Shiva embedded as a sub-plot. SP Prithvi Singh (Ronit Roy) wants to save his dying wife who is in need of a bone marrow transplant for which he plans to kidnap his wife's father who happens to be the Chief Minister of the State and has no knowledge of this daughter that he has, since she is born of a woman he raped many years ago. The wife is strategically voiceless and it is the Shiva-like Prithvi, occupying the liminal space of an officer of law enforcement and an outlaw, who has to settle the score with his corrupt father-in-law and right the wrong the latter has done.

Sati's defiance of her father/natal family and the patriarchal institutions he/it represents followed by the role of the father/institution in the daughter's misery and doom reflects in the 2016 Marathi film *Sairaat*, its Hindi remake *Dhadak* (2018), and much earlier, in films like Maniratnam's *Bombay* (1995) with intersecting tensions of caste, class, community and religion. In *Sairaat* the tension results out of an upper caste Hindu girl's transgressive love for a Dalit boy in a small town in Maharashtra whereas in *Dhadak,* the story is recontextualised to a Rajasthani setting and the difference is essentially a class difference. Both plots are based on honour killing of couples or sometimes one of the two, by families which deliver a kind of barbaric justice to their own daughter for her transgressive behaviour of falling in love with someone outside her caste, class, community or religion.

In Maniratnam's *Bombay* too, the film starts with this initial tension sparked by transgressive love between a Hindu man and a Muslim woman with severe opposition from both families. This however is part of a larger socio-political context and the union of the lovers does not end in doom the way it does in the other films. The subject of honour killing and the patriarchal family's single-minded obsession to save its honour by killing the transgressing couple is broached in the films *Love, Sex and Dhokha* (2010) and *NH10* (2015).

A film that allows Sati the agency to decide her fate is Sanjay Leela Bhansali's *Padmavat* (2018) which has the queen of Chittor, Padmavati (Deepika Padukone) initiating johar or a mass immolation with thousands of women offering themselves to the fire in order to safeguard their honour. The filmic depiction glorifies and mythicises the act of johar which is a historical truth. Women across India, especially from warrior clans through history, have been known to perform johar when their husbands were slain on the battlefield and it was certain that their side would lose. This was done with the intention of undermining the attempts of the marauding troops and the invading enemies who would soon lay claim on the women and ravage and exploit them in any which way they wanted. Just like the mythical Sati's body became the site of contesting ideologies, the fact remains that when wars are fought, land territorialised and borders of nation states drawn, it is the bodies of women, like land that become the site of extreme violence, the locus centre of conquest and victory and bear inscriptions of barbaric acts. It is these bodies, dead, alive or possessed that become markers of victory, defeat or surrender.

Veer Zaara (2004) is another film that allows some extent of agency to the Sati archetype depicted in a Pakistani national Zaara Hayat Khan (Preiti Zinta). She is in love with an Indian who in the eyes of the Pakistani state is an outlaw and indeed is relegated to the status of an outlaw when he visits Zaara in Pakistan. Zaara breaks her promise to her father to marry the man of his choice and instead chooses to come to India and settles down in Veer's village. Sati's anger is toned down in Zaara but the resolve is the same. Instead of choosing a high profile life in Pakistan, Zaara chooses to lead a nondescript existence in a small village in Punjab in India. Like Sati, she shuns her natal family, choosing a period of tapa for the man she loves.

The *Devi Bhagavatam* episode of the victory over the Halahalas and the role of the Shaktis in the military conquest of their husbands winning them glory in all three worlds echoes in the 2020 release *Saand ki Aankh* based on the true story of

Shooter Dadi and Revolver Dadi, two women from rural Uttar Pradesh who defied the primitive patriarchal village norms to become shooting champions well past their prime when they were in their mid-60s. Chandro Tomar (Bhumi Pednekar) and Prakashi Tomar (Tapsee Pannu) are these two elderly women who become sharp-shooters, win many national championships and in fact, ironically it is their feats and remarkable achievements that place their small nondescript village in Uttar Pradesh on the global map. At one point, one of the women even says, that outside their village, their husbands are known by their names – the names of their wives who are national shooting champions – thus implying that it is their feminine shakti that infuses the names of their husbands with glory and fame.

Humanising Sati

Sati's anger is directed inwards rather than outwards and in this she differs from Kali. Nonetheless, she has several archetypal commonalities with the Great Goddess. But the question which should be raised is – Being a personification of adiparashakti why does Sati leave the path of exemplary behaviour and take an extreme step like self-immolation? One reason could be that since she is the quintessential parashakti, rage is her predominant quality and she is consistent with her archetype when angered by her father's repeated assaults on Shiva, she chooses to immolate herself knowing fully well the repercussions her death will have.

Sati's act is symbolic of a woman's rebellion against her natal family and its patriarchal authority which fails to acknowledge or respect her decision. Marxist philosopher Louis Althusser and Black feminist writer and activist Bell Hooks, both have observed in their works that the family is the first ideological apparatus that conditions the individual's actions and is responsible for the social construction of identity, especially normative femininity and masculinity. Sati is any woman who takes an initiative to act on a decision and go to any extent to see it through, against every possible odd.

Sati is an independent decision-maker and can face and counter challenges very well. She is a woman who is deeply intuitive and trusts her instincts to tell her what she needs to do. She is also a woman who privileges the institution of marriage to a point where she considers it almost sacred. Sati is also someone who seeks spiritual fulfilment in her marriage. For her this one relationship is much more important than all the other relationships she may have in her life. She is a woman who is capable of extremes of emotional conduct and will go to any extent to safeguard and defend her marriage.

Sati is a woman who is stubborn and hard to convince or dissuade once she has made up her mind. This woman seldom looks back or has any regrets over the choices she has made and the steps she has taken to implement what she has decided. She is a woman who is ready to rough it out. Sati is an incurable idealist and a romantic who could be a little removed from reality. Her projection of her future is picture-perfect and she strives very hard to make it so. She is someone who can be unbelievably and almost blindly loyal to her partner and who is ready to take on the entire world for the sake of her partner.

For her this perfect marriage is the goal of her entire life. She takes a lot of pride and joy in seeing herself wedded to the person she loves.

If Sati is a woman wedded to her profession or her organisation, she will have unconditional loyalty and commitment towards it. Her topmost priority is her office and the responsibilities she has been delegated. She will not flinch from putting her life and reputation on the line if need be for the sake of her organisation. A professionally committed woman with a Sati archetype is excellent at what she does, mostly because she loves it more than anything else which prompts her sincerity and commitment towards it. At the same time it is very likely that she has an emotional stake in her professional role. Sometimes she may fail to follow protocol and make an individual call and resort to an unorthodox approach or strategy to fulfil her objective. This can have ramifications which might cast aspersions on her professionalism and sagacity but never on her integrity or intent.

The Sati woman is strong, feisty and impulsive. She is also generally trusting who would like to believe in the goodness of others. She is proactive and outgoing, the first to call truce after a fight. She believes in forgiving and forgetting and moving on. She has absolutely zero tolerance for injustice and dirty politics. She is someone who calls a spade a spade. Diplomacy is not her strength. Candour is. She does not give up the pursuit of what is true and fair and she does not mind making her entire life a statement about it. She is a woman who will rarely go behind people's backs to speak ill about them. She is not a backstabber and believes in taking her adversary head-on. She is fearless and will not be threatened.

The Sati-like woman is an idealist who would like to appeal to people's sense of right and wrong, who would like to address people's conscience rather than their social positions. She does not believe in institutionalised or social hierarchies and in that sense, has an egalitarian outlook. She is also often feared and misunderstood by friends, family and other people because of her unorthodox behaviour. As a result of this, she sometimes tends to feel a deep sense of alienation which is why she seeks out all the fulfilment and bliss in one relationship which can be in her marriage or if she is a committed professional, then her job. As a wife, she is extremely devoted, as a professional she is a workaholic with no personal life.

The Sati woman acts on impulses. She does not plan her moves. She is spontaneous and decides at the spur of the moment. She does not shy away from danger or cower under pressure and can look her enemy or adversary in the eye and speak her mind. Sometimes her actions might seem to be against textbook organisational ethics but in the long run, they are advantageous to the organisation. Her loyalty is always to the organisation first, not her colleagues. In the same way, her loyalty is always to her partner first, not her children or her natal family or her friends or her in-laws.

Sati in Brands

Brands can use the Sati archetype to foreground a woman's candour, fearlessness, and forthrightness in a crisis. Sati in a professional context could be a law enforcement or an intelligence officer who does not always go by the book. She is someone who can feel the pulse of outlaws and thus bring them to book. She is also someone who can bring about a change of heart in outlaws. In this effort of hers she is aided by a particular brand of sunglasses or a watch or a brand of jewellery. If it is jewellery she can be wearing it more as a souvenir, a family heirloom or something that reminds her of her natal family or her absent partner and gives her confidence and courage.

Sati's martyr archetype can likewise be foregrounded especially around the uniform. The products can be a washing agent, a fabric conditioner, a whitener, a starch and the like. It can even be a device related to health like a handy blood pressure or blood sugar monitor which goes around the construct of the fit and committed body in the service of the nation.

Sati's transgressive and slightly wild nature can likewise be highlighted and replicated comically with lovebirds outsmarting a suspicious parent who is on the prowl. The couple can be seen enjoying a soft drink or a youtube video together.

Sati can also be portrayed as a lawyer defending her partner or fighting a right cause and then an activist on the ground much like the character of Kareena Kapoor in *Aitraaz*. The product can be something that sharpens her mind or contributes to that look of confidence on her face. Sati's is the unusual case and situation where a woman stands up and voices her defence for her partner instead of the other way round which is typically the norm.

Conclusion

Sati is a rich and textured figure in mythology. As a goddess, she is exemplary and fierce. Even after being dismembered she continues to be worshipped. She is invoked as the sacred feminine through her multiple shakti-pithas and is a constant reminder of the trials women have had to undergo to put across their point. In contemporary times she may be seen as someone who is self-destructive. At the same time she can also be viewed as a martyr who believed in a higher objective. Most captivating of all in Sati's myth is her strength and her ability to stand up in an all-male space, face an all-male audience and deride them for their acts and the awakening and realisation this act led to. Sati's act of destroying her body, if read spiritually and symbolically, exposes the vile side of patriarchy. She does not accept defeat and promises to be reborn. In doing this, she is actually affirming her continuity. She is also speaking for all women promising to keep up the fight and the resistance.

Sati is reflected in the women who were part of the Khejarli[7] massacre, who stood for a cause and gave up their lives for it and the women who were part of the Chipko[8] movement, who defied powers of the patriarchal state and stood their ground, not flinching from the possibility of being martyred. Sati is visible in women who consider themselves as part of a bigger

7 https://feminisminindia.com/2020/09/11/when-amrita-devi-and-362-bishnois-sacrificed-their-lives-for-the-khejri-tree/

8 https://indianexpress.com/article/what-is/what-is-the-chipko-movement-google-doodle-5111644/

movement, a greater cause and think of themselves as foot soldiers and the many like them, their replications who will continue with the fight and keep up the good work. Women who will keep the trails blazing and the flames alive and make their voices heard and their presence felt above the din and clamour. That is the power of Sati and that is what the shakti-pithas should be a constant reminder of.

PARVATI: THE GODDESS WHO WASN'T

SHE IS FASCINATING. Like a breath of fresh air, she rejuvenates and breathes new life into people. She leads them by the hand and makes them see life the way it ought to be lived. She makes any place liveable and can be at home anywhere. Beautiful, bubbly and vivacious, she is full of ideas and pranks; she is life itself. She makes heads turn and people smile because she is an unusual presence. She is a break in the monotony of daily routine. She makes friends quickly and soon she rules over hearts. People begin to confide in her. She is the girl-next-door and the agony aunt. And she will always surprise you with her out-of-the-box solutions. She loves an afternoon of languor as much as she enjoys a morning of recreation. She seems impulsive and irresponsible and yet in a crisis, she is someone who can think on her feet. She is more than dependable and an excellent caregiver. She is free-spirited and independent-minded but with a deep sense of compassion and a great love for life. She binds people with real love when they are only existing in superficial harmony. She is fun-loving and recalibrates the dynamics of a hierarchical family structure. She is the inimitable Manju played by Rekha in the Hrishikesh Mukherjee directed 1980 comedy *Khubsoorat.* And she embodies the qualities of one of the most iconic goddesses of Hinduism, Parvati.

If there ever was an archetypal mother who creates, cares and nurtures, a wife who is as much a lover as a guide and a friend, a woman who likes her space, her autonomy and expects what she says to be heard and followed, then it would be Parvati.

The Myths of Parvati

Parvati, who was Sati in her previous life, is a peaceful manifestation of the divine feminine power or shakti and returns to earth on the repeated pleas of the devas who have been driven away from Amravati and are tormented by the atrocities of an asura by the name of Tarakasur. Tarakasur seems to be invincible as he is blessed with a boon which says that he can be killed only by Shiva's son. Since Shiva is a widower after Sati immolates herself and childless, the possibility of vanquishing Tarakasur seems remote. Also, ever since Sati's unfortunate and tragic death, Shiva has immersed himself in tapa or penance and the heat radiating from his body has turned the surroundings into a desolate heath where nothing grows and there is no life of any kind. His ganas feel orphaned and deprived of the joys of being cared for. Moreover the earth is unable to bear this steady emission of heat from Shiva's body as a result of his tapa. It is imperative that Shiva be awakened from his meditative state to prevent the destruction of all Creation. The devas thus approach the divine mother or adiparashakti who agrees to take birth as Parvati in order to marry Shiva and turn the hermit into a householder once again. She will also marry Shiva to beget the son so desperately needed to vanquish Tarakasur.

Shakti is born to the mountain King Himavat and his wife Mena who name her Parvati, coming from the word 'parvata' meaning 'she who dwells in the mountains'. Parvati is a lovely child – the favourite of her parents and outstanding in her accomplishments. Once the sage Narada visits the royal palace and predicts her future to her father: Parvati will grow up and get married to Shiva. Himavat is overjoyed to hear this as Shiva is Mahadev, the god of the gods and his glory and power is famed in all three worlds. From an early age, the maiden Parvati observes severe austerities and penance of immeasurable magnitude and intensity to please Shiva. Her parents are appalled by her self-inflicted suffering and hardships and try to demotivate her but in vain. Parvati also takes the help of her sisters Rati and Preeti and Rati's husband Kamadev, the god of love to woo Shiva as she is determined to marry him. Kamadev uses one of his arrows of love to pierce Shiva. When Shiva opens his eyes, the first person he looks at is Parvati and feels attraction towards her but he also glares at Kamadev and so intense is the heat that emanates from Shiva's blazing glare that Kamadev is instantly reduced to ashes. On Parvati's request, Shiva revives him and on her suggestion enables Kama to have a disembodied consciousness for free movement and a ubiquitous presence. From then on Kamadev is formless and moves around with no body, just like the wind.

After a lot of twists and turns and another series of austerities that Parvati observes to win Shiva, the two are all set to get married and there is great rejoicing all around. The royal palace immerses itself in wedding preparations but as the groom's procession approaches the palace, Parvati's mother Mena who is watching it from the window is aghast at the spectacle. She is repulsed by Shiva's matted locks, the snakes writhing and crawling over his ash-smeared body, the tiger-skin that covers him and the repelling hordes of the ganas who accompany him, each, a terrifying and revolting aberration. A horrified Mena beseeches Parvati to reconsider her choice and even goes to the extent of forbidding her to marry Shiva just like Daksha Prajapati had done to Sati-Parvati in her previous birth. Thus is accorded the name Uma to Parvati uttered as 'u ma' meaning 'Oh don't!' as Mena dissuades her daughter from marrying Shiva. Seeing her mother's plight, Parvati then requests Shiva to assume the form of a handsome groom which he does most willingly. Seeing him in this form, realisation dawns upon Mena who gives her consent to the marriage.

Shiva and Parvati make Mount Kailasa their new home. The *Shiva Purana* says that the world trembles and shudders when the two make love and engage in their 'excessive amorous play'. The earth is heavily weighed down by the erotic activity of the couple and unable to breathe. When the devas, led by Brahma and Vishnu, approach Shiva with discretion, gently alluding to the oppressed condition the earth is in and also reminding the latter of their piteous plight because of Tarakasur, a distracted Shiva sheds his semen, but not in Parvati's womb. Agni or the fire god who sees the semen dropping, takes the form of a bird and swallows it before it touches the ground but so intense is the heat, finds himself being consumed. This interruption in her erotic pleasure angers Parvati who curses the gods that since they had not allowed Shiva's semen to enter her womb, the wives of all gods forever would remain barren and incapable of bearing any children.

Meanwhile, a tormented Agni deposits Shiva's seed in the wives of the Seven Sages who come to bathe in the river, all except Arundhati who senses something amiss. The remaining six wives, the *Krrttkas*, not only become pregnant with Shiva's seed but also find it impossible to bear the heat. To add to their affliction, their husbands accuse them of adulterous involvement with Agni. The agonised wives leave Shiva's seed in the form of an embryo on one of the peaks of the Himalayas. But the mountain peak too can't stand the feverish heat and gives it to

Ganga, whose waters start boiling the moment it is deposited in her. Ganga, in her anguish and hurry to rid herself of the excruciating torture, tosses the half-formed seed into a clump of reeds by her side where it immediately takes the form of a beautiful boy and sprouts six heads. Thus comes into existence Shiva's first child who is incubated in multiple wombs.

The Krrtkas, or the six abandoned wives of the six sages, who had borne him for some time in their womb, start looking after him and nursing him. Eventually Shiva and Parvati come for the little boy. The Krrtkas hand him over to them and Parvati, with a stroke of her hand, fuses the six heads into one. Thus comes into being Skanda who will be the terror of the asuras, destroy Tarakasur and restore Amravati for the devas. Fair, handsome, brave and graceful astride his peacock, he will also be known as Kartikeya or Kartik because of his association with his surrogate mothers, the Krrtkas.

After the birth of Kartikeya, Parvati desires another child who will be born out of her womb. But Shiva is not keen as he believes that children are for householders with desires which they try to fulfil through their children and he, after all, is a hermit. Parvati has earlier discussed the longing for another son with her companions who tell her that she ought to create a child of her own. Once Parvati goes for her bath with a gana guarding the entrance, leaving strict instructions that no one should be allowed to enter. While she is having her bath, Shiva enters the chamber. Parvati is not too happy on her personal space thus being encroached upon and realises that the gana is after all Shiva's subject and will do his bidding. This further intensifies her desire for a child of her own who will follow her and obey her commands. It is said that one day, before her bath, Parvati applies a beauty paste on her body and when the paste is dried up, she scrubs off the dry clay from her skin and makes a child out of it. Thus is born Vinayaka (without the help of a man or nayak), a lovely boy made out of the beauty paste and dead skin of Parvati.

Parvati asks the boy to guard the entrance while she goes to have her bath. Shiva comes along and wants to enter her chamber but is surprised when he is stopped by the young boy and astounded when the latter introduces himself as Parvati's son. Several Puranic tales describe the terrifying battle that ensues, with all the devas and the ganas on the one side and the invincible boy guarding Parvati's room's entry on the other. Finally in a rage, Shiva beheads the boy and kills him. When Parvati emerges from her bath and sees her dead child, she is distraught and mad with fury. She threatens to destroy all Creation if her son is not brought back to life. Shiva immediately orders the gods to go in search of a living being and get the head of the first creature they accost which would fit the boy. The gods come back with the head of a majestic white elephant and this is placed on the body of the dead child. Shiva brings him back to life and thus comes into being Ganesha the elephant-headed god, the lord of the ganas or 'Ganapati'. Shiva blesses him and proclaims that he will be the first among the gods to be worshipped and will be known to symbolise wisdom and intelligence and famed as Vighnaharta or the remover of obstacles.

Puranic tales abound with accounts of Shiva and Parvati's married life. The couple engages in deep philosophical and theological discussions, squabbles over day-to-day household matters or relaxes by playing board games and entering frequent wagers. These tales are especially popular in south Indian lore. One such myth recounts the series of events that follow as Parvati leaves the mountain abode when Shiva refuses to provide her with a kitchen at Kailasa. Later, when the hungry ganas approach him for food, he is at his wit's end and goes searching for Parvati who he finally locates in Kashi. Admitting his mistake and addressing her as Annapoorna (the nurturer symbolising bounty), he implores her to return with him to Kailasa.

Another instance is when Shiva addresses Parvati as 'kali' or the dark-skinned one in jest and earns her wrath as she walks off in a huff and immerses herself in deep tapa. The heat generated whenever Parvati immerses herself in tapa is unbearable and so intense that the very gods have to beseech Shiva to ask the goddess to stop and go back to her family life. Once, when Parvati is away, an apsara by the name of Madhura engages in a sexual relation with Shiva. On her return when Parvati finds her husband's ashes on the apsara's body, she is enraged and curses her to turn into a frog.

One tale in particular conveys Parvati's significance and her indispensable role in ensuring the functioning of the world. As Parvati and Shiva indulge in a board game, Shiva keeps losing every round and has to give up his rudraksha beads, his ash and even his damru. Finally, he stops playing the game as he feels humiliated even as Parvati is amused. Then, Vishnu comes over and asks him to go back and resume playing, assuring him that he will enter the dice and control the movement so that Shiva doesn't lose and thus help him get back all his possessions. Shiva agrees and the game resumes. Parvati is surprised when she sees Shiva mysteriously winning every round. She senses something wrong and implies that he is cheating, at which Shiva flies into a rage. Seeing the couple fighting, Vishnu appears and discloses the truth to Parvati who is not too happy. Shiva tries to make an argument suggesting that it is a game, just 'maya' or mere illusion like the food one eats and one need not mull over gross material things to this extent. At this, Parvati feels insulted because *she* is Maya. She does not like the manner in which Shiva belittles the worth and importance of food and takes off from the earth.

Soon the crops fail and a famine strikes the land. The seasons cease to change and nature comes to a standstill. It is one long unbearable summer. Animals and plants die and people starve. Humans and demons come together and start praying for the season to change and for the earth to show her bounty. Seeing her children in this state of misery, Parvati descends from above on the city of Varanasi and in her Annapoorna avatar, starts distributing grains and food. Shiva comes seeking her forgiveness, realising his folly and the casual words spoken without thought.

Time and again, whenever the devas are threatened by powerful asuras, Parvati sends one of her warrior manifestations to destroy the asuras and restore peace in the world. She is also the mediator between the devas and Shiva, whose defining nature is that of the ascetic and who is often immersed in tapa and inaccessible to most.

A lot of regular tiffs and mundane bickering like in any husband-wife relationship is an aspect of the Shiva-Parvati relationship too. Sometimes the tiffs can turn into very serious differences and fights as well as is evident in the numerous instances when Parvati walks out of the marriage.

Buddhist feminist scholar Rita Gross says that the whole range of myths around Parvati cannot and do not exhaust the power, depth and intensity of the divine feminine in Indian mythology. While this is true, if Parvati is really the archetypal mother and wife, then there are a lot of qualities in her which she uses and exercises within the domestic space to assert her individuality and autonomy, besides fulfilling her expected role as nurturer and companion. She is every bit a goddess in her own right with or without Shiva despite her seat next to him. The myths bring out myriad qualities and characteristics in Parvati that, by today's standards, do not qualify as conventionally feminine. But if the myths highlight those qualities, it means that they were qualities that were culturally valued and qualities that were held as desirable in women once.

Analysing Parvati in the Light of the Myths

Known for her beauty, vivacity, generosity and domestic competence, Parvati is one among the Indian goddess trinity or Tridevi. She symbolises fertility, abundance and nourishment and certainly embodies the archetypal nurturing mother as she is not only concerned about the well-being of her own children but also those of the ganas, which is why she asks for a kitchen in the first place. She is effervescent and extroverted and depicted as enjoying an equal relationship with her husband. They share hobbies and an intellectual compatibility too. It is she who is instrumental in inspiring Shiva to assume the form of Nataraj and instils art and aesthetics in an ascetic.

In her more motherly appearances, she is usually imagined with her children around her and with flowers and eatables, or a cow in the vicinity or nearby, suggesting the Annapoorna aspect, the universal mother who keeps everyone nourished. She is also depicted as yoni or the female organ with Shiva as linga or the phallus erectus: suggesting the sexual power of procreation and regeneration and the equal role of man and woman in this process.

Parvati can be honey-coloured or yellow, which is also the colour of ripe crop standing for harvest and fertility. She is usually described as a beautiful, dark-skinned woman implying her possible assimilation in the Brahminical pantheon from the indigenous cultures. She symbolises perseverance and dedication as she has to perform extremely difficult austerities and tapa to please Shiva who has become a recluse and cut himself off from the world after Sati's demise. In other words, she symbolises the potential of the human to transform into a goddess or figuratively seen, to transcend one's ordinariness and attain the impossible. She is also the one who turns a hermit into a householder. In fact, she controls Shiva's ascetic heat and neutralises it by engaging him as a householder. She is known to complement Shiva's *rudra tandav* or the dance of rage with the soft and graceful *lasya*.

Addressed by a 1000 names in *Lalithasahasranama* created by Lopamudra and rishi Agastya, Parvati, in her many manifestations, negates the very idea of the essential woman or the essential feminine, a Western construct. She has an extensive iconographic presence across the Indian subcontinent and South east Asia. A lot of hasta-mudras or hand gestures in Indian classical dance can be attributed to the iconographic depictions of Parvati like tarjani (menace), kataka, hirana (antelope – elusive and graceful), chandrakala (moon - intelligence) and abhaya (fearless). Abhinay Darpan has a special Parvatimudra denoting her as divine mother.

There is no direct mention of the goddess Parvati either in the *Rigveda* or the *Kena Upanishads*. The first direct mention of the name Parvati is seen in the *Hamsa Upanishad*. She becomes more prominent and acquires a conspicuous presence in the epics Ramayana and Mahabharata and is further popularised through the Puranas and the play *Kumarasambhavam* by the poet Kalidasa. She could have been appropriated and mainstreamed from the tribal cultures as a goddess who dwelled in the mountains. Interestingly, The Lady of the Plants and of the Sea in Native American Navaho Mythology is seen as the Divine Creator who made the first human beings from skin rubbed from various parts of her body, which is very similar to the events that lead to the creation of Ganesha.

Parvati and her Archetypes

It is actually impossible to essentialise Parvati or to look up to her as depicting one essential or dominating or overwhelming feminine characteristic. Parvati is regal and reflects the Queen archetype in her concern for the well-being of the devas and the ganas. She is benevolent and concerned about the well-being of these people who she regards as her responsibility. Time and again she comes to the rescue of the devas fighting and winning battles with hideous asuras for them. She is capable of raising her own army as the *Devi Mahatmyam* suggests and take on multiple forms like Kali, Chandika, Ambika, Durga, Bhairavi and Kalaratri to protect the devas, destroy evil and maintain cosmic balance. She wages wars and wins them without the help of any man. She is equally sensitive to humankind and bestows her generosity as Annapoorna on them. She is also capable of raising worthy sons on her own as she is the one who teaches Kartikeya the art of warfare. She also creates Ganesha entirely on her own without any help from her husband. Her Queen archetype gives her a certain sense of autonomy which she exercises, whether it is to demarcate and guard her personal space or to create a child, or to protect those who seek refuge under her.

The act of creating Ganesha reflects the Pioneer archetype too, someone who is thrilled at the prospect of trying out something completely new. Parvati uses her dead skin and clay to create a child and seeks delight in it. In her mission to marry Shiva, Parvati reflects the Seeker archetype who is persevering and unrelenting in her efforts till she has accomplished what she sought out to achieve. She is also a good networker and resourceful, as she can get, not only her sisters but also Kamadev to help her in her mission. Parvati is also seen to embody the

Teacher archetype along with the Queen archetype where she takes charge of the situation, offers counsel, provides leadership and acts as a representative. This is evident in her advice to Shiva after the Kamadev fiasco, in grooming Kartikeya into a formidable warrior, in training Ganesha to show nothing but utmost loyalty to her, in mediating between the devas and Mahadev and also in her participation and inputs in the deep philosophical discussions she has with Shiva.

Parvati likewise embodies the Nourishing Mother and Earth Mother archetypes, especially in her manifestations as Annapoorna and as the symbol of fertility as she is the only one among the goddesses to have any children. If one were to consider the lesser known myth of Andhaka, Parvati also symbolises the quintessential mother, quite blindly loved by her son Andhaka, who gives up his life for her. A psychoanalytical reading of the myth would reveal quite a few interesting aspects of the Mother archetype.

Andhaka is born when Parvati closes Shiva's eyes in jest and he sheds his semen at the touch of her hand. But because his eyes are closed, darkness falls on the universe and the child that is born is blind. He has a terrible bearing and is of demonic rage and strength. Equally intense is his love for his mother, who he wants to possess and proclaim as his own. Symbolically read, it probably represents the blind and sometimes consuming love of sons for mothers which lead them to have a conflicted relationship with the father, which the psychoanalyst Sigmund Freud too elaborates upon in the theory of the Oedipus Complex. Literally and symbolically blind, Andhaka is that son who is unable to get over his initial attraction for his mother and succumbs to it.

According to scholarly readings by A K Ramanujan, a Tamil folk anecdote describing a conversation between Parvati and Ganesha also accounts for an Oedipal undertone. Once, Parvati asks Ganesha what kind of bride he would prefer. Ganesha instantly replies that he would like a woman just like his mother. This blatant confession of an incestuous desire for his own mother, earns him Parvati's wrath who curses him to remain a celibate his entire life.

Tracing Parvati in Popular Culture

Parvati, since she is the manifestation of several archetypes, has an extensive presence in Indian cinema. Aspects of her character and glimpses of the goddess can be traced in many characters which synthesise her antithetical characteristics and make her endearing and loveable. One of the most memorable characterisations which borrows from Parvati is, of course, the one mentioned at the start of this chapter, that of the bubbly, vivacious character of Manju played by Rekha in the comedy-drama film *Khubsoorat* (1980), who introduces art and fun within the domestic space of the family and has an ideological difference with a disciplining matriarch, Nirmala Gupta, played by Dina Pathak who runs the family with an iron hand.

Manju succeeds in reconfiguring the dynamics of the family and the stifled, stunted existence of the family members who live in the looming shadow of the matriarch. Manju forges the laws of the household anew and subverts oppressive

hierarchical patterns from within the system by undoing myths of perception. Instead of rebelling openly she uses tactics to circumvent the laws of the household so that others get a first-hand experience of a liberated life. *Khubsoorat* thus has the female protagonist Manju deconstructing the traditional notion of the ideal Indian *bahu* by humanising the bahu construct and according her a subject status. Moreover, Manju goes on to show how others too in the family are leading constricted lives and need to loosen up. She makes the Gupta family who she is visiting, her very own just as Parvati embraces Shiva's ganas and mount Kailasa. Just like Parvati, Manju breathes new life and new ways of being and living among the family members which leaves them liberated.

In another Hrishikesh Mukherjee directed film, *Angoor* (1982), glimpses of Parvati can be seen in the character of Sudha played by Moushumi Chatterjee. A perennially watchful Sudha, worrying for her unmindful and hot-headed husband Ashok (Sanjeev Kumar) and always sending his sidekick Bahadur (Deven Verma) to look out for him, typifies a slightly controlling Parvati overseeing an absentminded Shiva. The squabbles which Ashok and Sudha have, the card games they engage in, the amorous play, the hint of the erotic in a conjugal relationship, all allude to the Shiva-Parvati relationship with a not-so-intelligent but extremely loyal Nandi-like Bahadur, always on the watch and often failing. In fact, the film actually has a scene where Ashok, on returning home late one night after having a fight with Sudha earlier that morning, finds his entry barred. No one opens the door. Though it happens unwittingly and Sudha is not directly responsible for this, the scene nonetheless is reminiscent of the barring of Shiva's entry in Parvati's space.

The tough female character of Indu played by Hema Malini in the multi-starrer film *Satte pe Satta* (1982) also has strong shades of Parvati. Ravi (Amitabh Bachhan), the oldest of seven brothers who lives on a ranch along with his brothers in wild Texan style and whose lifestyle resembles that of horses rather than humans, woos Indu (Hema Malini) and marries her after a brief courtship. But Indu is in for a surprise even as she enters Ravi's house. She sees his brothers for the first time

and the sight of the wild, unruly, half-clothed, feet-stomping, clamorous men is not very different from Shiva's ganas with all kinds of aberrations and flaws. In course of time, Indu becomes more like a mother figure and a nurturer who civilises her brothers-in-law and teaches them the ways of the world. She is a strict disciplinarian and a kind nurturer at once. But she is capable of flying into a rage and losing her temper if her instructions are not followed. She is vocal about her needs in the wild house and makes sure that her demands are met. Her act of cleaning the kitchen and cooking for the family draws from the myth which relates to Parvati's demand for a kitchen at Kailasa. Clearly, Ravi has never bothered to have a fully operational kitchen before this and none of the brothers have bothered to cook proper meals. Indu's act of cleaning the kitchen, laying out crockery and serving a proper meal, positions her undeniably as Parvati among the ganas at Kailasa, symbolising her as Annapoorna or the one who nourishes.

The character of Tanu played by Kangana Ranaut in *Tanu weds Manu* (2011) has shades of Parvati as she walks out on her marriage over a tiff with her husband who keeps thinking of ways to get her back. Tanu is shown to tell the doctor how much she has given up to be with her husband in a foreign land, only to witness his complete preoccupation with his work; in other words she has problems reconciling with the ascetic and the recluse in him. She complains about his nature which is not fun-loving. Tanu's playfulness, her impish, mischievous charm, and her wisecracks set off against her husband's calm, low-profile and introverted demeanour alludes to Parvati's vibrant profile against the rugged backdrop of the mountain and its equally rugged dweller, the recluse Shiva.

Even though Parvati goes to mount Kailasa with Shiva after her marriage, which is far from civilisation and isolated, she retains her bridal attire. Most of the time she is depicted as wearing a red saree and bedecked in all her finery and gold jewellery. Unlike Sita she is not in the clothes of a forest dweller. In the film too, we see Tanu brightly clad in solid silks, florals and vibrant cotton fabric which stand in sharp contrast to the pastel-coloured and nondescript shirts of her husband Manu. Tanu exercises her autonomy and does not feel accountable to anyone for her decision. Full of wisecracks and street smartness, she really knows how to get her husband to come after her, retains her sophistication amongst small towners and makes friends with them so that she wins their goodwill.

There are other depictions of Parvati which focus on the other archetypes in her character like those of the devoted wife. Almost all films depicting vivacious, energetic, lively girls turning into coy brides after marriage, draw from the hegemonic archetype of Parvati which focuses on the 'princess' leaving her palatial lifestyle for a life of hardships in the mountains. Anjali, played by Kajol in *Kabhi Khushi Kabhi Gham* (2001), is a character that comes instantly to mind. From being bubbly and energetic, she goes on to become demure and comely and manages her household and her family in a far-off land, proving to be the ideal companion of her recluse husband Rahul (Shahrukh Khan).

Films that portray a strong woman in charge of her life and

pair her with a slightly unmindful, preoccupied man, easily angered or demotivated or easy to please who is still learning the rules of adult, heterosexual relationship in a domestic space, borrow from the Shiva-Parvati householder myth. Aisha played by Konkona Sen and the archetypal dynamics between her and Sid Mehra (Ranbeer Kapoor) in *Wake up Sid* (2009) is one such portrayal of this aspect of Parvati's character.

Many scholars have regarded myths as encasing life's truths and acting as models with messages for humankind. Myths tell us how life ought to be lived and how relations ought to *be* rather than what they are. In that case then, if there are so many myths that centre around fights and differences between Shiva and Parvati, their intention might be to tell us that this is actually how a marriage ought to be. An ideal marriage is not one that is an unequal marriage where partners are not comfortable voicing their true concerns but a marriage where partners are free, don't flinch from fights and from offering constructive criticism and express themselves if they have been hurt. An ideal marriage is where partners do not think they are perfect and neither pretend to be so; instead, they learn from each other and their own mistakes. They reflect on their behaviour and cement the relationship further. The numerous instances when Parvati walks away from Kailasa not only indicate her sense of strong individuality but also point to a deeper intention behind the action – that of making Mahadev realise that he is not above erring and thus humanising the god of the gods.

One film that borrows from this myth is the Anubhav

Sinha directed 2020 release *Thappad.* It centres around Ammu (Tapsee Pannu), who can be just about any married woman in a regular Indian upper middle-class family who has adjusted with the ways of her husband's household and who goes more than the extra mile to become the ideal wife and bahu but then does a very strange and unexpected thing. She walks out when she is unwittingly slapped by her husband - to make him realise… what? That she didn't really want him slapping her or that all would be well if he had not slapped her? Though it might seem so, the film goes way beyond making a statement on domestic violence. It is about the hierarchy in the marital relationship which is unmistakeable and entrenched, accepted and even endorsed. The silent compromises and the more silent transformation that the woman is expected to undergo in a marriage which is institutionalised and part of an indoctrination that starts early and never stops. And it is this hierarchy which is time and again contested by Parvati and her actions, the moment it tries to set in and stabilise itself. Parvati walks away without bothering to explain herself. It is the events that follow which reveal the significance of her actions and

make her husband Shiva realise why she did what she did. *Thappad* too is open-ended, suggesting that now the man is really going to have to go the extra mile to get his wife back since she is truly deserving and it is he who has undervalued her and taken her for granted in the relationship all long.

Parvati's determination to marry Mahadev symbolises a woman on a mission to attain the unattainable in the face of the severest of odds. All women-centered movies where the (often) self-motivated woman sets out on a hero's journey to attain the impossible, faces initial failures but finally emerges successful are conceived on the Parvati archetype. New York based choreographer Dia's (Madhuri Dixit) uphill and nearly impossible journey in the small town of Shamli in the film *Aja Nachle* (2007) is a reminder of Parvati's austerities in the face of insurmountable odds to attain her goal. Likewise, the women characters in films like *English, Vinglish* (2012), *Tumhari Sulu* (2017), *Toilet: Ek Prem Katha* (2017), and *Badrinath Ki Dulhaniya* (2017) have inimitable shades of the Parvati archetype. If it is Shashi Godbole's (Sridevi) resolve in *English, Vinglish* to do the unthinkable i.e. transcend her housewife role and cross the literal and metaphorical threshold to learn English, then in *Tumhari Sulu*, it is Sulu's (Vidya Balan) exuberance and confidence combined with her optimism and resilience that bring out the Parvati archetype so prominently.

All the women in the films mentioned above have one thing in common. They have a resolve, they are on a mission and they want to succeed. They take up different routes to succeed in their mission – some like Jaya played by Bhumi Pednekar in *Toilet: Ek Prem Katha*, leave their husband for a cause that will benefit the entire community. Jaya's demand for a toilet is exactly like Parvati's demand for a kitchen. In both cases, the husband shows indifference to the need and the wife walks away till he realises the significance of her demand.

Some like Vaidehi Trivedi played by Alia Bhatt in *Badrinath ki Dulhaniya (2017)* walk away because they fear their autonomy is likely to be compromised in a marriage. Only when Badrinath (which is incidentally another name for Shiva), the boy who loves Vaidehi and wants to marry her, acknowledges her potential and assures that no one will come in the path of what she aspires to achieve, does she return to him. The Parvati archetype is likewise traceable in the lead female characters in films like *Lagaan* (2001), *Soorma* (2018), and *Sui Dhaga* (2018) who don the roles of rescuer, healer, motivator and channelise the man's energy, acting as a source of inspiration to him and enabling him to be successful in his mission. Mamta (Anushka Sarma) in *Sui Dhaga* does the balancing act, managing the anger and frustration of her husband Mauji (Varun Dhawan) who is time and again misunderstood just like Shiva, while firmly navigating him to realise his true potential.

A glimpse of the lesser-known Oedipal myths of Andhaka and Ganesha and the shadow archetype of Parvati, the mother who commands uncompromising loyalty of the son can be found in the 1992 highest grossing Bollywood film *Beta* in which Raju (Anil Kapoor), is quite literally blinded by his love for his mother Lakshmi (Aruna Irani) and chooses to be oblivious of her ulterior motives till it is almost too late.

Another Andhaka in cinema would be Birju (Sunil Dutt), a dacoit and an outlaw in *Mother India* (1957) who loves his mother the most and is confident about getting away with the most heinous of crimes because he believes he has her on his side. A more toned down Andhaka, the shadow son-lover would be Vijay (Amitabh Bachhan) in *Deewar* (1975) who chooses the shadow path of crime and intrigue to get rich and famous and dies, first an emotional death and eventually a literal death in his mother's arms when he knows he has lost her because of the path he has chosen to walk on. He chooses death over estrangement and leaves, his love for his mother unreconciled.

The jealous and unforgiving lover archetype of Parvati which is foregrounded in the myth of the *apsara* Madhura who Parvati's curse turns into a frog, finds its way in the character of Safina Firdausi (Alia Bhatt) in *Gully Boy* (2019) when she very coolly and nonchalantly breaks a beer bottle on the head of Shweta 'Sky' Mehta (Kalki Koechlin) who has the potential of becoming the other woman in her boyfriend Murad's (Ranveer Singh) life.

Contemporarising and Humanising Parvati

Parvati epitomises the potential of a woman to attain superhuman abilities and extraordinary powers through diligent efforts, pure perseverance and an extraordinary level of commitment. It is said that to be able to marry Shiva, her ascetic heat needed to be on a par with him for which she had to perform penances and observe austerities of unimaginable intensity. So intense was her tapa that finally the devas had to devise ways to dissuade her from continuing her penance for fear that the earth would be scorched. She is a human incarnation of adiparashakti but in her human form, she is also a woman who awakens the adishakti in her; she is not endowed, she kindles it and taps into her dormant energy and power which means she has to work on it and not for a brief period of time but as per the Puranas, for several thousand years which metaphorically symbolises the extent of her perseverance and grit. She is not born a goddess; she becomes one through exemplary behaviour, perseverance, penance and a flawless execution of her plans. Thus read figuratively, it depicts Parvati as a woman of tremendous determination and will power, a woman capable of undergoing hardships and sustaining the severest of conditions. She is undoubtedly a go-getter, a woman who can seek help from outsiders to get the man she loves or wants, or the goal she has in mind.

Her uncompromised tapa not only leads to her union with Shiva but makes her a formidable force in her own right. The power she attains makes her autonomous and a transcendental force to reckon with. And yet, time and again, she reaffirms her faith in human earthly strengths. She is a woman capable of embracing the marginalised and of accommodating people following an alternative lifestyle and belief system symbolised by Mahadev's followers. She has been known to balance Shiva's ascetic heat which if extremely intense has the capability of destroying Creation. Thus, she balances the tension between over-absorption in a discipline or professional preoccupation on the one hand and erotic urge and domesticity on the other, in a man. Parvati is a woman who controls her husband's highly polarised and whimsical behaviour and balances his extreme eroticism and extreme asceticism. She makes Shiva realise time and again the importance of being a householder and a husband along with being a hermit and an ascetic.

Parvati is an extraordinarily independent woman who has the ability to birth and raise children without a man. Not only does she create Ganesha all by herself but it is also her own independent decision to bring forth another child in the family. Despite her husband's unwillingness for another child, she goes ahead and has one all the same. She is a woman who demands and succeeds in getting an equal position in the marriage, has philosophical and intellectual debates with her husband and is not merely relegated to the domestic sphere. She is also someone who values her space highly and feels offended when that which she values and seeks is not respected. She makes her displeasure very clear more than once, during her initial interaction with the devas when they interrupt her and Shiva in their dalliance and later to Shiva himself when he enters her chambers during her private time. She has an action-oriented approach and when she realises that this violation can happen time and again, she comes up with a solution by creating her own child who will be her personal guard. This action again brings out the Queen along with the Problem-solver archetype in her.

Parvati is a woman who questions stereotypes and dismantles tradition as she marries a man who is not an elitist ruler or a king with material possessions like her father. Thus, her act of marrying Shiva is symbolic of doing away with the status-quo. Not only does she marry the man of her choice, after having successfully devised and implemented a fool-proof plan of acquiring him, but she also resists all kinds of opposition to her choice. However, she chooses to be resilient rather than rebellious. When her choice is objected to, she resorts to tactics and negotiation, requesting Shiva to change his appearance which will assuage her mother. She is successful in having her groom's ear and convinces him to prove himself and his worth in order to put all the apprehensions of his in-laws to rest. That is the kind of compatibility and understanding she has developed during her courtship period with Shiva and the kind of influence she has over him even before she is actually married to him.

Parvati is not merely beautiful. She is glamorous, sexually attractive and does not discard her royal and queenly attire, neither her Queen archetype on getting married to Shiva who exists outside the pale of material and worldly possessions. Despite living in Kailasa, she does not embody the Recluse archetype. She is the one to mediate with the devas and the ganas and widely respected by all of Mahadev's followers who frequently seek her counsel. Her advice is highly sought and esteemed and as a mediator, she is someone who can get work done for others from her husband or can convince her husband to take unprecedented measures when required. Likewise, she is ever wary of her husband crossing the line in his absent-mindedness: like the instance when she places her hand on his throat to prevent with her maya, the poison ingested from the samudramanthan to enter his stomach. Parvati also has the Warrior, Shape-shifter and the Rescuer archetypes in her and sends manifestations of her 'self' to vanquish her adversaries.

The Shiva-Parvati relation is the archetypal heterosexual relation which is a model of mutual respect for and acceptance of each other. Neither tries to change the other. Parvati never tries to change Shiva's appearance or is seen to complain about his ungainly looks. Neither does she judge the followers he has who are symbolic of the non-normative in society, comprising the strange, the ugly, the repulsive and the marginalised, when seen through a Brahminical lens. Neither does Shiva ask Parvati to give up her queenly bearing. Parvati is the force of culture and civilisation in existence. At the same time she is also symbolic of the bounteous side of nature. Shiva and Parvati are the idealised realisation of the fusion and simultaneity of ascetism and eroticism, both of which are required in existence.

The Parvati Archetype in Brands

Parvati and her various aspects can be used in different ways to highlight one or a combination of the archetypes she embodies for more empowering projections of women. Though Parvati has been conventionally regarded as the symbol of fertility, domesticity and motherhood, all three notions acquire different connotations when one regards her in the light of the lesser known myths. She is the symbol of fertility, yet she does not actually receive Shiva's seed and birth children from her womb, thus subverting the notion of fertility and biological motherhood. Neither is she the hegemonic version of the compliant wife who will always conform to her husband's wishes without having a voice of her own. Parvati is far from passive and farther from being a conformist. She has the Rebel archetype which manifests strongly in every act of hers whether it is her marriage, or the way she begets her children, or her married life. She uses the Rebel archetype in her to question stereotypes and conventions that can cause more harm than good.

Women today would like to identify with someone who is not stereotyped as totally domesticated and operating only in the domestic sphere and for this, brands, while presenting the feminine construct need to turn to a more humanised archetype of Parvati. Brands working on positive projections of women might want to depict the empowered homemaker; for instance a wife who has a say in her partner's career choices and can offer counsel to her spouse when the latter makes professional decisions. They might also be inspired by the construct of Parvati and want to project the wife as this woman who can navigate her spouse's life in a way that the latter attains work-life balance. A partner who engages with her spouse in financial, political, social matters and through it, senses or experiences a participation in the public sphere.

Drawing from more of Parvati's qualities she could be depicted as someone who is friendly and nurturing towards her spouse's family and relatives, but at the same time as a woman whose life is not confined with concerns about what is happening in her immediate family alone but who also has an interest in and understanding of what is happening in the world. She can be projected as a mother who is the right combination of authority and approachability. Her partner's colleagues and subordinates might often come to her for her counsel regarding some official matter and her partner's opinion on it which they may not have direct access to. A homemaker who has the autonomy in her marriage of making independent decisions, deciding for her children and is respected by her partner for her decision-making ability and her wisdom.

In her unmarried version, a construct with Parvati's archetypal qualities would be a woman who can resort to *jugaad* and who convinces others to help her get the person she loves because after all she is not only determined and resourceful but also a go-getter and someone who excels at whatever she takes up. A woman in the professional sphere on the lines of the Parvati archetype would be someone who is as good as her boss and has the ability to make her boss see the sagacity in her decisions.

A married woman when depicted, does not have to be situated only in the kitchen or stand to represent only the archetype of the caregiver. There are homemakers who have a strong housewife archetype in them and find it empowering to manage the house and be in charge of the well-being of the family members. But that by no means makes their work or their choice less meaningful than their spouse's responsibilities as a breadwinner or those women who choose to work outside the house. The archetype of the housewife has undergone a lot of bashing and has come to have diminutive connotations today.

The need is to have an empowered positive projection of the homemaker who has a say in family matters, who is not merely relegated to the kitchen or confined to the work of caregiving. She is entitled to having fun with the other family members and to a position of respect in the house. She needs to sit at the dining table with the rest of the family having dinner or lunch, rather than standing by it and serving others with a ladle in her hand. She could be shown making informed choices related to finance and investment, looking up better career opportunities for her partner or for classes to enrol for the children.

She could be shown as having an autonomy over her space, having her 'me' time and enjoying it too and engaging in other kinds of constructive occupations that do not concern the house but are prompted by a concern for the larger community for instance. One of the Britannia Marie biscuit advertisements, which shows the homemaker conducting fitness classes for the elderly in the neighbourhood, is one such example of a positive projection of a homemaker along the lines of the Parvati archetype.

Though Parvati has always been predominantly associated with wifehood and motherhood in the mythological narratives, her life, before she is married to Shiva also deserves attention. The ascetic Parvati is the symbol of endurance, depicting the ability to bear physical suffering of unimaginable proportions.

This Parvati negates and deconstructs all the notions associated with relatively modern, later-sanskritised and West-inspired depictions of the white/upper-caste woman who is weak/frail, needs to be protected and is primarily a sexual being. Parvati is not protected but rises as the protector instead.

A depiction on these lines which focuses on the enduring side of the ascetic Parvati would be the protagonist of the web series *The Test Case* (2020) streaming on Alt Balaji. Centred around a female army officer Shikha Sharma (Nimrat Kaur), it shows her impossible journey of becoming the first female combat officer and situates her in an exclusively male space where women are strictly denied any form of entry. She is the first, the first female test case in a combat role. Her journey embodies the myth of the unmarried Parvati's physical endurance. Captain Shikha Sharma's journey not only symbolises the unimaginable level of endurance and physical stamina required to train and qualify as a combat officer but also the trials involved in transcending an identity overdetermined by her gender and hegemonic patriarchal perceptions about a woman's threshold for handling physical pain and resolving mental challenges.

Shikha's situation in many ways is different and more difficult as compared to that of the mythological Parvati as no one really believes that Shikha Sharma will be able to withstand the pressure of the training while everyone believes in Parvati's capacity to endure. This is because today's woman has to battle the *Bhartiya nari* construct which resulted out of colonial discourses on womanhood and femininity influenced by the values of the Indian cultural revivalists on the one hand and Victorian standards of femininity on the other (informed by the colonial government and West-educated Indian intelligentsia, all men) and stands dissociated from the divine feminine archetype of the East which originally symbolised unbridled energy and power that inspired fear and awe.

While films today, more than ever, want to stand the reality test and, therefore, prefer honest and mostly hegemonic depictions of constructs, advertisements have always allowed people to escape into the realm of fantasy because they needn't always be seen through the prism of reality. Thus, advertisements have more scope to work on and incorporate positive, empowered depictions of an archetype thereby bringing in a new sensibility amongst viewers and also reshaping the discourse around gender roles.

LAKSHMI: THE GODDESS ON THE MOVE

SHE IS QUEENLIKE; stately in her bearing and composed at all times. She exudes power, brilliance and has a strong presence even in a crowded room. People stop to acknowledge her and then feel drawn to her. She has a charismatic bearing. She is deep and she is magnetic. She has the perfect manners and the perfect charm that leave her audience spellbound and in awe of her. She has a strong individuality and yet she complements her husband perfectly. People begin to like him and notice him because they like *her*. He is the one in power and she is the one who has made it happen. She is the one who makes it happen every day, like bread that needs to be freshly baked every day. It is her untiring efforts, her unwavering presence by his side and her complete and undivided support of him in front of the world that makes him popular, even likeable. The optics change. People stop seeing him like a tyrant and start softening to him. If he can have a wife like her and her unquestionable devotion, surely he *must* be a good man. Till power makes him heady and he humiliates her and she leaves him.

Not one to retaliate violently, not one to create a scene, quietly, decisively she simply leaves him. She is not one to be with a man who does not have her best interests at heart, who uses her as a prop to further his power and who is so utterly blind that he completely fails to acknowledge that it is *she* who has made him and without the projection of their combined strength, their complementary presence, he is nothing. She is Claire Underwood, the lead female protagonist of the extremely popular American political web television series *House of Cards,* with 33 Primetime Emmy Award nominations to its credit, including outstanding lead actress and Golden Globe Award for Best Performance for Robin Wright. Claire epitomises Lakshmi and her marriage and partnership with the ambitious and power-hungry Democrat Congressman Frank Underwood, that of Lakshmi's partnership and marriage with the king of the devas, Indra.

Widely worshipped in different manifestations across regions, continents and religions, if there was a goddess that fits into a universal archetype of the savvy, smart, suave, self-assured, go-getter who has a strong, positive animus driving her, makes informed choices and deft moves promising her influence and affluence to those who respect her worth, then it is beyond the shadow of a doubt, the Indian goddess Lakshmi, one of the trinity of the divine feminine.

The Myths of Lakshmi

The myths of Lakshmi are many and they bring out different aspects of her, justifying the many names and adulations that describe her and the at-times ambivalent adjectives that qualify her. Known by names like Indrani (wife of Indra), Vishnupriya (Vishnu's beloved) and Chandrasahodari (consort of Chandra or the Moon), Lakshmi's association with several men of power and repute including Kubera, the God of wealth and the *asuras* Prahlada and Bali have also earned her the name of Chanchala or the fickle-one, with literal and metaphorical connotations. If Lakshmi symbolises affluence and good fortune, men shouldn't let it go to their head as they may not possess it permanently.

Lakshmi stands for wealth in all its forms. She is the fertile earth, the moist soil which unites with the rain god Indra on which seeds are sown and harvests reaped. As Indra's wife (which finds mention in some Puranas and the Taittiriya Brahmana and is indicated in the Rigveda), she is the queen goddess Sachi or Indrani. It is her fortunate and blessed presence which defines Indra's power and affluence and the unrivalled prosperity of

Amravati. But Indra is forever paranoid and insecure that his kingdom will be usurped by the asuras and that leaves him in a permanent state of anxiety. Sachi's words and presence fail to calm him as he has forgotten her true nature. He oscillates between extreme pleasure and extreme paranoia. Sachi excuses him his distractions, his drunken stupors and occasional flings but when, in his arrogance he humiliates her publicly she knows it is time to leave him.

Myth has it that once, a wise sage called Durvasa offers Indra a garland of lotus flowers. Indra, in his arrogance, throws the garland around the trunk of his mount, the elephant Airavat who throws it on the ground and tramples it. Durvasa is enraged and Indrani who witnesses this hubris, takes it as a personal humiliation as it is she who dwells in the garland. The furious sage curses Indra that he will lose everything to the asuras since he has failed to respect Lakshmi.

By allowing the garland to be crushed, Indra has symbolically disparaged Sachi. She leaves his heavenly abode and disappears in the milky ocean. Indra, driven by his desires – women, gold, riches, throne, wine, pleasure – is indifferent to her, so Lakshmi leaves him and all that she had brought along with her vanish. Barrenness takes over all three worlds. Once she leaves, good fortune and prosperity also leave Indra and Amravati becomes vulnerable to the attacks of the asuras. Indrani or Sachi will emerge only much later, during the churning of the ocean and this time choose Vishnu over Indra and be hailed as Lakshmi.

The second of the Dashavataar (the ten incarnations) of Vishnu is the Kurmavataar or the incarnation of the Lord as a tortoise at the time of the samudramanthan or the churning of the ocean. According to the *Bhagavata Purana*, tired of defending themselves against the asuras, the devas led by Indra, approach Brahma for a solution who takes them to Vishnu. The devas can become immortal if they drink from the amritkalash or pot of ambrosia buried in the depths of the milky ocean or the kshirsagar. But to obtain the pot the ocean must be churned.

Vishnu concedes to assume the form of a great kurma or a tortoise which will support mount Mandhar on its back for the ocean to be churned. The great serpent Vasuki will serve as the rope that will be tied around mount Mandhar to rotate it for the churning. Vishnu also advises the devas to make peace with the asuras as the task will be impossible to accomplish without the combined efforts of the devas and the asuras. The asuras and the devas, both desirous of the ambrosia, agree to a truce and join forces to perform this magnanimous task.

Once the churning starts, various treasures emerge from the depths of the waters including Kamdhenu the wish-fulfilling cow, Parijaat the wish-fulfilling tree, Chintamani the wish-fulfilling jewel, Halahala or the poison that Shiva ingests, the goddess Lakshmi and finally Dhanwantari with the pot of ambrosia. Once the ambrosia is procured, Vishnu assumes the form of Mohini, an enticing maiden and makes away with the ambrosia which has always been meant only for the devas. Lakshmi, enamoured of Vishnu and his guile, decides to be his consort. In him, she sees a preserver and someone who is empathetic to a just cause.

Lakshmi, in subsequent Puranas, is seen dwelling at Vaikuntha which is Vishnu's abode. She is charmed by the archetypal shape-shifter in him and in his human incarnations she is by his side as Sita when he incarnates as Rama and as Rukmini, Satyabhama and Draupadi when he incarnates as Krishna. She is his daughter, wife, lover and consort.

In the myth of Prithu, Lakshmi is Vishnu's daughter Prithvi. Prithu is the son of the evil king Vena whose reign spells anarchy as he fails to observe the Vedic rituals and curse befalls the land. Vena is killed by the sages who then churn his corpse, out of which emerges a dark dwarf that is symbolic of his evil or shadow self. Out of his remains which are now pure, rises Prithu who is also regarded as a part incarnation of Vishnu as he is born of a man's body without a woman. Prithu's birth is primarily to negotiate with Bhudevi or the earth, a form of Lakshmi who has taken the form of a cow and run away to escape the atrocities of Vena. Prithu chases her but she refuses to return saying she cannot bear to be exploited any further. Prithu convinces her to come back with him, promising her that she will not be exploited and be 'milked' on his watch.

Prithu then 'milks' the earth by summoning Manu in the form of a calf for the earth to be replenished with vegetation and natural resources once again. Thus guarded and assured of her safety by Prithu, the earth comes upon being regarded as Prithvi, the daughter of Prithu. In her identification as the Earth Goddess and the metaphor of the cow to symbolise her, Lakshmi comes very close to the Greek goddess Gaia who is also the Earth mother with the cow as her symbol, indicative of the Indo-European continuum in the realm of myths.

There are many myths that account for Lakshmi's origin. Lakshmi has more than one father. In fact, she is believed to have five fathers – Varuna, the sea god since she emerges from the churning of the ocean, Prithu who vows to protects her as Prithvi, Brahma who births her through meditation and Bhrigu according to *Garuda Purana*, *Linga Purana* and *Padma Purana* but no mother (except for Bhrigu's wife Khyati who does not get much of a mention). Lakshmi is also believed to be the daughter of the asura Puloman who rules over patala or the netherworld and thus is also called Pulomi. On a symbolic level this would refer to the mineral reserves, fossil fuels and precious stones all amounting for the immense wealth found under the earth.

In Greek mythology, the wealth on the surface of the earth and the wealth below the earth are represented by Demeter and her daughter Persephone respectively. In the theology of the Eleusinian mysteries, Plutus, who is either the son of Demeter or of Persephone personifies the god of wealth. Initially associated with the wealth generated from the surface of the earth that is through agricultural means, Plutus gradually came to stand for wealth of all kinds symbolised by the Cornucopia or the horn of plenty he holds.

According to the *Shatapatha Brahmana*, Lakshmi is supposed to have emerged from the mouth of Brahma as a result of his deep meditation on his creation of the universe. She is a shimmering entity, trembling with energy and blinding brilliance and when the gods see her, it unnerves them. They feel drawn to her and want to possess her but at the same time they are wary of her powers. So they approach Brahma expressing their desire to kill her and then appropriate her talents, her powers and her gifts. Brahma forbids them from doing this as it is a sin to kill a woman and advises them to appeal to her benevolence instead, and seek her blessings.

Each god goes to her with a certain lakshya or objective in mind which is fulfilled by her as she bestows her power to each of the gods including Agni, Soma, Varuna, Mitra and even Brihaspati, the guru or the teacher of the devas. Thus she becomes Lakshmi or the goddess who fulfils one's desires, objectives and goals in life. She is also someone who enables one to become more knowing, insightful, observant and understanding as lakshya also means concentration.

As the daughter of Puloman she is Pulomi, the princess of the netherworld or *"Pataal Nivasini"* and the source of all wealth and buried treasures. Puloman is attacked and killed by Indra and Pulomi taken as his wife after which she comes to be known as Sachi or Indrani. Symbolically, this myth possibly alludes to the violation of the earth by the devas or 'light-skinned migrants' and their pursuit of extracting natural resources from the earth, especially metals and minerals. Her asura lineage could also imply that Lakshmi may have been an indigenous deity. In another myth, once Indrani leaves Indra and immerses herself in the ocean of milk, she becomes the daughter who has come to seek refuge in her father's (Varuna or the water god) realm. As the daughter of Bhrigu, one of the Saptarishis, Lakshmi is Bhargavi of supreme intellect. Thus she is associated with three asura fathers – Varun who is believed to be an asura in many texts, Bhrigu, the teacher of the asuras and Puloman, an asura himself.

According to some myths, both Lakshmi and Saraswati, are Vishnu's wives and they are always competing with each other for his attention. Vishnu is so tired of this squabble that he places Saraswati on his tongue and Lakshmi in his heart or near his feet, as far away as possible from Saraswati. Though Saraswati gets a more prominent position, it is actually Lakshmi who is visible and comes to be associated with Vishnu.

Though Lakshmi is often projected as the subservient companion of Vishnu, especially through her positioning at the feet of the semi-recumbent Narayana, there are several myths that foreground her sense of self-respect and individuality. Once all the sages come together to perform a maha yajna on the banks of the river Saraswati, but they are unable to come to a consensus as to who among the trinity, Brahma, Vishnu and Mahesh is the greatest of all to be accorded the position of the presiding deity of the yajna. The sages request Bhrigu, famed for his knowledge, intellect and spiritual powers to find out the greatest of them all.

Bhrigu sets out on his journey and reaches the abode of Brahma first. He announces his arrival but Brahma is in a meditative state and does not respond. Bhrigu, full of the pride of his knowledge and scholarship, is furious and leaves to go to Kailasa. When he reaches Kailasa and announces his arrival, Shiva does not respond as he is engaged in lovemaking with Parvati. Bhrigu is even more infuriated than before and leaves

Kailasa in a huff and arrives at Vaikuntha. When he announces his arrival, he finds no response as Vishnu is sleeping. An enraged Bhrigu kicks Vishnu on the chest. Vishnu wakes up immediately and instead of lashing out at Bhrigu for the latter's insolence, expresses his concern and wants to know if Bhrigu hasn't hurt his toe while kicking him. Bhrigu realises his folly and his false sense of pride leaves him as he begs Vishnu to forgive him.

Lakshmi, who resides in Vishnu's heart, however, takes offence at this action and is not pleased that her husband has failed to show any concern about *her* being hurt and instead is worried about Bhrigu. She walks out of his heart, out of Vaikuntha and comes down to earth and starts residing on earth.

Unable to bear his separation from her, Vishnu too leaves Vaikuntha and follows Lakshmi to earth. But he realises that he cannot make two ends meet without her. He starts living as Srinivasa but most of the time he is badly off. Lakshmi who is looking out for him, has a cow arranged for him who will give him milk and help him sustain. Meanwhile, Vishnu decides to marry the local princess Padmavati, the daughter of the king of Tirupati, but the king demands a huge bride price. So he takes a loan from Kubera and marries Padmavati. When Lakshmi hears this news, she is not too happy and comes back to reclaim her place and reaffirms her position as the first claimant to Vishnu. So Vishnu places the princess Padmavati to his left and Lakshmi to his right and becomes Venkateshwara. According to legend, even today, devotees throng the Tirupati Balaji temple with money and gold to help Vishnu repay his loan to Kubera which he had borrowed for his wedding in return for spiritual guidance.

In another popular myth in Odisha, which women narrate on the day of Kaumudi Pournima, they describe Lakshmi's disappearance from the temple of Jagannath at Puri where she dwells in the kitchen that serves food to thousands of devotees who come every day. She ensures that the kitchen is always stocked and no devotee goes back hungry. One day Lakshmi goes to visit a Dalitbahujan woman's house. When Jagannath's (Vishnu) brother Balabhadra (Balaram) comes to know about this, he orders the temple doors to be closed and does not allow Lakshmi to enter the temple precincts as she has violated a rule. When Lakshmi sees the closed door she leaves Puri for good. Soon there is no food and the crops fail. A terrible famine strikes the land. Jagannath realises his mistake, begs her forgiveness and she finally relents.

In her human incarnation as Sita in some versions of the Ramayana, Lakshmi is the obedient wife of Rama, the prince of Ayodhya who is abducted by the asura king Ravana and kept captive in his kingdom in Lanka. When Vishnu is believed to have incarnated as Krishna, Lakshmi incarnates as his wives Rukmini and Satyabhama. While Rukmini stands for unconditional love for Krishna, Satyabhama symbolises wealth and influence.

A lesser known myth is that of Satyabhama and the fierce battle she fights with the dreaded demon Narakasur who she finally slays. Narakasur is the child of Vishnu in a former *avatar* of his, the Varaha avatar, when Vishnu incarnated as a boar to free Bhudevi from the clutches of the demon Hiranakshya who had hidden her in the depths of the ocean. Narakasur is invincible and has a boon by Brahma that he can be killed only by his mother. His reign of terror increases as he vanquishes and overthrows king after king, slaying people and taking the princesses of the defeated kingdoms captive who he hides on top of the mountain Maniparvata which is guarded by Mura, a five-headed demon.

His audacity reaches new heights when he not only attacks Indra and his kingdom but also steals the earrings of Aditi, the mother of Indra. A livid Aiiti, who is a relative of Satyabhama, comes to her seeking her intervention in destroying Narakasur. Satyabhama agrees and wants her husband Krishna to assist her who readily agrees to be her charioteer. The two fly on Vishnu's mount the majestic eagle Garuda to the fortress where Narakasur holds all the princesses captive.

Narakasur deals a near fatal blow to Krishna who falls unconscious. Mad with fury and bloodlust, Satyabhama attacks Narakasur and slays him, thus fulfilling the condition of Brahma's boon that he could be killed only by his mother. A dying Narakasur begs his mother's forgiveness and expresses his last wish which is to be remembered well and for his deeds to be obliterated from memory. Satyabhama grants him his wish and tells him that the day he died will be commemorated as the festival of lights. This day comes to be known as *Narak Chaturdashi* when people celebrate Diwali, the festival of lights.

Analysing Lakshmi in the light of the Myths

In the *Rigveda* Lakshmi is a disembodied entity hailed by the name of Sri standing for good fortune, and all that is auspicious. She is believed to be located in the cushion of the royal throne. She is also more concerned with the qualities that go into making a just ruler rather than the position, power or authority the ruler enjoys or the ruler himself.

Lakshmi appears prominently in the 1st millennium BC. The *Saubhagyalakshmi Upanishad* gives an exhaustive description of the full extent of her qualities, power and characteristics. She acquires the position of a major Puranic goddess and the presiding goddess who oversees the act of Creation in the *Pancharatra* texts. A detailed interaction between Lakshmi and her husband Vishnu on matters of ethical and moral issues related to one's political, social and personal life is compiled by Venkateshwara in South India and divided in 30 chapters called Niti in what comes to be referred to as the *Subhashita* or the *Punarartha Samgraha*.

Lakshmi is worshipped by different names in Tibet, Nepal, Bali, other South East Asian countries and even Japan and China. Graeco-Indian gems and seals have her form imprinted on them and she can be also traced on coins in circulation in Afghanistan and across India. Lakshmi is worshipped, both as a consort of Vishnu and as an independent goddess. She is worshipped in the western part of India and some parts of Odisha in the form of cowdung. The *Pancharatra* texts acknowledge her supreme divinity and power with the *Lakshmi-tantra* actually attributing the work of all Creation to her and undermining the role of a somnambulant Vishnu. She is worshipped as *Mahalakshmi*, the divinity governing all Creation. Fertility, bounty, abundance, growth, fecundity, prosperity, wealth, affluence, excellence and success in all spheres of life-social, cultural, financial, intellectual, emotional and professional are universal desires of the unconscious and projected on the goddess by imagining her as the giver of all these in the form of Ashtalakshmi.

Lakshmi is matter and energy both, that which is stationery and fluid in Creation. Lakshmi symbolises wealth, both on the earth and under the earth. Besides symbolising fertility and the wealth and abundance present in nature, she also symbolises the wealth that is in the pot or is collected and assigned the status of wealth in a culture. She is sometimes seen as holding a wheat sheaf which connotes her close association with the earth and its resources, symbolising a good harvest and food. She also has a jar of gold coins which is symbolic of worldly riches.

Lakshmi is bedecked in finery and jewels which communicates her royal lifestyle. In fact, her attire and iconography make a very powerful statement and reveal the mysteries of nature's abundance and the power of culture to project material wealth. Her red saree and gold jewellery speak of her queenlike position. Lakshmi is also Padma or Kamala, both names for the lotus flower. The lotus is believed to be the symbol of the ever-expanding universe. Lakshmi's close association with the lotus probably stands to represent ever-increasing and ever-expanding wealth, growth, abundance and prosperity that is desired by all. Just like the lotus, Lakshmi has risen from the primordial waters but has attained a transcendental position. She rises from the mire but is immaculate herself. This suggests the spiritual connotation of wealth, which implies that Lakshmi is not merely the symbol of material wealth but also that of spiritual bliss. Additionally, the lotus stands for fertility as well, as it gets its nourishment from always available water.

Lakshmi is flanked by majestic white elephants on both sides which are again symbols of fertility and rain. The white elephant is also a sign of wisdom and thus Lakshmi's relation with the intellect and the god of wisdom Ganesha who she enters with, in the domestic space as a household deity. Interestingly Durga is worshipped twice a year, Saraswati only once but Lakshmi is a household deity who is the most popular if not the most powerful and most frequently invoked and is worshipped every day and in some parts, every Thursday. In the state of Bengal and its adjoining regions, it is customary to read the *Lakshmi Panchali* every Thursday which has stories of the goddess that are contextualised and resonate with the trading community. Lakshmi, thus, manages to capture the popular imaginary. In the eastern part of India, the owl is a part of the iconography of Lakshmi, symbolic of age-old wisdom and a penetrating vision that cuts through the darkness.

Lakshmi is the presiding goddess of abundance but she also stands for the ephemeral nature of material gains. Her mythology is a constant reminder of how, all that is material is also temporal. How it takes a moment for things to change. As long as she is in Vaikuntha, Vishnu is relaxed and sleeping. The moment she leaves Vaikuntha, it results in despair in Vishnu. Without Lakshmi by his side, even the most powerful preserver of Creation is reduced to penury. He has to take a loan from

Kubera. Indra meets with a similar fate when Lakshmi leaves him and so do Bali and Prahlada. Thus, it is evident that even the greatest and wealthiest of men can be reduced to nothing without Lakshmi by their side.

Lakshmi personifies the idealised image of the woman who has the power to be the harbinger of good fortune and prosperity for the man she is associated with and also the household and the family she is married into. This is a common Indian belief. The daughter-in-law in India is seen as *Grihalakshmi* or Lakshmi of the house, a human manifestation of goddess Lakshmi who will bring abundance, good fortune and material prosperity to the family after marriage.

Lakshmi and Her Archetypes

Like Parvati, Lakshmi too has a strong Queen archetype in her which is evident from her bearing, her attire, her mount, (the elephant – the mount of kings) and her disposition. She is benevolent and concerned about the well-being of those who depend on her for sustenance. In the *Sri Vaishnava* texts, she is repeatedly described as someone who takes the pleas of devotees to Vishnu and mediates between the two.

The archetypes of the Critic and the Judge reveal themselves through Lakshmi. Lakshmi is drawn to valorous, courageous men of principles who rule righteously and who have earned their position. Therefore, she abandons Indra because his fortune is more like a windfall. She does not discriminate between devas and asuras and can be companion to either if they are righteous and just. David Kinsley in his book *Hindu*

Goddesses observes how Lakshmi in fact, lives with both Bali and Prahlada for a long time before Bali is sent to the netherworld by Vishnu in his Vamanavatar and Prahlada is tricked by Indra into parting with his fortune and success. Both are asuras but righteous rulers and therefore dear to Lakshmi.

The lores that have Lakshmi leaving the side of Vishnu present her as an independent woman who desires to be respected and wants no control or authority over her. She is critical of men who make an obscene display of their wealth, knowledge and possessions. She is as repulsed by Indra's flamboyance as she is by Bhrigu's arrogance. She regards the actions of these men critically and takes extreme steps for her displeasure to be known and for them to realise their folly, but not by reacting violently. Instead, like a true teacher and critic, she forces them to introspect and reflect on their misdoings.

Vishnu is her husband but her urge for fairness to prevail is so intense that she has to leave him to make him realise that she is not really appreciative of his diplomatic and sly tactics. The myth says that while expressing his concern over Bhrigu's toe, Vishnu touches the latter's toe and drains all his intellectual and spiritual knowledge through his touch. Similarly she does not want anybody dictating terms to her, even if it is Jagannath's elder brother Balabhadra who is a family elder. She has a strong sense of justice and an overriding benevolent nature which is why she goes to the humble dwelling of the poor woman.

Lakshmi's association with various men of power, all of them rulers or influential gods, show that she is more invested in the position and the power of the throne or the chair rather than the individual seated on it. This would explain her act of leaving her husband Indra, the king of gods who apparently is not above reproach and making errors. She goes to Vishnu instead of Indra after she emerges from the ocean because behind the householder, she can perceive a hermit who actually does not plan on hoarding her. She does not like to be held captive or be possessed or hoarded.

In several myths, however, Lakshmi also foregrounds the Victim archetype, especially as Mother Earth or Bhudevi, when she is abducted by the daitya king Hiranakshya and as Prithvi who takes on the form of a cow and escapes exploitation at the hands of king Vena. Apparently Vishnu has taken a vow to protect Lakshmi whether it is Bhudevi or Sridevi connoting natural and material wealth. In his avatar of Parashuram too, he slays all the kshatriyas to free the earth of all evil doers. He starts with the kshatriya king Kartavirya Arjuna who steals Surabhi the cow from the ashram of rish Jamadagni, who is the father of Parshuram. The cow symbolises the earth as she is an inexhaustible source of sustenance for the ashram dwellers. Parashuram kills the king and returns with the cow.

As Satyabhama, Lakshmi embodies the warrior and the Devouring Mother archetype who slays her son Narakasur. She also has the archetypes of the Strategist and the Negotiator as is obvious through the myths that describe her rivalry with Saraswati and also, where she lays her terms and conditions as Prithvi, before she returns with Prithu. She attracts people to her and thus embodies the archetype of the eternal Seductress whose very presence and aura inspire men to desire her. But the nature of her seduction is not sexual. They value her as an asset, an auspicious presence who will usher in and ensure their continued good fortune.

If one had to consider the unnatural and unfair distribution of wealth and entitlement, then Lakshmi seems to wear the Trickster archetype. She is Chanchala after all, who can be unpredictable and leave you just when you think you have her secured. She will outwit you and slip through your fingers even before you realise what is happening. She is restless and always on the move. Through a deft move she can remind you of your true place and worth in this world. She will not do your bidding. She has a mind and a will of her own and if she is forced, she has the ability to replace herself with her shadow or her sister Jyeshtha or Alakshmi who will bring misfortune upon you and destroy you.

On the other hand, she is also someone who can make you feel safe if you give her space. She will offer you sound counsel and good advice and impart some of her penetrating insight so that you can benefit from it. A figurative association of Lakshmi to the Nurturing or the Devouring Mother archetype can be traced in her reference as Bhagyalakshmi and its opposite, 'fate'.

Tracing Lakshmi in Popular Culture

Lakshmi's close association with natural and cultural wealth, fertility, abundance, growth and good fortune make her a universal archetype. She is a woman with many fathers and is in every way guided by a strong animus or masculine principle and every bit a father's daughter, ready to navigate her way through a man's world. She values qualities like courage, strength, leadership and excellence that are highly valued traits in a patriarchal culture and she is a patron goddess of material and masculine pursuits of attaining power and glory through wealth. In this she comes close to the Greek goddess Athena who identifies with her father Zeus as she is born out of his head while through her symbolic association with fertility, Lakshmi is like the earth goddess Demeter.

Lakshmi resembles the Egyptian goddess Isis in that the latter personifies nature at times and also embodies the archetype of the Magician. Isis, like Lakshmi, also has an owl by her side and her crown is the symbol of the throne of the king, which implies her association with the seat of power just like Lakshmi. Lakshmi's Magician archetype comes through when in order to prove a point or make people see what is just and fair, she resorts to being the White Magician. She turns princes into paupers and confers sudden good fortune on some poor soul steeped in penury.

Thus, we find Lakshmi-like characters extensively and across cultures, universally bearing her archetypes and depicting the many shades of her persona. Claire Underwood in the *House of Cards* (Seasons 1-4) is the archetypal Lakshmi who complements her husband in every way even overlooking his occasional flings (like the way Lakshmi tolerates Indra's womanising) knowing fully well, he will return to her. Claire is financially independent, runs her own very successful NGO, goes international and helps her husband whenever he is in a spot, till she feels she is not an equal in the marriage.

Claire emblematises the Lakshmi who attaches herself to the man who has grit, gumption and brilliance – the potential to be king. Claire, like Lakshmi, symbolises wealth and prosperity and it is her money that launches her husband's political career. Frank Underwood the man she marries, goes on to become the President of the United States but he is a dark soul. And when Claire begins to realise that he has been flaunting her and using her to further his political career compromising her interests and her ambitions at every juncture, denying her the office, in other words the position she rightfully deserves, she feels conflicted.

When Frank humiliates Claire after she has stood by him like a pillar of strength, she decides it is time to leave. This has echoes of the myths of Lakshmi every time she leaves the side of a king because the king has lost his vision and the qualities that make him worthy of the throne and is especially a reminder of the Sachi-Indra myth. With Claire's departure, Frank's goodwill and reputation quickly begin to vanish and his ratings start to drop. This is exactly what happens to all the kings who Lakshmi abandons – they eventually lose their kingdom and their power.

Lakshmi's archetypes of the Counsel and the Queen resonate in Olivia Pope, the protagonist of the political thriller *Scandal*, yet another television web series based on White House politics aired on ABC from 2012 to 2018. Rich, professionally occupied, successful and independent, Olivia Pope (Kerry Washington) is the best lawyer in DC, quite queenlike as she is on top of her game. She has been hired to manage the election campaign of a presidential nominee. She is

attracted to men with the potential to rule and command and thus she is attracted to Fitzgerald Grant III (Tony Goldwyn), the Governor whose campaign she manages and who goes on to become the President of the United States.

Olivia has no difficulty navigating her way in a man's world and offering counsel, making tactical decisions and almost always saving the day for the President. She is competent, she thinks on her feet and she is fiercely independent. She is extremely resourceful and ensures a constant flow of money in the law firm she runs with her formidable team. She has a remarkable foresight, can anticipate political moves well in advance and nip problems in the bud even before they have had a chance to rear their head. She makes her moves with the same self-assuredness as Lakshmi and for difficult clients and trouble-makers, she always has a trick up her sleeve. She is a tough negotiator and manages the best deal on the table. She has her magical secrets too which she uses as leverage to get to the truth and sometimes as a negotiating tool.

People see the magic, the seemingly effortless charm but

underneath the magic is a lot of dedication, hardwork, gift and grit along with superb networking skills which always gives her an edge over her competitors. Anyone Olivia walks out on, suffers, because along with her, she also takes away their means to power and glory. She is a king-maker, the backbone of any campaign or a case that seems hopeless and therefore she is highly sought. She is capable of turning the tables which again seems like magic but is only a result of thorough research, optimal utilisation of resources and deft networking.

Another woman embodying the Lakshmi archetype would be Kendra Daynes (Zoe McLellan) in *The Designated Survivor* (Season 2) streaming on Netflix, also based on White House intrigue. A lawyer and a woman of firm conviction, she is driven by her sense of fairness and she agrees to work for the White House only because in President Tom Kirkman (Kiefer Sutherland), Kendra sees a true visionary and leader who has the nation's best interests at heart and is more of a statesman than a politician. Kendra brings to mind Lakshmi's decision to go to Vishnu rather than any other god because in him she sees someone who is capable of maintaining the cosmic balance. The asuras have the secret of Sanjeevani vidya which enables them to come back to life once killed and Vishnu has ensured that the devas get the ambrosia or the elixir of immortality. He has acted in all fairness. Though Kendra's relation with the President is strictly professional, her choice is informed and prompted by a similar observation of Kirkman.

Criminal Lawyer and Professor of Law Annalise Keating (Viola Davis) in the second phase of *How To Get Away with*

Murder has unmistakeable shades of Lakshmi when, phoenix-like, she rises from the ashes and rebuilds her reputation presenting herself as a brand. In fact Keating, after hitting rock bottom, reinvents herself. She is stately and poised even in adversity and her second innings recall Lakshmi's emergence from the kshirsagar to start life afresh, with none of her powers dormant or compromised.

Another Lakshmi-like figure would be Catherine Fox (Debbie Allen) in *Grey's Anatomy* (introduced in Season 8), the Chairman of Fox Foundation and the owner of Grey-Sloan hospital, who is prosperous, creative, an ace surgeon, a seductress of sorts with an inimitable zeal for life and works round the clock to keep expanding her chain of hospitals. She has an aura that is quite overwhelming and makes her presence felt in the room.

Though many Indian films attempt to capture and depict the daughter-in-law or the housewife as Lakshmi, because that is what her position in the Hindu household traditionally connotes, most films fail to project the many shades and archetypes of the goddess which go much beyond her power to ensure abundance and prosperity. The archetypal Lakshmi in the form of the exploited or victimised Grihalakshmi is one recurring characterisation in a number of Indian films. Lakshmi in many Indian films symbolises 'Sri' or the presence of the auspicious element in the domestic space. She is invested with the qualities of a good housewife. She looks after the house, is devoted to her husband, is often a loving mother and all in all, part of a happy family till something goes wrong and she becomes a victim.

Films like *Basera* (1981), *Nikaah* (1982), *Akhir Kyon?* (1985), *Akhree Rasta* (1986), *Sindoor* (1987), *Tezaab* (1988) and *Pratibandh* (1990) have projections of the Grihalakshmi and valences of Bhudevi with the Victim archetype. While in *Akhree Raasta* Mary (Jaya Prada), a loving mother and wife, gets raped and kills herself as a result, leaving her wrongly convicted husband David (Amitabh Bachhan) to avenge the death of the Grihalakshmi, in *Tezaab* the archetypal Lakshmi, Mohini (Madhuri Dikshit) endowed with beauty and talent is regularly exploited by an alcoholic father to earn a living. She is saved from her predicament by Munna (Anil Kapoor) and will go on to become the Grihalakshmi. In *Pratibandh*, Shanthi (Juhi Chawla) is similarly saved from the clutches of the villain Rama Reddy ('Spot' Nana) by Inspector Siddhant (Chiranjeevi) who then marries her just like Vishnu saves Bhudevi time and again.

One also encounters repetitions of the archetypal situation in the Indra-Sachi myth of the Grihalakshmi being humiliated and either removing herself or being ousted from the house followed by a spell of misfortune. In *Sindoor*, Laxmi (Jaya Prada) who is a devoted housewife, is wrongly accused by her husband Vijay (Shashi Kapoor) of having an adulterous relationship with a man and leaves the house as a result. In *Aakhir Kyon?*, Nisha (Smita Patil) is happily married to a wealthy, good-looking man Kabir (Rakesh Roshan). She, in every way, symbolises the Grihalakshmi through her gentle demeanour, her traditional appearance and her devotion to her husband. However, she is gradually displaced from her own house when her own sister Indu (Tina Munim) starts having an affair with Kabir. The two

lead a hedonistic life style as a tearful and humiliated Nisha is forced to leave the house.

The 1982 blockbuster hit film *Nikaah*, under the movie genre of the Muslim Social, has a storyline similar to that of *Aakhir Kyon?*. A damsel-like woman Nilofar (Salma Agha) is married to Wasim (Deepak Parashar) who is a nawab. The picture-perfect marriage slowly develops cracks and fissures as a devoted Nilofar feels increasingly neglected by a workaholic husband who apparently wants her only by his arm as a trophy wife once the initial romance of newly-weds fades off. When a depressed and perturbed Nilofar confronts her husband on this issue, in a moment of heat he, utters the forbidden word 'talaaq' three times and divorces her.

These are all archetypal instances when the Grihalakshmi has been displaced from her position as wife and mistress of the house thus spelling the end of good fortune, harmony and happiness in the domestic space as she leaves behind Alakshmi in her space. Some films in fact even have the personification of the Alakshmi or the shadow archetype of the Grihalakshmi like Indu in *Aakhir Kyon?*. After Nisha leaves, Kabir's financial condition worsens as if on account of the archetypal presence of Alakshmi in Indu.

The misfortune that can strike a person and result in his downward spiral once he is abandoned by the prospective Grihalakshmi is evident in the 2002 epic romantic film *Devdas* when Paro (Aishwarya Rai Bachhan) walks out of Devdas' (Shahrukh Khan) life who, in an angry spate humiliates her. Not only does he end up losing his emotional strength but he also forfeits his good will, his reputation, the property he is entitled to and finally his life. Though her name is Paro invoking Parvati in the film, she is more of a manifestation of the Lakshmi archetype who decides to walk away from the man who insults her, never to return and moves on in life marrying another man, leaving behind destruction in the wake.

A slightly modified version of the archetype of the Grihalakshmi-turned-Victim would be *Basera*. Sharada (Rakhee) married to Balraj (Shashi Kapoor) returns home after having spent 14 years in a mental institution where she had been admitted, following a head injury in an accidental fall. In her absence and in the light of her uncertain recovery from her condition, her younger sister Nima (Rekha) has stepped into the role of the Grihalakshmi, taking charge of the house and the children. Ironically, Sharada fell off the stairs and injured her head when she heard the news of the sudden death of Nima's husband. A fully recovered Sharada now wants to take over as Grihalakshmi which Nima concedes to, without even letting her sister know that she is married to the former's husband.

But when Sharada accidentally discovers the truth, she chooses to go back to her victim state and pretends to have a relapse so that she can be taken back to the mental institution.

There are also the Grihalakshmis like Maya (Padmini Kolhapure) in *Woh Saat Din* (1983) and Nandini (Aishwarya Rai Bachhan) in *Hum Dil De Chuke Sanam* (1999) who feel trapped and victimised in an arranged marriage which has taken place without their approval or under unavoidable circumstances while they pine for the love of their life. The narrative of these movies is a gradual domestication of the woman into the Grihalakshmi mode as she is rid of her fickle nature and made to realise where she truly belongs. In this, more than the Grihalakshmi it is the stable and understanding archetype of Narayana in the spouse which needs to be foregrounded as he passively awaits a change of heart in the Grihalakshmi.

The husband's absolute non-interference and absence of coercive measures to lay claim over his wife, giving her the space and time, she wants to think through and reflect on her course of actions is what makes her realise the selflessness of the man she is married to. Eventually the woman gives up her 'fickle', 'free' self which craved for the lover and romanticised an impossible and impractical union and settles down in the role of a mature and responsible Grihalakshmi, the truly deserving and appropriate wife of a husband – the archetype of Narayana who is a firm believer in fairness and justice and embodies an empathetic and sensitive masculinity.

The protagonists of *Tumhari Sulu (2017)* and *Sui Dhaga*

(2018) have positive valences of the Grihalakshmi and bring out the Entrepreneur archetype in Lakshmi as they think of enterprises from within the confines of the house and not only make a mark for themselves but also make it a financial success. In *Sui Dhaga*, Mamta (Anushka Sharma) is the ideas person who wants her husband to be independent and encourages him to start small but be self-reliant when he loses his job. Like Lakshmi, she is resourceful and with her networking and envisioning skills, she chalks out the trajectory of their professional success. She is the one who comes up with the brand name of 'Sui Dhaga' to give their garments an identity and it is also she who uses her public relation skills and acumen to convince the dying fraternity of weavers to work for them. It is her indispensable assistance and presence by her husband's side which paves the way for his professional and material success.

In *Tumahri Sulu*, Sulu (Vidya Balan) thinks of an out-of-the-box job and in fact creates a position for herself with her convincing abilities. In this, like Lakshmi, she is inherently gifted with qualities and talent and thus is a brand by herself.

The Devouring Mother archetype, which is an aspect of Lakshmi and comes through in the mythological character of Satyabhama who is her human incarnation, finds its onscreen presence in the formidable and awe-inspiring Sivagami (Ramya Krishnan), the queen mother in *Bahubali 2: The Conclusion* (2018) who orders the execution of the son she loves more than her life because she is led to believe that he is a threat to the kingdom. Like Satyabhama, Sivagami has the posture of a warrior and is unrelenting, once her decision is made. The difference is while Narkasur is mythologically depicted as really an evil king, Amarendra Bahubali (Prabhas) is a just prince and is a victim of conspiracy.

The devouring mother may seem like the shadow of the mother archetype but it has a light side. Whether it is Sivagami in *Bahubali*... or Radha (Nargis) in *Mother India*, they are invested in the kingdom/community and sacrifice their sons as they perceive the son-turned-rogue to be a threat to the people. While Radha has known about her son's exploits for quite some time and makes an informed decision when she ends his life, Sivagami reacts in haste. They are both strong women and leaders in their own right. However, the true test of leadership lies in showing one's wisdom and sagacity, especially when it is a decision as monumental and difficult as executing one's own son. In this regard, Radha's character reflects the archetypal decision-maker, problem-solver in Satyabhama while Sivagami's posturing and staging is more of a reflection on the Warrior and Queen archetypes in Satyabhama.

Other than her manifestation as Satyabhama, Lakshmi is not usually identified or regarded as a warring goddess like

Durga or Kali. In case of a conflict, she uses a tactical rather than a combative approach as is evident from the myths that surround her. She simply leaves the conflict zone and does what she has to do without an irreversible fallout or fight. She leaves a route and a door open with the possibility of returning if she is sincerely appeased.

Contemporarising and Humanising Lakshmi

Lakshmi is any woman who believes in having a refined lifestyle within available means and who believes in keeping herself well-groomed and attractive. She displays qualities and an idealised staging of the self that make her enviable. Her positive projection draws people to her and everyone wants to know her, be near her and connect with her. In that sense she is a seductress with a magnetic appeal. She is someone who values the importance of material success. She is also someone who is self-reliant and perfectly capable of looking after herself and others she cares for. She is mostly even-tempered. She may not be an intellectual or an expert authority on any particular subject but she certainly has a range of talents that make her far more popular. She can look out for herself and put her talents to best use which will bring her fame, success and wealth. She has a positive frame of mind and that is why others associate good fortune with her. Her presence is refreshing, energising and motivates people to perform.

She is a woman who is an asset for the household which she runs, or the organisation where she works and certainly someone who has smart ideas about starting profitable ventures; in other words, someone who knows how to get the moolah for the organisation. She is a woman who can breathe life into a household or an organisation making it richer and more prosperous by her sheer energy, vibrance and presence. Lakshmi has an aura of hope, opportunity, progress, growth and she is a person with a vision and clarity who can anticipate and speculate well in advance and plan her moves accordingly. She is a woman who knows the importance of ranking high in the social order and having a strong organisational presence. She is someone who is a role model and inspires other women to be like her. She is a woman who enjoys holding high offices, being in the limelight and on the front page of magazines but for the right reasons.

Lakshmi is as much a king-maker as she is attracted to men in power but expects full respect, attention and reverence from them. She values her autonomy and walks out regally and with dignity whenever she deems it appropriate to do so. She is self-sufficient. She does not need support from the outside but she can offer valuable support to men and women, both. She is someone who has an indisputable brand image and her very presence is enough to elevate the worth of the person she is with or seems to be endorsing.

She is clearly a woman who men are initially intimidated by because of her radiant presence, because they feel overshadowed by her but eventually are drawn to when they realise that her qualities could benefit them. A woman who clearly has arrived, a woman who is fond of wealth, riches and a lavish lifestyle herself but does not depend on a man to give her all this, she is also someone who absolutely desists being chased and instead appreciates generosity and magnanimity of heart in men. She feels comfortable when she has autonomy in decision-making and is not treated as a prized possession or someone to be flaunted. She is a woman who will be munificent and generous only to those who do not obsess with her and give her, her space and acknowledge her individuality and supremacy. She can prove to be resilient and a tough negotiator even if she is cornered. She is a go-getter and will always get the best deal.

Despite being rooted in materialism, Lakshmi is detached enough to leave, even the most powerful man if she feels he is getting complacent or if she perceives a threat to her self-esteem from him. She can inspire both envy and respect in men and thus play them to her advantage. She rises fast and is quick to associate herself with people at the top, benefitting them with her ideas, her qualities, her worldly wisdom and her smartness. She is a woman whose loyalty can be easily won and retained if she knows she has a say in matters. Lakshmi is an independent-minded woman who believes in an equal relationship. She does not compromise on that front till she has found the right man and finally settles down. And when she finds true love she will not flinch from complementing her partner in every possible way. She values her autonomy and walks out regally and with dignity whenever she considers appropriate.

She is a proud woman who can become vain at times because she is supremely talented. She is competitive and can outsmart others, sometimes manipulate just a little using her appearance and her assets to rise higher. She will take steps necessary to attract eyeballs and make her presence felt but she is also a woman who believes in collaborative work that will bring rich returns just the way she unites with Indra to bring prosperity on earth.

The Lakshmi Archetype in Brands

The several positive archetypes of the Entrepreneur, Creator, Negotiator, Networker and Initiator in Lakshmi can be variously assimilated and projected through contemporary feminine constructs by positioning them within the domestic sphere or the workplace. Brands, when using the archetype of Lakshmi could depict women with an aura of well-being, prosperity, autonomy and material success, both at home and at work. She can be conceived as a woman entrepreneur who uses her qualities as a means of sustenance. For instance, the woman in the Britannia[9] Marie Gold ad who comes up with an idea of a small start-up to sell the artefacts she makes at home is a projection of Lakshmi whose values or qualities or assets are at the core (*rasa*) of what she creates and markets.

Lakshmi's archetype could be projected through women pioneering Startups, MSMEs or operating from SOHOs where their initiative reaps commercial benefits. Likewise it can manifest in women conceptualising and laying out the blueprint of a business plan or venture. Women consumers today would like to identify with feminine constructs who take an initiative to think, who bring people on board and finally implement a

9 https://www.youtube.com/watch?v=eEGDMifjQS4

plan, who are shown to procure funds or successfully handle a project that will bring profits to the organisation. It could construct women as engaged in the image-building process of the organisation along with increasing their own visibility.

An advertisement could be conceived showing a woman turning around a friend's business which is in loss with a brilliant idea or capitalising on an unforeseen opportunity so that loss becomes gain. Narratives could trace the journey of a woman who is innovative enough to come up with new ideas and smoothly navigate tough negotiations making her look like an institution and her company look like it is the best and the biggest in the market. A more charitable depiction would be that of a woman who also looks at giving back to society, or who urges her organisation to be more focused on the nature of its CSR (Corporate Social Responsibility). A professional who can be shown as prosperous, commercially driven and yet against over-exploitation of labour or resources for overtly capitalistic or commercial gains.

The pot of Lakshmi could figure as a symbol in an advertisement or a motif in a series of advertisements for the same product where the woman holds the secret to material success. It can be depicted as an 'ideas' pot to keep the organisation from bankruptcy, the pot thus becoming a metaphor for immortalising the reputation and ensuring the sustenance of the organisation. Or the figurative association of the woman with the cornucopia (since Lakshmi is also associated with the akshay patra) which never runs out of ideas and says, 'There's always a way out'; a woman embodying an action-oriented, problem-solving approach.

An alternative narrative, positioning the woman in the domestic sphere and working on the Grihalakshmi archetype could be that of a housewife who can be shown encouraging her recently widowed mother-in-law or father-in-law to start a venture, use their skills or to become a dealer or a trader so that it gives them a sense of being productive and also confirms tangible returns.

A woman dreaming of or visualising a successful venture and then working towards it could also be a desirable narrative which resonates with women with an entrepreneurial bent of mind. A woman devising a plan to build her own brand or working on herself as a brand, a woman inspiring other women to start a venture, financing them or assisting them with ideas could be other motivating narratives. Likewise, a woman who is calculating risks and anticipating problems and has a backup plan to fall back on, could also be a possible construct embodying the Lakshmi archetype. A woman coming up with a brainwave to save the organisation from bankruptcy, promoting teamwork, taking a radical decision and turning around a business, all of these can be developed into narratives positively projecting the Lakshmi archetype.

SARASWATI: THE GODDESS WHO HID

SHE IS THE quiet kind. Demure, and with a demeanour that seems to suggest that she would like, not to draw too much attention her way, she tries to keep a low profile but ends up doing the exact opposite. She may not be eye candy but she certainly is a show-stealer. She can mesmerise people with the mellifluous notes that flow effortlessly out of her, like free-flowing, crystal-clear water in the mountains. She sings easily without thinking of the unique gift she has. She is gracious and charming in accepting the praises that her rapturous audience has to shower on her. But she is an ascetic. She has a simple lifestyle, wears simple fabric and very little jewellery. She is almost nondescript that way. She loves her gift because it comes naturally to her. It is who she is. She is not out to flaunt her gift and that is perhaps the reason why she is so sought after. Her singing is beautiful precisely because it is so simple, honest and pure, unsullied by ambition or pride.

For her, music is her very being, the air she breathes, the light surrounding her. She simply does not know any other way of being, than through music. Gently, simply, lovingly she flows, till she realises the pain and the agony she is causing her husband and freezes. What she thinks is a delicate morning light, is her sheer brilliance which overshadows and scorches her husband, affecting his gift. He is restless, because people like to listen to *her* more than him. He pretends not to mind, he frets inside, till one day he snaps. And thus assaulted by a man's ego, she stops flowing. Not one to show her pain, she simply ceases to flow, just like the river which changed its course and hid itself. Shying away from all adulations and invocations, she vanishes from public eye to go back to the small village she came from. She is Sudha (Jaya Bhaduri), the simple yet supremely gifted protagonist of the Hrishikesh Mukherjee 1973 blockbuster *Abhimaan* and the very embodiment of the Goddess Saraswati as much in her appearance, bearing and temperament as in her attributes.

The river Saraswati's disappearance underground has often been symbolically interpreted and attributed to the undermining of arts and aesthetics in the face of rising materialism in the Vedic period which indicated a preference for Lakshmi, the goddess of wealth over Saraswati, the patron goddess of wisdom and arts. Sudha's journey can be traced on the lines of the journey of the river Saraswati which simply disappears from the face of the earth when she is undermined, to continue with her life underground.

The goddess of institutions, whose worship meant that communities had changed their primitive way of existence to go beyond surviving and consuming, to dwell on more refined and intellectually stimulating pursuits like music, art, science, aesthetics and literature, Saraswati, in her many cultural and regional manifestations invokes the seeker, the artiste and the scholar in us.

The Myths of Saraswati

Saraswati is regarded as either Brahma's wife or his daughter and sometimes both. According to the most popular Creation myth in Indian mythology, Brahma splits himself into two parts - male and female and falls in love with the female half which is Saraswati. This results in a conjugal union out of which evolves the whole of Creation. Saraswati is thus the mother of all Creation. However, Saraswati is apparently not too happy with this union as she sees it as unethical and therefore is believed to have subsequently shied away from Brahma.

The *Devi Bhagavata Purana* and *Brahma Vaivarta Purana*

also validate the hegemonic incest myth though they say that the female half (prakriti or matter) splits further into five feminine forms of which one is Saraswati. She is supposed to be the most sattvic, in other words the most spiritual, the most pure, the most chaste of all the femininities. In many sects she is believed to be single. There are also myths which describe Shiva's beheading of Brahma following Saraswati's ravishment by the 'Creator' of the Universe. Shiva as Rudra intervenes and beheads the Creator who tries to possess that which he has created. Legend has it that this is also one reason why Brahma is not worshipped by earth-dwellers unlike Shiva and Vishnu who have temples across India dedicated to them. An anthropological reading will trace the diminishing popularity of Brahma to the decreasing importance of the Vedic rituals of yajna and sacrifice and their gradual replacement by Puranic rituals around idol worship.

The earliest association of Saraswati is with that of a river. Saraswati originates in heaven and flows down to the earth. She is a turbulent, fast-flowing, surging river with waves whose power can thwart and destroy mountains. She is believed to have descended on earth on the suggestion of Mahadev and at the request of Brahma who wants her to consume a raging fire by the name of Vadavagni which has threatened to consume all of creation. When Saraswati descends, Mahadev hands over the fire to her and she bears it in her, carrying it all the way to the ocean through Pushkar where the fire is finally subsumed in the great waters.

There are myths that talk about the origin of Saraswati on

the tongues of gods like Brahma, Vishnu and Krishna. A myth describes the incessant rivalry and one-upmanship between Saraswati and Lakshmi who, in the Vaishnava sect are believed to be the wives of Vishnu. An exasperated Vishnu places Saraswati on his tongue and Lakshmi in his heart or near his feet to keep them as apart from each other as possible. It is a popular presumption that Saraswati and Lakshmi cannot dwell in the same place together. It is also said that if one chases Saraswati, Lakshmi is bound to follow, but if one chases Lakshmi, Saraswati ceases to favour that person. Symbolically read, pursuit of knowledge, wisdom, art and aesthetics may prove to be materially advantageous as one capitalises on one's gifts and abilities but material pursuits will not enlighten one, increase one's scholarship or make one an authority over any discipline.

Saraswati, at the request of the devas, is known to have sat on the great asura, Kumbhakarna's tongue when, after inordinate penance, the latter seeks a boon from Brahma. Saraswati twists the words that come out of his mouth and instead of Indrasan or the seat of Indra the king of Gods, Kumbhakarna finds himself asking for the boon of nidrasan or an extended state of sleep which makes him go into a state of deep slumber for six months at a stretch. Another episode from the Ramayana related to Saraswati describes how the devas, worried about the growing power of Ravana, approach Saraswati for help. Saraswati enters the mind of Kaikeyi's maid Manthra in her dream. The next day she makes Manthra suggest the unthinkable to the queen – Rama's exile and Bharata's coronation. This is an initiative by Saraswati at the request of the devas as, in order for Rama to vanquish Ravana, he will first have to go into exile which will set off the series of incidents that will eventually lead to a clash between Rama and Ravana.

In the Vedic period, rituals and yajnas were often held on the banks of the river Saraswati. In certain Vedic texts like the *Satapatha Brahmana*, Saraswati is also associated with healing and medicine. Saraswati, along with the Aswins, was beseeched to heal Indra when he was fatally wounded in battle and is known to cure people of ailments.

In some texts, Saraswati is also associated with Gayatri or the goddess of hymns who is also the personification of the Vedas. Saraswati is also known as Vedagarbham or the mother of all the Vedas originating from her womb. In one shloka of the Rigveda, she is described and invoked as the slayer of the serpent demon Vritra.

Analysing Saraswati in the Light of the Myths

Saraswati seems like a fuller personification of the Vedic goddess Vac or Vagdevi, meaning speech. Her association with speech and thought is the reason why she is given the status of the goddess of knowledge, arts, sciences and music. Saraswati is worshipped as Tara in Buddhism and highly revered in Jainism as the goddess from whom all source of learning originates. It is believed that Saraswati enabled the spread of Jain teachings through the sermons of the Tirthankaras. She is also worshipped in other South East Asian countries and even China and Japan which see her as the goddess of learning, knowledge, music and wisdom.

The high regard for Saraswati in Vedic times and deifying her through a river in North West India suggests that the Aryans had probably begun to transition from a nomadic community into a pastoral one, gradually settling down and identifying with a specific geographical location. In fact the deification of the river Saraswati and her invocation as a goddess heralds a long tradition of deification and mythologising of rivers like Ganga, Yamuna, Narmada and Godavari.

Saraswati is the first river or goddess metaphor to introduce the idea of water as holy, sacred and capable of removing impurities and sins. The river is the source of nourishment for an agrarian community and civilisations are known to have come up primarily near rivers. Once a community is settled, it has a steady source of subsistence; only then can it look at or focus on evolving its culture and developing its own music, art and literature.

Saraswati, the river, becomes a metaphor for that nourishing source or the goddess which enables and brings about the higher, more transcendental nature of cultural prosperity resulting out of material stability. Saraswati also symbolises flow and absence of stagnancy which is how true knowledge and wisdom ought to be. The whole metaphor of crossing the river in one's spiritual journey in the religious discourse of eastern religions like Hinduism, Jainism and Buddhism could seem to have sprung or evolved from this initial association of sacredness, purity, the ability to heal and bring prosperity through fertility with Saraswati. Her mythical origin in heaven attributes a celestial identity to her and her material manifestation on earth is only part of her divine identity.

According to some myths, Sarswati is believed to be born on the tongue of Brahma, and sometimes on the tongue of Vishnu. This imagery of a woman originating on a man's tongue or the presence of a feminine power on a masculine being is symbolic of vocal expression by a woman or a feminine mediator to convey male divine authority and commands. The persistent imagery of Saraswati born on the tongues of gods can also be interpreted as a patriarchal order's desire for patriarchal control over speech and knowledge as it replaced goddess cults. So, though the initiator is a feminine power, she is seen more as a mediator of the divine idea or the concept in the mind of the Creator (a Father God) bringing it to humans and making it comprehensible for the human faculties. This whole process could indicate the introduction of a new theology and a new world order informed by patriarchal logic but validated because of its mediation and dissemination through a feminine voice to make it acceptable to hitherto goddess cultures.

Vedic Brahmanism centres on, '*shabda brahman*' or the ultimate power of speech or creative sound. Saraswati's close association with it indicates the important role of the feminine principle in the dissemination and comprehension of knowledge. She is not merely seen as the manifestation of thought but that which underlies speech too. So she is in fact thought or intelligence itself. The myth that has Saraswati slaying Vritra, the serpent dragon, is a deflection from the more hegemonic myths in which the serpent is slain by Indra. This myth of a serpent-like dragon-like demon slain by a god is a universal myth found in almost all Indo-European myths. Even Zeus, Indra's Greek counterpart is known to have slain a serpent demon. At one level, this myth is a metaphor for the destruction of the Goddess culture (represented by the serpent as the goddess was closely associated with the serpent) by a more masculine religion believing in the 'Father God' represented by the king of gods like Zeus or Indra. The deflection of the myth however, where Saraswati is regarded as the slayer and subsequently praised for her courage, is an effort to validate the replacing religion and ideology as the older religion in the form of a serpent is decimated by Saraswati, a female divinity.

Saraswati is consistently associated with images of water in any natural manifestation. This suggests that she goes much beyond the association with just one river. Saras means water and if water is a metaphor for thought or imagination then it could be visualised in any form, like water in a pool or a lake or water that flows corresponding to thought or imagination that remains still and contained, or that which flows and changes. As water, Saraswati is all pervading and becomes as much a symbol of fertility as of spirituality also suggesting the harmonious fusing of the two.

Saraswati has no negative side to her. She is ascetic-like in her bearing and purely one dimensional if one were to disregard the incest myth of Brahma. Myths keep her unsullied as she is described to flee from Brahma when he seeks her sexually. She assumes a more pragmatic and activist role in Buddhism as Tara, who is credited with softening Buddhism's rigid stand towards women. In certain parts of Tibet and Nepal,

Saraswati is worshipped as Nila Saraswati, an aggressive and violent or ugra roop of the calm, passive, and peaceful goddess. She is worshipped in this manifestation as a Mahavidya in Tantrashastra.

Saraswati is always clad in immaculate white which suggests her almost virgin-like, pure status besides her close association with water. The *shubra vastram* or the white garment suggests qualities or elements like purity, peace, wisdom and bliss. The absence of warm colours in her sartorial depiction indicates an absence of warm emotions like passion, anger, sensuous love and valour in the goddess. The absence of jewellery suggests her ascetic and detached nature, also simultaneously symbolising the true pursuit of art or knowledge detached from material things, leading to spiritual enlightenment. The presence of crystal beads reinforces purity and transparency as also elements of healing, as crystal is supposed to be a healing stone. Saraswati sits on the lotus, a flower that symbolises enlightenment and detachment as it rises well above the waters with the help of its stalk.

Saraswati's iconography includes a book standing for knowledge, the veena, an Indian string instrument standing for music, and two birds, a goose and a peacock. While the goose is immaculate white just like the goddess, a probable reason of its inclusion would be the popular belief in its peculiar discriminating ability to separate milk from water and also pick up pearls from the floor of a water body with the help of its beak. Just like the goose, a true seeker of knowledge and an artiste needs to have this quality of knowing and being able to separate the relevant from the irrelevant. The strutting peacock is regarded as a symbol of pride and vanity but the peacock near Saraswati does not flaunt its plume. This indicates that the worth of a true artiste or a scholar lies in their modesty and not a blatant exhibition of their abilities.

Academic and cultural programmes in India normally commence with the lighting of the lamp and garlanding the idol or the picture of the goddess. In eastern India, there is a practice of worshipping books and musical instruments at homes on the day of Vasant Panchami along with the goddess. The goddess is also worshipped in schools and colleges as she is the presiding goddess of academic institutions. It is also believed to be auspicious for children to hold the pen for the first time in the presence of the goddess on Vasant Panchami and write the letters of the alphabet on this day, thus solemnising their life-long contract with the written word.

Drying up of the river Saraswati to the point of its disappearance can be seen as symbolic of the drying up or diminishing importance given to knowledge and the arts and the rise of business, trade and commerce, leading to increasing materialism and scientific and technological pursuit with a focus, mostly on materialistic rather than altruistic or humanistic goals.

Saraswati may have an African archetype in Oshun, The West African Goddess of love, art and sensuality who enlightens one about beauty and creativity. Lusiah Teish, a priestess of Ishun in the African tradition of Yoruba Lucumi, describes her as , 'the river waters meet the ocean. She is…the love that gave the original impulse for creation...she embodies everything that is beautiful, that inspire people to have great imaginations to create exquisite works of art and to really use their senses'. This metaphor of the river to describe the goddess, is similar to the myth of the river Saraswati, swiftly flowing to meet the ocean and immerse the fire in it.

Saraswati and her Archetypes

In her bearing, her attire, her persona, her iconography and the way she dominates the popular religious and cultural imaginary in the region of the Indian subcontinent and other East and South East Asian countries, Saraswati is the veritable embodiment of the Sage archetype who is the source of all knowledge, wisdom, theoretical rigour and artistic fervour, and deeply invested in intellectual pursuit. Her flowing nature and close identification with a river and water bodies, likewise, the suggestion of sacred activities happening on the banks of the river are a reinforcement of the Sage archetype. Like the Sage, Saraswati's being exudes simplicity and asceticism. She believes in dissipating the darkness by the light of knowledge and not in vanquishing the enemy through bloodshed. She symbolises that which is true and pure. She has the unrelenting energy of the Seeker archetype as she crashes through the mountains to carry the fire all the way to the ocean meandering through thousands of kilometres. As the swift and unstoppable river on a mission, she mirrors the archetypal Researcher, Scholar, Investigator and Disciple who is on a mission and has dedicated their very existence to the cause.

Saraswati has the archetype of the Pioneer and the Creator as both ancient Indian scripts, Brahmi and Sharada, are attributed to her and she is the presiding deity of speech. She has the Mediator archetype too as she gives voice and expression to the commands and directives of the gods. Equally strong is the Teacher archetype in her, as not only does she personify abstract thought but also devises the means of breaking philosophy into comprehensible nuggets which can be absorbed by the seeking intellect.

The goose or the hamsa by her side reflects the Critic archetype which can discriminate and sift the important from the trivial and extract the essence of a text or an experience. The Artiste archetype is reflected through the presence of the ornate yet humble peacock who like a protégé, sits by her feet in reverence and realisation instead of strutting about in full glory and splendour. Saraswati is the archetypal 'Voice of Creation' and its very inception since 'In the beginning was the word'. Also called Subhaga, she reflects the Mother archetype symbolising fertility in her form as the nourishing river. She is the metaphorical mother who gives birth to all disciplines, religious scriptures, aesthetic schools, philosophical worldviews and art forms on her sacred banks. She embodies the Healer archetype too in several myths where she and her medicinal waters help in restoring life and vitality.

Saraswati personifies the Judge or the Justice archetype as in the *Ramayana* after she has appeared in Manthra's dream, she is once again requested by the devas to manipulate Bharata's thoughts and turn him in favour of Rama's exile. It is said that Saraswati refuses to do this. Though Saraswati has been appropriated by Shaktas (worshippers of Shakti) and presented along with Kartik and the Shaivas (worshippers of Shiva) who present her with Ganesha and the Vaishanvas (worshippers of Vishnu), who regard her as Vishnu's wife, she is the archetypal Recluse since she is not known to cohabit with any particular god and functions on her own. She is worshipped as an individual goddess. Her association with Ganesha is only because she is the goddess of wisdom and so is he. With Kartik she is associated more as a goddess of art where he is the reflection of the affluent and handsome feudal lord of colonial Bengal and symbolises the patron god or connoisseur of all art forms and musical genres. And her association with Vishnu too is ambiguous as she is hardly seen with him.

Saraswati's aggressive manifestation or ugra roop in the persona of Nila Sarswati and her Buddhist counterpart Tara embody the Advocate and the Activist archetypes as she champions the rights of women to enter the Buddhist order. As one of the Matrkas, Brahmi and as the slayer of Vritra, she might be imagined as wearing the Warrior archetype.

Tracing Saraswati in Popular Culture

Films that portray the Saraswati archetype in the lead female actor or protagonist generally focus on qualities of commitment, ethics and principles which are uncompromising. The women are dedicated to a cause, a calling or a duty which is beyond the boundaries of self-centered goals. For them what they are involved in or the work they do, the profession they follow is not a job or a career or a means to attain success or define their upward mobility. It is something they believe in with all their heart and are ready to lay their lives for. It is what defines them. Such portrayals take the character beyond the predictable confines of heterosexual romantic plots and storylines. In fact, such protagonists are mostly single and even if they have a love interest, it is not foregrounded. It is the cause and their relationship with the cause that is the focus of the narrative.

In Hindi films, Rani Mukherjee with her nondescript, girl-next-door looks and appearance is quite the archetypal Saraswati whether she is a lawyer, a reporter or a teacher. Mukherjee in the 2004 period romance *Veer Zara* is a stellar example of the Saraswati archetype. She is diligent, believes in a righteous cause and most importantly does not take the case assigned to her casually. She plays the lawyer Saamiya Siddiqui who really believes in the innocence of her client. Saamiya is an upcoming Pakistani lawyer who is given the case of convict 786 who is the protagonist Veer (Shahrukh Khan) and the victim of a malicious conspiracy. She has to prepare a defence. Her challenge is not merely to get the convict who hasn't spoken in 22 years to speak, because only he knows the truth but also to dig into his past, gather facts and concrete and irrefutable evidence which will cement the case and build a fool-proof argument and then present it with conviction and confidence as she is pitted against a renowned and very senior prosecutor Zaakir Ahmed (Anupam Kher) who is determined to prosecute her client and prevent his acquittal. Saamiya is persevering and determined in her pursuit of truth and even undertakes a journey to India from Pakistan to get to the bottom of it. Mostly attired in pastels and spotless white, sporting nude makeup, burning the night oil in her preparation, without any love interest in her life, Saamiya makes for the perfect Sage. Her gritty disposition combined with her infallible belief in the credos of truth prevailing and good triumphing also bring out the archetype of the Innocent in her who is driven by her unshakeable faith in poetic justice and the benevolence of the universe.

In the 2011 biographical thriller *No One Killed Jessica*, Rani Mukherjee plays a reporter Meera Gaiti who wants to expose the truth of Jessica's murder after the court has pronounced its verdict and released the prime suspects who are also her murderers. While the character of Saamiya brings out the archetype of the Innocent through the Sage, Meera embodies a combination of the Justice, the Activist and the Critic archetypes along with that of the Sage as she is just not ready to believe in the court's verdict and decides to conduct investigations on her own. She goes about it professionally and meticulously with utmost care and caution so as not to leave any stone unturned until she has enough to expose the institutions of the law and enforcement for being irresponsible and by leveraging her position in the media, garners support to pressurise the system. She even reaches out to the highest offices of the land for reopening the case. In this she is the Sage along with the Hero because she is committed to fighting evil even if it means taking personal risks. Meera has a professional appearance in the film and it is her professional training as a reporter that helps her lay her groundwork. Like Saraswati, Meera's love life is never foregrounded and she is shown as single-mindedly dedicated to the cause she takes up of bringing justice to a dead woman.

The 2018 production *Hichki,* adapted from Brad Cohen's autobiographical work *Front of the Class: How Tourette Syndrome Made Me the Teacher I Never Had*, essays Rani Mukherjee in the lead role as Naina Mathur, an aspiring teacher who faces rejection as she suffers from Tourette syndrome. The syndrome causes her to produce intermittent sounds like hiccups which make her an awkward presence and a laughing stock in the classroom. However, it is Naina's dedication to her vocation which she has chosen, her passion for teaching, her sheer resolve and also her unconventional style of interacting with her students that lead to her acceptance as a teacher. The character has very strong Sage and Teacher aspects of Saraswati combined with the Hero archetype, as Naina is asked to handle class 9f of St Notker's School, a class infamous for its notorious and troublesome students. Naina steps out of the shoes of the conventional teacher and welcomes their pranks. She even celebrates them because what she appreciates is the planning and the execution of the pranks which requires collective group effort. She brings about a paradigmatic shift in her pedagogical approach and turns the class around into a group of hardworking students by respecting them. In her journey as their class teacher who helps them study, she becomes an enabler and a facilitator maximising learner autonomy.

Throughout the film, Naina has an easy demeanour and is dressed in pastels with very little makeup and minimalistic jewellery which make her every bit the archetypal Saraswati who situates herself not only in an institution of learning but also amongst the most academically and socially backward group of students who have been ghettoised in the school and are therefore hurting. Like Sarswati's hamsa, Naina displays the ability to differentiate the good from the bad and realises the true potential of the students, eventually succeeding in her mission of mainstreaming them. In her commitment and her endeavour to make the school accept the students of 9f as its own, Naina is also disseminating the true philosophy underlying learning – knowledge and wisdom is for everybody, not merely a privileged few. The plot interestingly also shows Naina's father's opposition to her choice of profession as he believes it is not lucrative enough and Naina's resistance to this opposition symbolises her preference to identify with Saraswati rather than Lakshmi.

The Sanjay Leela Bhansali directed 2005 film *Black*, drawing from the life of the deaf and blind academic and activist Helen Keller, was a huge commercial success and had Rani Mukherjee playing the character of Michelle McNally, showing her journey to self-actualisation as a person with disabilities. Michelle's character again has elements of the Hero, given her journey and reconciliation in which she is assisted by her teacher Debraj (Amitabh Bachhan). He invokes the image of the ancient Creator Brahma who is father, teacher and lover of Saraswati. The incest myth is inverted as it is Saraswati or Michelle who seeks an intimate moment with her teacher, operative father and mentor Debraj to which he reluctantly concedes. Barring one intimate exchange with her teacher, Michelle, like the archetypal goddess she epitomises, is an ascetic seeking fulfilment in her existence through her artistic abilities and academic avocation.

The journey with her teacher initially brings out the archetype of the Rebel and then the Disciple in Michelle who is determined to learn and overcome the roadblocks in her road to realisation. This determination is evident in Michelle's repeated attempts to get her degree and become an accomplished singer and an expert dancer. 'Black' looms heavy as a symbol in the film, indicating the darkness around Michelle and the rapidly gathering dark clouds in the mind of a mentally deteriorating Debraj afflicted by Alzheimer. However, it is 'white' that captures the imagination and prevails at a symbolic and transcendental level. The presence and persistent prevalence of white is symbolised by the softly falling snowflakes that dissipate the darkness and usher in hope and happiness. The contact with white, its downy presence, its soft feel on the skin lights up the faces of the characters and the frozen frame becomes the archetypal core of the entire film as it is replicated through film posters and promotional teasers.

Another female actor who has embodied the Saraswati archetype from time to time is Kareena Kapoor Khan. In the 2016 release *Udta Punjab*, a critically acclaimed yet commercially unsuccessful film, she plays the character of Preet Sahni, a doctor and an activist who runs a rehab centre in Punjab. She emanates the Sage archetype in her relentless pursuit of the truth and her resolve to expose the drug mafia which has destroyed the lives of so many young people in

Punjab. She is assisted in her mission by Sartaj Singh (Daljit Dosanjh), a junior policeman who is personally affected by the menace as his own brother is an addict. Preet lives and dies for the cause, succumbing to an attack by Balli, a recovering addict and the brother of Sartaj who tries to escape her rehab facility. The Sage and the Hero archetype come together yet again along with the Healer archetype in Preet's understated glamour, only accentuated by her doctor's white apron which she dons most of the time and which is a constant reminder of her profession and her cause.

The archetypal Saraswati manifests briefly in a sedate and composed Kareena Kapoor Khan through the character of Geet Dhillon, otherwise a gutsy and feisty Punjabi girl in the 2007 Imtiaz Ali directed romantic comedy *Jab We Met*. Otherwise reflecting the Hero and the Trickster archetype, Geet transitions into the Sage when she disappears into anonymity after running away from home, only to be turned down by her boyfriend. A rejected and hurt Geet takes up a job in another town and leads a self-effacing existence keeping a low profile and sticking to her job as a school teacher till she is revisited by her past and transitions back to her former self.

Likewise in the 2009 film *Kurbaan*, Kareena Kapoor Khan is an academic by the name of Avantika Ahuja living in the United States who is smitten by Ehsaan Khan (Saif Ali Khan), an Islamist radical in the guise of a University professor. The rest of the film is about Avantika's heroic effort to bring down the terrorist outfit which her husband is a part of and mar his plans. The film projects her as a highly intelligent and capable woman who can think on her feet. Her academician identity is used by her husband to get an entry into the United States where he can carry out his terror attacks. Avantika, however, is smart and takes calculated risks to undermine his plans.

In the 2004 Govind Nihalani directed critically acclaimed film *Dev*, Kareena plays the character of a Muslim girl Aliya who stands up for the truth while in the romantic thriller courtroom drama *Aitraaz*, released the same year, she unflinchingly dons the mantle of the lawyer and enters the courtroom as lawyer Priya Malhotra who fights and wins a sexual harassment case for her husband Raj Malhotra (Akshay Kumar) class who has been molested by his CEO's wife Sonia Roy (Priyanka Chopra). As she wins the case, Priya is a combination of the Sage, the Warrior and the Activist archetypes, which are all archetypes associated with Saraswati and also the construct of Nila Saraswati and manifest in the various myths surrounding her.

Glimpses of Saraswati and Nila Saraswati can be seen in numerous films where the female protagonist is committed to a cause or in pursuing the truth or uncompromisingly dedicated to a vocation. Meghana Dixit played by Dimple Kapadia is a news reporter in the film *Krantiveer* (1994) who lives modestly in a chawl and rallies against injustice. Dressed in white, she has taken to the Sage archetype, choosing the power of the pen to agitate against evildoers after having undergone traumatic experiences herself. She is idealistic and also embodies the Teacher archetype, who is trying to educate ignorant readers through her articles and enlighten them about the unimaginable acts of corruption and crime committed in society.

The 1986 T Rama Rao directed *Naache Mayuri* is a biopic that traces the arduous and painful journey of a classical dancer-actress after she loses her leg in an accident and her heroic comeback as a dancer. The character played by Sudha Chandran is actually based on her life story. The dancer met with an accident in which one of her legs was irreversibly damaged so that the doctors had to amputate it which left her with a stump for a leg. The prosthesis she resorted to by taking the support of a Jaipur leg was not just difficult but painful and alien to her being. The rest of the story shows her journey with her artificial leg and the ordeal she undergoes as she resumes her dancing with this foreign body part. Mayuri the protagonist embodies the Struggling Artiste archetype as she loses her ground and faces the threat of dissolution and anonymity after her accident. It is her dedication and unwavering love for her vocation, along with her steely resolve, bringing out the Hero archetype in her that help her accomplish her goal.

The healer Sudha Sen (Rakhee) a doctor, mostly wearing pastels and white in *Kala Patthar* (1979) who is more like a therapist to the tormented Vijay (Amitabh Bachhan) and guides him towards light, Shivani (Nafisa Ali) in her cameo in the Anurag Basu directed *Life in a Metro* (2007) – a very positive, self-sufficient, single woman who finds absolute joy in dancing and in her interaction with her shishyas (disciples) – and Minister of Defence Shraddha Pandit (Juhi Chawla) in the Alt Balaji series *The Test Case* (2020) as a well-meaning, benevolent politician almost accorded celestial authority to identify the first lady officer in the Indian Army to undergo training to join the Special Forces and thus paving a new path for women despite resistance from the high commands in the army, are some other female characters in supporting roles who conspicuously embody the Saraswati archetype.

The very urbane Simi Garewal, always dressed in white and reinventing herself for her show *Rendezvous with Simi Garewal,* which makes us oblivious of the promiscuous and slightly negative roles she played in films, is a Saraswati-like immaculate figure giving us access to lives of celebrities and stars in a soft, fluid, mellifluous and lyrical voice. Her avatar has more of the Saumya Saraswati to it. In more recent times, the qualities of the benevolent Saumya Saraswati are projected on Sakshi Tanwar in Epic TV as the host of *Tyohar Ki Thaali* as she demonstrates and lucidly takes us through recipes and their religious and cultural significance, thus enlightening us about several aspects of Hindu tradition.

A particularly striking manifestation of the archetype of Saraswati which brings out the combination of the Sage, Mediator, Writer, Scribe and Activist archetypes in her is the character of Subhashini Saigal played by Shabana Azmi in the 1989 vigilante thriller drama *Main Azaad Hoon*. This film, also starring Amitabh Bacchan in the lead role of Azaad, was a colossal failure at the box office but can be seen as one of the very first films that highlights the power of the fourth estate in spinning and circulating certain narratives that then acquire hegemonic status with the full potential of defining the subsequent course of events and also veering out of control, leading to catastrophic consequences.

Subhashini portrays aspects of the shadow Saraswati who uses the power of her pen as a journalist to create a voice which attacks the corrupt and unjust institutions of the country and the political patronage they enjoy. She ascribes a factual and borrowed identity to this fictitious voice giving him a name, 'Azaad' and making him seem like a real individual. This idea of hers which she puts into action is initially in order to save her job in the face of rapid layoffs and mounting competition. However, when the story picks up, she has to scout for a person who will be ready to play along and pretend to be Azaad. She does find a vagabond-like man who agrees to play the part and very soon becomes a rage as she has been building his image and his ideological positioning for some time now.

Azaad has a face as he starts addressing public gatherings but more than a face, he is a voice that has risen from the masses and addresses the masses but in truth, he is a figment of Subhashini's imagination and most of what he says is written and edited by her. It reminds one of the myth of Saraswati sitting on divine tongues to pass divine ordinance, and is a classic example of the lethal effects of the manipulative voice of the media which in today's times we often consider to be an usher of the age of post truth. The film reaches its predefined climax because Subhashini has already decided the fate of the character before she has even identified him to play the role. In one of her very first pieces which she wrote as Azaad she had stated in the first person in Azaad's voice, that he will be jumping off a building and ending his life on Republic Day to show his disillusionment and make a statement against the establishment. The film ends with the pseudo Azaad actually jumping off a building because by then he has started identifying with the ideology of the fictitious Azaad.

The character of Subhashini Sehgal brings out shadow aspects of the Writer who encapsulates imagination and presents it as fact, and the good side of the Scribe who organises information and presents it through a fictitious but powerful voice. She has elements of the Survivor, the Trickster and shadow of the Planner archetype as she devises this ploy to safeguard her job. Her columns that are Azaad's fulminate criticism against an indifferent system oblivious of the plight of the disadvantaged and marginalised in society. Though the content is sincere, Subhashini and Seth Gokulchand (Manohar Singh), the owner of the newspaper are hand in glove in this deception to increase the sales of the paper and their machinations eventually cost Azaad his life. So powerful and effective in its intent is the voice that it ends up subsuming and finally consuming Azaad.

The Sage and Seeker aspect of the Saraswati archetype

is depicted very strongly through the character of Maureen Robinson played by Molly Parker in the American science fiction television series *Lost in Space* (2018) available on Netflix. Maureen is an aerospace engineer who makes a call to take her family to another planet Alpha Centauri as she envisions pioneering the task of building a new and a better world. The journey is rife with unimaginable threats and difficulties. Maureen is singularly dedicated to the success of the mission and stands out in her intellectual capabilities, her problem-solving and critical thinking abilities and her calm disposition in the face of impending and immediate terror.

Maureen and her husband together make a great team but she very clearly dominates the cerebral and intellectual scene as she knows way beyond anybody else on board about the spaceship since she is actually the one to have designed it. She has a slight tilt towards people who show a scientific and analytical bent of mind. This also leads to an estrangement between Maureen and her younger daughter Penny who is inclined to literary pursuits. But Maureen is quick to realise this and assumes the Teacher archetype from that of the Scientist and the Researcher to train her daughter in also getting her head around the futuristic equipment and their predicament.

Erin Brockovich, the legal clerk in the American biographical film by the same name played by Julia Roberts, brings out the Researcher, Sage and Activist archetypes in the character. Erin goes on to uncover a major corporate misdemeanour on the part of the Pacific Gas and Electric Company which costs residents their lives as they succumb to different kinds of cancer owing to the toxicity in the ground water, which is because of the effluent the company releases. The corporation tries to cover this up by providing doctors to the ailing residents at their expense. Erin's investigation results in a major expose and an apparently inevitable class action lawsuit. It is owing to her unabated efforts, her deep digging and her persuasive and negotiating skills that the company is forced to pay a compensation to the amount of 333 million dollars to the plaintiffs.

Contemporarising and Humanising Saraswati

Saraswati's association with the Sage, Seeker, Creator and Teacher archetypes give her a universal dimension. The archetypal Saraswati manifests through women – professionals, scientists, artists, teachers, who have dedicated a lifetime to their profession or vocation, who pursue it with single-minded devotion and who draw the very sap of their existence from this unequivocal and incontrovertible commitment. These women are mostly single and even if they are married, it is undermined and overshadowed by their pursuit and commitment to their field. Their distractions are few and they have uncompromisingly trudged on this solitary journey. They are all recluses in their own right because they are in the company of their vocation, their art, their pursuit.

In the Indian popular imaginary, the famed singer Lata Mangeshkar is often seen as the embodiment of Saraswati because she is single and the most enduring female voice of India. She is also always dressed like the goddess in immaculate white and has led a long life free of controversies devoted to her musical gift. Female social workers, doctors, activists, NGO workers working in remote areas away from their families (so metaphorically single) to spread awareness amongst the socially and economically backward evoke the Saraswati archetype. Writers, academicians like Romila Thapar, Nivedita Menon, Mahashweta Devi, who committed their lives to research or to being the voice of others, who are only spoken about or remembered in the context of their work likewise wear the Saraswati archetype. In fact, these women can be sometimes regarded as Nila Saraswati too in their unrelenting pursuit of the truth and their steady resistance to the hegemonic and authoritative voices of the establishment which often brands them and their works as unsavoury and harmful for the sensibilities of traditionalist and conservative groups. Nonetheless, they are all dedicated to causes higher than themselves.

Female lawyers, journalists, environmentalists, human rights activists, RTI activists like Aruna Roy, Vrinda Grover, Barkha Dutt, Nidhi Razdaan, Vandana Shiva and Shabana Azmi, offering a different perspective or insight into a case or a story have the unmistakeable Nila Saraswati archetype in them which believes in action, an audience to address, a stage to enact their resistance, and in being heard and noticed. A distinct archetypal manifestation would be the Indian writer and mental calculator popularly called 'the human computer' Shakuntala Devi. Not only does she symbolise the Sage and Creator archetypes, but her pioneering work *The World of Homosexuals* positions her as an advocate and champion of gay rights too.

A woman who has the Saraswati archetype is committed to the cause of spreading knowledge and awareness even at the expense of personal danger and is usually of unquestionable integrity. Women who often take up the task of educating other women, making them aware of their rights but in a non-violent, affirmative, assertive and non-aggressive manner are also embodiments of the archetype. As Saraswati symbolises civilisation and perfection, the archetype is manifest in women who have a refined sensibility and superior intellectual capabilities. These women are generally socially and financially independent and usually do not need a man to identify with. Even if they are associated with a man or men, the men will usually be known by their association with these women and not the other way round.

Saraswati-like women may have mentees and students as they believe in tutoring. They can be research guides and professional mentors and even acclaimed artistes who have scores of disciples under their tutelage. The Kathak maestro of the Jaipur Gharana Late Pandita Rohini Bhate, who dedicated her life to dance and groomed many disciples under her who carry on her legacy, is reminiscent of the Saraswati archetype. So is Sonal Man Singh, Indian classical dancer and Guru of the Bharatnatyam and Odissi dance forms. Throughout the active years of their life these women have been single. Vandana Shiva, the writer, public intellectual and ecofeminist activist advocating for the rights of farmers and biodiversity and fighting an intellectual and legal battle with corporations involved in monopolising and corporatising agriculture is symbolic of Saraswati fighting for the rights of Lakshmi or Bhudevi.

Highly driven, self-motivated women focused on creative, artistic, scientific and professional pursuits likewise remind one of the Saraswati archetype. Professionals like Indra Nooyi (former CEO of PepsiCo), Arundhati Bhattacharya (Former Chairperson, the SBI), Naina Lal Kidwai (CEO and Country Head – India, HSBC) and Sudha Murty are some of the women in the corporate sector prominently embodying the Saraswati archetype. In fact, Sudha Murty's transition into a writer in recent years is a further extension and reinforcement of this archetype reflecting another valence of Saraswati.

Saraswati comes through any woman who is not merely engaged with but dedicated to the cause of dissemination of knowledge and someone who offers intellectual, professional and artistic support and enlightenment to others. A teacher, preacher, educator or mentor-like figure who can be trusted, and who is benign, benevolent, giving, pure, kind, knowledgeable and wise, of any age, could be associated with the archetype of the all-knowing wise and evolved Sage in Saraswati. Saraswati is also any woman who appreciates and values the Sage and Seeker archetypes in her mentee or protégé.

Saraswati is not of a combative nature. Instead, she believes in collaborative work. She can take orders from superiors but if the ordinance is unjust then there is a fair chance that she may back out on ethical grounds. She is capable of manipulating and distorting the truth but she will not do so unless for a noble cause. She is not someone who will work in her own self-interest but rather focus on the benefit of the community or humankind through her pioneering research. She usually has no duality in her character and no secrets that can make her vulnerable. She is highly respected and revered in her field and is primarily known for uncompromising work ethic and her intellectual or artistic brilliance. She is balanced, good with her choice of words and welcomes opposing worldviews and ideologies on the table as a true intellectual is one who strives towards no bias and can accommodate all viewpoints and is informed by all kinds of observations before they arrive at a conclusion or an inference. Therefore, the woman with the Saraswati archetype does not make many personal enemies. She has enemies because she may inspire envy and people might want to pull her down because her honest dedication and non-negotiable work ethic may not be in their best interest. So at times, she may be sidelined or undermined because of her refusal to leave the path of truth. She comes across as objective and mature while expressing her views on a subject and her efforts are always towards offering a 360 degree perspective on any issue.

The Saraswati Archetype in Brands

Saraswati's numerous archetypal aspects like those of the Artist, the Scribe, the Investigator, the Seeker, the Writer, the Researcher and the Pioneer can be projected through feminine portrayals constructed on the lines of any one or more than one of these archetypes. This could happen through the construct of the single working woman and her identification more with her work or her vocation, her contributions in the field of technology, science, medicine, law and research. She could be depicted as a professional, not too glamourous, possibly with glasses, professionally clothed, preferably in pastels or white and cotton fabric accentuating a pure and pristine appearance and situated in her workplace like a lab, an office, a boardroom or on the field. The Tanishq ad which was discussed in the introduction and which situates the woman in a corporate boardroom is an example of a manifestation of some aspects of the Saraswati archetype.

If she is an artiste then she needs to be captured in her element in the act of performing or practising (riyaz or sadhana) or imparting her art form. The narrative could focus on her busy routine, the many commitments she has and the futuristic or the community outreach aspect or the progressive side of her work. If it is an art form or yoga or something to do with aesthetics, it can even focus on healing abilities. The thrust has to be on the power of the particular vocation and the archetypal Saraswati's role as knowledge resource or subject expert and the teacher or the mediator of this vocation. If it is an outdoor setting then, the backdrop needs to be serene and lush to convey the healing and invigorating side of nature which she is in sync with.

The woman in the narrative has to come across as a proliferator of knowledge, pathbreaking research, creative endeavours or as a healer. On the other hand, if the narrative of the ad needs to bring out the Activist or Advocate archetype, then she could be projected as a woman committed to issues like climate change, environmental awareness, social inequalities, poverty, illiteracy, child abuse, domestic abuse, women empowerment, etc. This could be combined with the Magician archetype as the narrative describes the monumental transformation resulting out of her tireless efforts or some miraculous breakthrough.

The narrative of the ad can focus on developing the archetype in the context of an institution so that the product or the brand gets institutional sanction/ratification too, something like the Colgate and Sensodyne ads where dentists are shown to recommend the use of the product. The same message can be conveyed through someone who embodies the institution. It can be a sophisticated, educated, mature, sensible looking woman who seems self-reliant and self-assured without being arrogant or pompous. A middle-aged or an older woman will certainly be more convincing. A woman who through the narrative comes through as very focused on her work, not career but work; selflessly and resolutely committed to a bigger, nobler, transcendental cause.

Images of younger women as budding Saraswati archetypes who are embarking on a journey can be empowering too. These narratives can be particularly contextualised for health drinks and food items which ensure her health and fitness (whether a student or an artist), the light bulb (that allows her to study) a mattress (that ensure a good night's rest), a watch (that reminds her of home and also helps her to keep time and follow discipline) or shoes, backpacks or a deo that support her long hours on the field. Any of these products can be inserted in the narrative of the budding Saraswati.

The possibilities of projecting the Saraswati archetypes are both promising and immense because women consumers would want to identify with these constructs which go beyond conventional sex roles and gender stereotypes and add value to the feminine. Likewise, relatively unconventional and traditionally perceived as non-lucrative and, therefore, undesirable fields related to art, aesthetics, academics, social service and writing can be promoted through the Saraswati archetype in progressive feminine constructs.

MATRKAS: THE GODESSES WHO ARE MISUNDERSTOOD

SHE IS THE mistress of the house and yet, she climbs trees. She lives in a time and place in colonial Bengal when women were expected to observe purdah and yet, she is nocturnal and goes around semi-clad, prowling like a leopard meaning business. She hangs upside down from trees, walks with feet turned backwards and secretly loves the legend of the witch that is attributed to her. She was denied love and agency and yet, she succeeds in getting back both, in her own dark and macabre way.

By day, she is the regal mistress of a sprawling mansion lending a kind ear to subtly passed on direct and indirect accounts of women oppressed by their men folk; by night she is the predator catching these men unawares and bringing them to swift justice. Sunshine by day, nemesis by night, she is an unseen terror that gets under the skin of men making them want to cross the jungle as fast as they can and not daring to even venture near it by night, for each man in his heart carries the guilt, the shame and the fear of having been an oppressor one way or the other. She operates outside the pale of normative right and wrong and so people liken her to a witch while for those she saves, she is Kali the goddess.

She is two beings in one – sedentary and lithe, graceful and fearsome, seductive and predatory, stately and wild – she is her own conjoined twin. She is Bulbbul (Tripti Dimri) in the 2020 critically acclaimed Crime Horror Netflix original by the same name – a woman who goes straight for blood to assuage her ravaged and tormented soul and embalm her scarred and mutilated body.

Though Bulbbul does not have the big teeth and the low hanging lips and breasts or the bloating belly and disheveled hair of many of the Matrkas, she could be any of them – Hariti, Jara, Jyeshtha, Putana, Brahmani, Indrani, Chamunda – because she shares their bloodlust and unbridled power and energy that so unnerves patriarchy leading it to condemn them because it can't control them.

The Myths of the Matrkas

Matrkas are a group of seven (Saptamatrka) or eight (Ashtamatrka) or sixteen goddesses who are varyingly presented in epics, religious texts and Puranic literature. According to the *Devi Bhagavatam*, they can be even up to as many as a hundred in number. Some texts like the *Devi Bhagavatam* and the *Devi Mahatmyam* depict them as warrior goddesses who help Durga in her battles against the asuras, especially in her battle against Sumbha and Nisumbha. As Ambika and Kalika fight the asura brothers Sumbha and Nisumbha in the snow-capped Himalayas, the mountain ranges suddenly start glowing as if bathed in the resplendent light of a thousand stars like the sun. Apparently, the light is emanating from a hundred goddesses, the Matrkas, each a shakti of a god, a reflection of her male spouse with a different persona, and bearing her own unique weapon, who charge into the battlefield.

Amongst the Matrkas are Brahmani, the wife of Brahma, mounted on a swan with her ayudhas and her kamandalu, Vishnu's shakti Vaishnavi on Garuda's back carrying all of Vishnu's weapons, Shiva's shakti Sankari mounted on the bull Nandiswara with the crescent moon, the trident and the coiled cobra, Kaumari, the shakti of Kartikeya mounted on a peacock, Indra's shakti Indrani on Airaavat the white elephant who is Indra's mount and even some shaktis of incarnations of Vishnu like Varaahi and Narasimhi, the shaktis of Varaha or Vishnu-as-the-wild boar and Narasimha Vishnu-as-half-human-half-lion respectively along with the shaktis of other gods like Kubera, Soma, Varuna, Ganesha, Agni, Vasus, Surya and Yama.

All the goddesses have one thing in common. They are bristling for battle and eager to wield an attack. They plunge into the bloodbath almost with erotic excitement and start slaying the massive army of the demon kings Sumbha and Nisumbha. The Matrkas are described as resorting to combative strategies and techniques specific to them. Indrani wields the thunderbolt while Brahmani reduces asuras to ashes by sprinkling her sacred water over them even as Sankari's mighty bull tramples thousands of asuras under its hooves. Narasimhi guts the demons and Chamunda drinks the blood that spills from their gaping injuries, especially that of Raktabeeja as he is swiftly decimated and prevented from cloning himself from the drops of his blood.

The mythology around the god Kartikeya is also dotted with the presence of the Matrkas. The epic Mahabharata has a reference to the Matrkas in the context of the birth of Shiva's son Kartikeya. In the vana parva of the Mahabharata, Indra is said to have sent a band of Matrkas to kill the new-born Kartikeya, but on seeing him the Matrkas find their maternal instincts activated and instead, start nursing and looking after him. In another myth, the Matrkas are born out of Kartikeya when Indra strikes him with his thunderbolt.

Sometimes these Matrkas are also conflated with the Krrtkas or the wives of the seven sages barring Arundhati who are accused of infidelity by their husbands, thus leading to the birth of Kartikeya from Shiva's semen which Agni has ingested and which is part fertilised by the Krrtkas. Since they are spurned by their husbands, they take up the task of bringing up Kartikeya.

The Matrkas beseech Kartikeya to give them the boon of living off other people's children since they cannot have any of their own, having been disowned by their husbands. The Matrkas also desire to be revered and respected. Kartikeya grants them both the boons and gives them a free hand to afflict children till the time they reach the age of sixteen, thus bringing out the ambivalent nature of the Matrkas that embodies both nurturing and destructive tendencies. In his blessing to the Matrkas, Kartikeya also makes it very clear that the Matrkas will not have to transform or forego their violent and excessive nature in order to be worshipped, thus decreeing the acceptance of their wild, volatile, predatory and devouring nature.

There are many more episodes in the Mahabharata that mention and give accounts of the Matrkas in various contexts. There is Jara in the sabha parva who feeds off children and collects the halves of two infants birthed and abandoned by two sisters, joins the halves and hands over a whole child to the king of the land in return for being venerated and worshipped. There is Putana who tries to kill the infant Krishna in the guise of an attractive woman under the pretext of nursing him but is killed instead, revealing her true, monstrous self. Likewise there is Jyeshtha or Alakshmi of repulsive bearing and countenance who lives in places where there is no love or amicability among people and who is often held responsible for family fights, disputes and material misfortune.

These are some of the earliest representations of the Matrkas with their image being subsequently cleansed in the medieval times. From child-stealers and afflicters they become warrior goddesses. In the *Matsya Purana* in fact, they are supposed to have aided Shiva in his fight against the demon Andhaka and even owe their creation to him. In the *Varaha Purana* where the Matrkas come into existence as a result of a tapa gone wrong, they are created because goddess Vaishnavi gets distracted and loses her focus during her meditation.

Buddhist texts talk about a certain Hariti whose name literally means 'stealing children' and she is regarded as so. And yet there is also Sasthi Devi, one out of the 16 Matrkas and the sixth part of the Devi Bhagavati, hence the name Sasthi who is regarded as a protector of children and a giver of sons. The *Devi Bhagavatam* gives her the epithet of Devasena and refers to her as Kartikeya's wife. When king Priyavrata's wife gives birth to a stillborn, Sasthi comes to him and promises to revive his son only if she can take the child with her. A desperate Priyavrata agrees and she breathes life into the still-born. Seeing the lifeless body regain the colour and vigour of life, Priyavrata is overcome with immense happiness and immeasurable grief at once for he will soon be separated from his son. Sasthi devi, sensing his torment gives back the child to the king, saying that he is a part of Narayana and will be called Suvrata. She asks Priyavrata to start and spread the tradition and custom of her worship across the land, especially for the long life and well-being of children.

Analysing the Matrkas in the Light of the Myths

According to David Kinsley, the earliest description of the Matrkas appears in the Mahabharata, believed to have been recorded in sections added later to the epic, somewhere approximately around the 1st century AD. In the epic, the Matrkas are vile creatures and clearly embody the irregular, deformed, vicious and wild construct of 'the feminine other'. There is nothing apparently divine about Putana or her intentions in her earthly manifestation since she is very often confused as a rakshasi and not a Matrka. Stated simply, she is evil, she means harm and she is eliminated by Krishna himself so that she attains salvation and can be free of her cursed life. Objectively read, the story as part of a text that is one among many trying to lay the foundations of a religious pantheon, is yet another instance of a relatively new and outsider 'Father God' theology, establishing its hegemony by maligning the indigenous goddess and thereby assimilating its cults in its ever-expanding ideology.

It is interesting just how many Puranas refer to the Matrkas as emanating from male gods or as the female personification of the shakti residing in the male gods, and as taking orders from male gods to fight evil and to be kept in check. Special avatars of male gods of the Hindu pantheon are delegated the duty of keeping the Matrkas in check. Sometimes the Matrkas are even attributed a dubious and unholy origin like the episode in the *Varaha Purana* where they are created because goddess Vaishnavi gets distracted and loses her focus during her meditation. So they symbolise the distracted mind, not the composed and focused mind of the goddess.

Matrkas are often categorised in many Puranas as dangerous beings and grouped along with dakinis, pishachinis, pretas and rakshasas. The Matrkas' relation and association with children is ambiguous and multivalent. Some Puranic texts describe Matrkas as evil-mongers out for children's blood while some look upon them as protectors of children. The myth around Kartikeya's boon to the Matrkas further problematises this.

The association of Shiva and Kartikeya with the origin myth of the Matrkas seems to be a sweeping attempt to justify all gods outside the Vedic pantheon and simultaneously establish their hierarchy. Various scholars have argued that both the male gods are indigenous to the land and very likely non-Aryan if not pre-Aryan. They are, however, assimilated in the Hindu pantheon through Puranic tales.

The battle between Indra and Kartikeya is perhaps symbolic of the clash between the Aryans and the indigenous people. Similarly, the Matrkas, who are in all likelihood, non-Aryan indigenous gramadevatas are included in the Vedic Brahmanical theological economy through their depiction as subordinate to the male gods or by presenting them as consorts of the male Vedic gods despite foregrounding their excessive and wild nature or as having been created by Shiva or Kartikeya for a specific purpose.

Perhaps it is the following of these indigenous goddesses and their popularity amongst the local populations that prompts the narrations in the Puranic texts to exaggerate their harmful disposition, excessive ways and wild aura and depict the Matrkas in a negative light thus enabling patriarchal Vedic Brahminism to project its fear and anxiety on these deities. Nonetheless, some of the more benevolent and life-giving attributes of the Matrkas reveal themselves unwittingly here and there like in the myth of the Krrtkas.

In Greek mythology, one comes across the story of Lamia, a beautiful maiden loved by Zeus and destroyed by his jealous wife Hera who turned Lamia into a monster who fed on the flesh of children. This is yet another instance of the generally pervasive misogyny that colours all mythology, projecting patriarchal anxiety on the monster Lamia, a woman and on the agent of the unfortunate curse, Hera, also a woman.

When one studies the Matrkas, an interesting parallel can be drawn with the Valkyries who occur in Norse mythology 'as a number of Destroyer demigoddesses who serve as handmaids to the Scandinavian All-father'. David Leeming and Christopher Fee in their book *The Goddess Myths of the Great Mother* point out that these goddesses are presented as unpredictable and can harm the people they have bestowed favours on.

They are all aspects or multiple forms of the Great Goddess, say the Scandinavian myths, thus making us want to recall the Devi's declaration in the *Devi Mahatmyam* in front of Sumbha that all Matrkas are but her multiple forms and her subsequent act of having them converge in her when Sumbha complains that the Devi is aided by too many allies in her fight.

There are several other instances in Puranic texts of one, two or multiple goddesses emerging from one goddess. For instance, when Gauri is angered, she turns black as thunder and emerges as Kali who later becomes Kaushiki. The Dasamahavidyas emerge from the brow of an angry Sati at the Daksha yajna, in the battle against Sumbha and Nisumbha the fair Ambika turns dark and the form of Bhadrakali emerges from her while earlier in order to kill Chanda and Munda and Raktabeeja she summons other Matrkas while leading to the form of a fury emerging out of herself who slays the demons and is called Chamunda. According to the *Devi Bhagavatam*, the *Vamana Purana* and the *Varaha Purana*, the Matrkas emerge from the goddess, in the *Matsya Purana* they are Shiva's handiwork, while the *Bhagavata Purana* attributes their creation to Vishnu along with other dangerous creatures like rakshasis, pishachas, dakinis and bhutas.

These tales make it very clear that the 'cult of the Goddess' was seen as something formidable. The wildness, aggression, lack of restraint and bloodlust associated with the Goddess as much as the emphasis on the dark, revolting, ugly appearance of some of the Matrkas was perhaps because the goddess culture was alien to Vedic theology and yet was too formidable and pronounced to be dismissed.

It needed to be accommodated and validated which the later Puranic tradition does. In fact, the earlier Vedic triad of Brahma, Indra and Agni is replaced by Brahma, Vishnu and Shiva and even later by Vishnu, Shiva and the Devi which is represented by the devotional theology of Puranic literature and the three schools or sects of Vaishnavism, Shaivism and Shaktism respectively.

Several phenomena like ailments and natural calamities which affected human lives led people to worship gramadevatas and regard them as protectors of the village or the community. It was believed that failure to appease the gramadevata would lead to disastrous consequences. It is easy to trace this anxiety projected on the Matrkas who are possibly the gramadevatas, only this time with Puranic identities and juxtaposed against Puranic gods.

Undoubtedly, infant mortality rates would have been extremely high in those times. Thus, in subsequent sections of the Mahabharata, which may have been added later, a new list of ten Matrkas like Putana, Raksasi, Diti, Revati, Kadru, etc. surfaces who are known to be the child devouring types and believed to, as Kinsley points out, lurk in the 'confinement chamber (where birth takes place)'. The myth, thereby, justifies the high death rate of infants following the week after they are born. Similarly, it was a popularly held belief that Matrkas could be women who could not have children of their own and therefore eyed the children of others. Such beliefs were reinforced through myths like the one about the Krrtkas who Kartikeya allows to torment children till they reach a certain age.

In the Buddhist tradition similarly, the child-stealing ogress Hariti and her subsequent transformation into a benign child-protecting goddess is an interesting account and has parallels in the Japanese and Chinese traditions. Hariti has a hundred children of her own and she steals other people's children and kills them to feed her own. The Buddha, with an intention of making her realise the agony of losing a child, steals one of her hundred children and hides it under his rice bowl. Hariti looks for her missing child throughout the universe and finally comes to the Buddha for help. He then asks her to reflect on the pain she has caused parents by stealing away their children.

Hariti pledges to never steal children from that day and in fact swears to protecting them. Hariti's parallel in Chinese tradition is Pinyin Guizimu (shen) and Kishimojin in Japanese tradition. Both goddesses are venerated and regarded as child-protectors in their benign aspect and merciless in their fearsome aspect towards unruly parents.

While not all of the Matrkas are widely worshipped in India and may remain regionally relevant despite being mainstreamed in the Puranic texts, Hariti is extremely popular and widely worshipped in Nepal.

All in all, the Matrkas are a group of goddesses who are revered but feared more, who are believed to be untamable and who are depictions of nature's raw and unharnessed energy. They can be prone to all kinds of excesses and lack in regulatory behaviour. They can be pleased with offerings of flowers, clothes, wine, meat and ritual sacrifice. They are believed to live near crossroads, in forests, in caves and caverns, on treetops, in crematoriums and in all other remote and inaccessible places which are removed from public thoroughfare. They are important deities in the Saivite and Shakta traditions and even in Tantric cults. The Matrkas appear quite prominently in the cave sculptures of Udaygiri in Bhopal, and in the Elephanta and Ellora caves in Maharashtra. In Ellora, each Matrka appears with a child in her lap, resembling the iconography of Hariti and invoking the universal image of Magna Mater. However, the presence of kala or death in the form of a skeleton alongside them, insinuates their darker nature and their close association with death and destruction.

Yoginis who are important in the Tantric tradition are believed to have evolved from the Matrkas. The number of Yoginis are believed to be either 64 having evolved from Ashtamatrka, or eight Matrkas or 81, having evolved from nine Matrkas. While the Saptamatrka are popular and widely worshipped across India by pregnant women and mothers of new born, their shrines are mostly found deep inside the forests.

The Matrkas and their Archetypes

The Matrkas symbolise the fearsome and gruesome aspects of the goddess and thus naturally embody the Outlaw archetype. They are transgressive constructs defined by their excesses. Their semblance, actions and intentions are nowhere close to prescriptive or normative femininity in a patriarchal society. This is undoubtedly the cause of the general dread and anxiety they inspire in scribes who have written about them and in devotees who worship them. In their depictions as child-stealers, child-devourers, afflicters of diseases and bringers of misfortune and calamities, the Matrkas symbolise the destructive side of nature and epitomise the archetype of the Devouring Mother standing for the darker side of Nature. Whereas in their commitment to protect the village and children from danger, they also embody the archetype of the Nurturing Mother depicting the benevolent side of Nature.

In later depictions, they represent the archetype of the Warrior as they take the battlefield by storm and sometimes destroy friend and foe alike. They are often depicted as acting on or following instructions of a superior god or goddess in Puranic myths and also in the epics. This also makes them archetypal Martyrs who plunge into a mission without any apprehension about the consequences. This is evident in the case of Putana who gets slain by Krishna. The Matrkas are endowed with the power of beguiling sometimes even the most discerning. They embody the Shapeshifter archetype and are known to assume different forms and guises in different myths, especially when they are out to steal or harm children. Likewise it is their shape-shifting ability that enables them to emerge from the goddess and then converge in her. Similarly, they embody the Spell-caster archetype too, as they are successful in enchanting and seducing people they want to, under a cleverly thought guise.

The Matrkas may be seen as goddesses prone to changing their dominant archetype and letting another archetype take over. This is evident from the stories of the Krrtkas who, on Indra's orders come to kill Kartikeya, but end up nursing and looking after him and also in the episode of Hariti who is transformed by the grace of the Buddha. While the Krrtkas turn from warriors into nurturing mothers, Hariti turns from a devouring mother into a protector. Almost all the Matrkas wear the Protector archetype as they are in charge of the protection of an entire city or the well-being of its inmates. In the battlefields they are also responsible for protecting male gods.

Tracing the Matrkas in Popular Culture

The character of Bulbbul in the Anvita Dutt directed and Anushka Sharma produced 2020 Netflix original film *Bulbbul* brings out the archetypal Matrka who has taken upon herself to guard her village and ensure the safety of its most vulnerable. She has brought upon herself this responsibility, for she has paid the price of being vulnerable herself. Raped by her mentally ill brother-in-law and brutally beaten by her husband, Bulbbul shape-shifts into a goddess as the ones who she saves would like to believe, and a witch for the ones who she comes after. Like a Matrka, she dwells in the forest at night and quenches her bloodlust by hunting out sexual predators and domestic abusers, starting first with her brother-in-law and finally coming after her husband with several successful kills in between.

As a little girl, Bulbbul is married to the eldest of three brothers, a man several years older than her who practically sees her grow into a young woman from a child in front of his eyes. Bulbbul's solitary life turns into a veritable nightmare as she pays the price for being emotionally attached to the youngest of the three brothers, her childhood playmate for he is closest to her in age. She grows up on tales and legends of a witch in the forest fed to her by her friend and youngest brother-in-law who is efficiently removed by her husband from the scene and sent abroad for higher studies once he senses Bulbbul's affection for the former. But this is not all. The poker her husband uses to hit Bulbbul for her supposedly transgressive behaviour cuts through her flesh and the bone of her feet, leading them to remain unhinged and free to swivel like a witch's feet are fabled to be. The narrative is refracted through a lens of fantasy and Gothic imagery as Bulbbul walks on branches and jumps from treetop to treetop with feet turned backwards just as a witch is fabled to do, killing offenders and saving women. Like a Matrka she is gruesome in this terrifying aspect of hers by night, which is nothing even remotely close to the heavily ornamented and regal 'badi bahu' or the elder daughter-in-law of the family which she roleplays by day.

But the Matrka archetype needs to be contained and is acceptable by normative society only in shrines and texts, obviously not in action and therefore it is only structurally appropriate that Bulbbul is finally ratted out and killed by her youngest brother-in-law, whose fictive tales she inhabits but who has failed to understand her. Transported to the realm of the supernatural from the earthly, Bulbbul like a Matrka shape-shifts one more time, this time to destroy her husband who has returned to the village after a long absence.

The 2018 award winning comic-horror film *Stree* likewise depicts the archetypal Matrkas in the characters of the witch 'Stree' and the mystery woman (Shraddha Kapoor) who comes to the town of Chanderi to unravel the mystery around Stree. Stree is rumoured to be a witch who comes to the town during the four days of the 'Devi festival' and abducts men from the streets.

The legend goes that once Stree was a famous courtesan who had a true lover and wanted to marry him but the townspeople, outraged by the idea of a courtesan becoming a part of normative, mainstream society and leading a married life, kill her and her lover even before the marriage is consummated. Ever since, Stree raids the town every year for men, in search of her true love. When some people take upon themselves to unravel this mystery, they realise that Stree is not merely looking for love but also respect which people never had for her. Stree's desire resonates the mythical longing of the Krrtkas to be acknowledged, respected and worshipped which they express to Kartikeya. Stree's powers are excessive and dangerous – exactly like those of the Matrkas and her wrath and desire for vengeance unplacatable. It is only when the townspeople acknowledge her by erecting a statue of her and pleading to her to protect them that Stree, like a true Matrka, takes upon herself not to plague the town anymore and leaves.

The mystery woman in Stree also has qualities that bring her close to a Matrka. No one knows her name or where she lives, where she comes from or where she goes after the festival. The narrative, however, makes her desire to acquire the power of Stree quite explicit as she is shown to merge the braid of Stree with her own and then disappear from a running bus in the concluding scene. Like a Matrka, she is a shape-shifter who beguiles undiscerning and unsuspecting people to help her in her mission. She plays the seductress for achieving her objective, settling for a gullible man Vicky (Rajkumar Rao) and making him believe that she loves him and getting him to run her odd errands. But she embodies the archetype of the benevolent Matrkas who can keep their power in check and use it for a good cause. In this manner she dons the garb of the protector Matrkas when she saves Vicky not once but twice from the clutches of Stree and is also instrumental in bringing back the men Stree has abducted, safe and sound. In this act then, the mystery woman is the archetypal Matrka who guards and protects the village and keeps its inmates out of harm's way.

The killer-mom trope in films is one embodiment of the archetypal Matrka who unharnesses her repressed powers in crisis and takes upon herself the task of killing to keep her family, her community and her village safe. The character of Devki (Sridevi) in the 2017 crime thriller film *Mom* is one such instance where a schoolteacher goes to unimaginable and horrific ends to find and kill the man or men responsible for raping and brutalising her step-daughter. The 2016 thriller film *Maatr* starring Raveena Tandon as Vidya is another instance of the killer-mom trope. Vidya, who is abducted by the son of the Chief Minister of her state along with her daughter and brutally raped, devises an elaborate plan to kill the offenders to avenge her daughter's death.

Another prominent work that has aspects of the Matrkas archetype through the killer-mom trope is the crime drama web television series *Aarya* (Season 1) streaming on Hotstar with Sushmita Sen playing the lead protagonist Aarya Sareen who is compelled to unleash her darker powers and her ruthlessness to safeguard her children after her husband is mysteriously shot by an unknown assassin. She embodies the

Warrior, Protector, Devouring Mother and Nurturing Mother archetypes of the Matrkas as she charges headlong into a full-blown confrontation with her husband's partners on the one hand and a dreaded druglord on the other. She resorts to excesses when required, makes strategic use of the weapons and people at her disposal just like the Matrkas did in the war against the asuras and finally manages to save the day for her children. The character of Aarya played by Sen is reminiscent of one of her earlier films *Samay: When Time Strikes* (2003) in which she essayed the same killer-mom trope playing a police officer, ACP Malvika Chauhan, on the heels of a serial-killer who she takes down after he has killed her own daughter.

The warrior archetype of the Matrkas as battle furies foregrounded in medieval texts, is captured and resonates in films like *Mirch Masala* (1987) and *Gulaab Gang* (2014). It is interesting to note that these films have only one or two notable faces and the total number of women is uncertain just as the total number of Matrkas is unknown and widely debated. In the Ketan Mehta directed psychological thriller *Mirch Masala*, the women of the village who pound chillies at the factory unite to attack the lecherous subhedar (Naseeruddin Shah) who has eyes for Sonbai (Smita Patil), one of them, thus maiming the sexual predator who is also the symbolic asura. Smita Patil's performance in the film was included by Forbes magazine in 2013 in its list of '25 Greatest Acting Performances of Indian Cinema'. Matrkas at times also feature independently in films like the 2019 period drama *Manikarnika: the Queen of Jhansi* for instance in the aiding warrior goddess avatar of Jhalkari

Bai (Ankita Lokhande) who joins Rani Laxmibai's army and sacrifices her life.

The 2014 Anubhav Sinha produced action drama *Gulaab Gang* centres around members of Gulaab Gang who act as vigilantes and activists in the Bundelkhand area and take up issues related to women like domestic abuse, rape, dowry as well as social issues like education, safety and health and electricity. The plot replicates the mythology of Durga and her Matrkas on a mission to oust evil and evil-doers through the characters of the leader of Gulaab Gang, Rajjo (Madhuri Dikshit) and the members of the gang. The much earlier 1997 Prakash Jha directed drama *Mrityudand* which makes a statement about social and gender justice also has the Matrka archetype in its lead character Ketki, again played by Madhuri Dixit who, inspired by her sister-in-law's worldview, tries to overthrow the exploitative pattern of gender oppression in the village.

The 2001 multi-starrer *Lajja* has glimpses of the Matrkas archetype in its female characters who engage in actions that are unacceptable by normal standards. Vaidehi (Manisha Koirala), who has left her house to escape being tortured and killed by her husband, has a Matrka like shape-shifting and warrior persona as she surfaces here and there and tries to stand up for women in exploitative conditions. Maithili (Mahima Chaudhary) walks out of her own marriage while Janki (Madhuri Dixit), objectified by her employer and doubted by her boyfriend, abandons him after undergoing a miscarriage. Ramdulaari (Rekha) puts up a brave front in being vocal against atrocities on women but is burnt alive.

All these women are the archetypal Matrkas, warrior goddesses, some of who become martyrs in the process. They are not regarded kindly by the people around them as is evident from the violence these women's bodies are subjected to. Vaidehi has to flee her own house as her husband is plotting to kill her, Maithili's wedding can spiral into a bride burning case as her in-laws adamantly pressurise her father for a dowry, Ramdulaari is actually burnt alive by the village goons while Janki is assaulted by the theatre audience and suffers a miscarriage. Each woman's body thus becomes or has the

potential to become a site of violence and is symbolic of a social issue related to women in an unequal society.

The 2015 critically acclaimed drama film *Parched*, set in rural Rajasthan, also has characters with the Matrkas archetypes and makes a strong and resolute statement against oppressive patriarchy. Rani (Tanishtha Chatterjee) a widowed mother of an irresponsible son, Lajjo (Radhika Apte), a woman in an abusive marriage and Bijli (Surveen Chawla), the village prostitute are best of friends and their bonding is symbolic of the manifestation of the Outlaw archetype of the Matrkas. The women, in their defiance of patriarchy and oppressive regulations in the village system which aim at thwarting women's basic rights, engage in transgressive behaviour and fierce action to seek a solution to their problems. The narrative is structured in a way that it makes us empathise with the same sex love and intimacy between Rani and Lajjo, the sexual excess of Bijli and finally Lajjo's involuntary orchestration of her husband's death. Both *Lajja* and *Parched*, belonging to the commercial and art genres respectively, are films that foreground a sisterhood and forge a common ground for the Matrkas making their cause a universal one.

Since Matrkas is an archetype prone to inspire anxiety and fear, it does not often find its way through a positive or justifiable depiction in the narratives that are a part of popular culture. Narratives of Hindi films that show dangerous mothers, women stealing children, meaning to harm them, mothers abandoning children, women in the guise of contract killers having come to kill or abduct children, women teaming up to work on the wrong side of the law, resonate the darker aspects of the Matrkas archetype and their earlier depictions in the epics.

The devouring mother who uses her children to further her prospects or who is abusive towards them or symbolically ingests them by thwarting their dreams and desires and disabling their free spirit is a common trope in popular culture. The Devouring Mother archetype of the Matrkas features very prominently in the film noir Austrian-German crime television series *Freud* (2020) streaming on Netflix through the character of the Duchess Sophia von Szapary (Anja King) who exploits her foster daughter Fleur Salome (Ella Rumpf) for the latter's psychic powers. Under the guise of a well-meaning mother figure, Sophia uses her spell-caster archetype to compel Fleur Salome to participate in sinister seances and gory rituals to gain cultural capital for her larger political motives which worsens the latter's already fragile state of mind, causing her to eventually snap.

A memorable instance of the devouring mother is the character of Laxmi played by Aruna Irani in the commercially successful film *Beta* (1992) in which Laxmi is all set to destroy her step-son Raju's (Anil Kapoor) family by killing his unborn child who she fears will inherit the family wealth, but has a change of heart like the Matrkas, Hariti and the Krrtkas when she sees the unconditional love Raju has for her and turns into a nurturing mother. In the 2015 crime thriller film *Jazbaa*, Garima Chaudhary (Shabana Azmi), a powerful politician, gets her own daughter kidnapped who is killed by her drug-dealer.

The grieving mother assumes the Devouring Mother archetype and gets her daughter's rapist and murderer acquitted through a lawyer so that she can burn him alive for what he has done to her daughter.

In the 2017 epic action film *Bahubali: the Conclusion*, the queen of Mahishmati, Sivagami (Ramya Krishnan) inadvertently turns into the devouring mother as she passes an order to kill the son she has raised as her own, Amarendra Bahubali (Prabhas), who she fears will assassinate her biological son. Sivagami also wears the Protector archetype of the Matrkas as she rules over the city with an iron hand ensuring the well-being and safety of her people. The 1993 suspense thriller *Khal-Naaika* has shades of the Matrkas archetype in Anuradha (Anu Agarwal) who comes as an imposter to destroy a family who she secretly blames for her husband's suicide.

Women who either show an unnatural obsession towards another's offspring or who mean harm to another's offspring are standard replications of the shadow aspect of the Matrka archetype. Mahamanga (Ila Arun) in the 2008 historical romance *Jodhaa Akbar* is a Matrka who lays an unnatural claim over Jalal/Akbar (Hrithik Roshan) who she has nursed and raised like her own son. Her unconditional loyalty to the emperor leaves her unflinching even when Akbar kills her biological son for treason. So possessive is she over Jalal that she orchestrates an elaborate plan to create misunderstandings between Jodhaa and Akbar for the marriage to fail as she wants to retain her position of influence in the emperor's life. A western parallel would be the lead protagonist Greta's (Isabel

Huppert) pathological obsession with younger girls in the psychological thriller film by the same name.

The trope of the scheming mother-in-law or stepmother conspiring to kill her stepchildren or daughter-in-law or any other person who carries in him or her a potential threat to replace her child in some way are manifestations of the Matrkas who are believed to harm other people's children to safeguard the interests of their own. Radhabai (Tanvee Azmi) in *Bajirao Mastaani* (2015) and Gopika Bai (Padmini Kolhapure) in *Panipat* (2019) are scheming mothers and examples of the Matrkas archetype who go to great lengths to destroy other people's children with the intention of safeguarding their own.

The shadow archetype of the Matrkas manifests in the character of Rani Sahiba (Simi Garewal) in the 1980 blockbuster suspense thriller *Karz* in which Kamini kills her lover to acquire power and position and becomes Rani Sahiba. She is a foster mother to a girl whose father knows her secret and has blackmailed her into giving his daughter a good upbringing and education. More shadow archetypes of the Matrkas surface in the films *Sadak* (1991) and *Sangharsh* (1999) through the characters of transgender/crossdresser antagonists who are devouring mothers, stealing and sacrificing children. In *Sadak*, Maharani (Sadashiv Amrapurkar), a transgender, is the dreaded madam of a brothel who runs a formidable syndicate of flesh trade after having girls abducted from their homes or handed over through small-time pimps. She is ruthless and fierce and enjoys an excess of violence and gore. In *Sangharsh*, Lajja Shankar Pandey (Ashutosh Rana) is a cross-dresser who abducts children and sacrifices them with the belief that this will make him immortal. Both films demonise the transperson, thus reinforcing society's prejudicial and hostile attitude towards the community and implying the presence of inherent antisocial and psychopathic traits in transpersons, thereby validating normative society's transphobia and anxiety towards the marginalized community.

If one considered the earlier depiction of the Matrkas in the epic *Mahabharata*, one could infer that they are a group of goddesses largely misunderstood and misrepresented. They are attributed epithet after negative epithet but many of the myths fail to give their side of the story. They are undoubtedly women of excess and therefore perhaps unfavorably looked upon. Popular culture likewise tends to depict women who resort to excesses or who are indifferent to violence, in a negative light just as the Matrkas. One such example would be the characters of Meghna Mathur (Priyanka Chopra) and Shonali Gujral (Kangana Ranaut) which got them the National awards for Best Actress and Best Supporting Actress respectively in *Fashion* (2008) where the women apparently are unable to handle their fame and glory and take off on a self-destructive path which is depicted through their excessive behavior whether it is drug abuse or random sexual relationships.

The negative portrayal of women who resort to an economy and logic of excess, in other words women 'who lack self-restraint' and try to lead a non-normative life style has always been presented in popular culture through a patriarchal lens and is shown as a sign of weakness rather than a conscious choice that has a possibility of empowering the woman and making them sexually and emotionally autonomous. More examples of such portrayals of women destroying themselves by indulging in excess and transgressive behaviour are the characters of the lead female protagonists Nikhat (Soha Ali Khan) in *Khoya Khoya Chand* (2007), Reshma/Silk (Vidya Balan) in *The Dirty Picture* (2011) and Mahi Arora (Kareena Kapoor) in *Heroine* (2012). In all three films the women hit rock bottom in their personal lives and their success, instead of empowering them, destroys them even as they realise that the real power does not lie in them and despite their celebrity status they are mere cogs in a wheel which turns relentlessly crushing people in its cycle. The films thus deny the women true power which will enable them to transcend their situation and assert themselves. This is a standard patriarchal depiction of women resorting to excesses in films – either they succumb to their own doings or they are demonised. In both cases it is the Matrka-like woman who is singled out, marginalised for her non-normative behaviour and punished for her excess.

In the 2007 comedy horror film *Bhool Bhulaiya*, the character of Avni (Vidya Balan) is a highly misunderstood one and epitomises the Matrkas and the tendency to typecast them without trying to delve deeper into their stories. Like Bulbbul, she is two selves in one, the repressed unconscious self taking over the conscious complying one, the moment Avni physically and metaphorically enters the alternate world of the dead dancer Manjulika by stepping into her room.

In the Emmy nominated web series *Sacred Games* streaming

on Netflix, both Jojo Mascarenhas (Surveen Chawla) the pimp and the dreaded don Gaitonde's (Nawazuddin Siddiqui) girlfriend and Kantabai (Shalini Vatsa), Gaitonde's surrogate mother are Matrka-like characters who live on the edge and operate from the shadows. They have courage that can unnerve the most courageous and laugh in the face of death or go about their lives as if nothing has happened. The goddess Kali, who in many myths has been depicted as one of the Matrkas, is believed to absorb the pain and suffering of the world. This metaphor resonates in the character of Jojo in the series who is in eternal pain which makes her invulnerable and fearless for she has no intention of shying away from the prospect of enduring pain, torture or suffering.

Matrkas were generally feared and worshipped so that they could be kept at bay. They were considered as an inauspicious presence. This is not surprising as some of the few goddesses the Vedas mentioned were also regarded as inauspicious entities who needed to be kept away. Their very presence was supposed to bring bad luck. Common amongst these deities who were considered inauspicious was Nrriti who is also regarded as proto-Kali by some scholars. While the Matrkas trigger anxiety amongst most devotees, prominent among them as a bringer of misfortune and conflict is Jyeshtha or Alakshmi who is spurned by all.

This misogynistic myth of women being inauspicious and unlucky and therefore somehow repulsive and unholy, permeates the narrative of the Netflix dystopian drama web television series *Leila* (2019) where all women are considered inauspicious and vile creatures and are taught by the state to understand that they are cursed and lowly beings. The same ideology reflects in Margaret Atwood's dystopic works *The Handmaid's Tale* (now turned into a web series on Prime) and its Booker Prize winning sequel *The Testaments* where women internalise deeply misogynistic beliefs and are indoctrinated to be suspicious about themselves and other women.

Humanising the Matrkas

A woman has the Matrka archetype in her if she bonds with other women and believes in a shared and empowering sisterhood without applying rules of prescriptive patriarchy to judge her fellow women. On her own, the woman with the Matrka archetype is fearless, assertive and bold. She is not bound by traditions. She lives by instinct. She paves her own way and though unceremonious in many ways, she has a fan-following of her own. She can get under some people's skins; on the other hand she can make some trust her blindly.

In the subsequent seasons of the thriller web television series *Homeland* (Seasons 4 and 5), after the lead male protagonist of seasons 1 and 2 Nicholas Brody (Damien Lewis) is killed, CIA agent Carrie Mathison (Claire Danes) shape-shifts from a Sati into a Matrka archetype. Carrie pursues her mission relentlessly and unapologetically, literally heedless to the collateral damage she is causing. For her it's not about right and wrong anymore but about unswerving commitment to the CIA's mission and America first, even if it comes at the expense of others and with a lot of brutality at the individual and collective level. She is on a rampage and can go to any extent as the boundaries between ethical and unethical, good and bad, right and wrong become increasingly blurred, so much so that even her most trusted ally Peter Quinn (Rupert Friend), who disapproves of many of her ploys and strategies, asks her if she ever considers drawing 'a line'.

So a Matrka can also be a woman who has been terribly hurt or is recovering from an irreversible loss but chooses to come out strong and not be shattered by it. She can then be uncompromisingly strong and uncannily determined once she has made up her mind. The woman with the Matrka archetype is a lot like Kali, almost unstoppable. She is also stubborn, one who does not listen to anyone. She is of unshakeable resolve and there is a ferocity about her will and promise which she keeps at any cost. She is an absolutely great ally to have since she will never back out or shy away or leave one's side. At the same time she is a formidable and lethal adversary.

As a professional she is good at following orders and flawless in the execution of the mission given to her. She can leave people dumbstruck and overawed by her efficiency and professionalism and succeeds in accomplishing tasks that no one had imagined could be done. She has no material interests and is independent of men. She does not need any emotional support or a shoulder to cry on when things go wrong. Instead, she plans on moving ahead and covering bases. She is good at roleplay and especially adept at beguiling people and winning their trust. She is someone who upholds her end of the contract and will never let down the organization she works for. She may go an extra mile and sometimes take things in her own hand to execute things her way. There are chances that she is more competent than the superiors she takes her orders from and sometimes she may ignore them leaving them with a feeling of being blindsided.

The woman with the Matrka archetype is full of steam and rearing to go under her silently assertive exterior. She is a dangerous enemy to have and can wreak havoc with her scathing attacks. She has an aura and commands universal respect from friends and foes alike. She is protective and maternal if need be, especially towards her own. She will not flinch from making a decision or two if that means ensuring the safety of her own family or people even if it involves harming others or causing collateral damage. For a professional the same may be applicable in case of the safeguarding of her organisation or her country.

The Matrka woman desires and commands respect. For her, her stature and the cult following she has is of prime importance. Whether it is her reputation at work, or it is her professional caliber or her ability to keep her wits together and take the responsibility of others, the Matrka woman values these strengths in her more than anything else and would like to see others respecting her for these very qualities. As a wife she can be very loyal and fight on behalf of her husband. She will turn her husband's adversary into a common adversary. But she is not a woman who her husband can control. She needs to be acknowledged and appreciated for her strength. What leaves her hurt the most is the lack of appreciation from the men she loves. If someone entrusts the Matrka woman with a responsibility she will put her life at stake to complete the task.

A Matrka woman can also be someone who changes her mind and sees reason when she is made to. She does not flinch from admitting her shortfalls and is ready to start over without any grouses. She can adapt to circumstances and transform herself overnight and make something that was totally alien to her till now, her life's topmost priority. She does not care if she is being judged and often ends up paying the price for her sometimes impulsive actions. She is feared because she is often misunderstood or perhaps because the ones who fear her haven't cared to actually look inside her. The Matrka woman, because of her non-conformist behaviour, often runs into the risk of being alienated and misrepresented. Her authenticity and genuine intentions are often misunderstood. Sometimes she might be targeted and unable to cleanse her own image because a woman with this archetype is generally not diplomatic.

The Matrka woman, however, does not succumb under pressure and is ready for as many blows as may come her way. She is a survivor who hardly ever bites the dust. Even when everything seems to have failed she comes up with a plan to outwit people at their own game. She is crafty and a smart strategist. She is a trickster, shape-shifter and spell-caster all rolled into one and knows exactly when to use which strength to achieve her goal. The Matrka woman generally has been through a lot which is why she has a strong Matrka archetype. Her posturing is combative. At the same time she can show a range of mixed traits. She can be benevolent and ruthless at once.

Even if she has no biological offspring, it is generally her strong maternal instinct and her protective urge that prompts her to take charge of ensuring the safety and well-being of others. She is a situational leader who rises to the occasion and lives up to her commitment. She often plays with fire and takes uncalculated risks, her bravado costing her more than what she had anticipated and yet, she is never bogged down. She can go to unimaginable amounts of hardships and physical and mental pain to finish what she started. She is an adventurer who likes traversing unexplored and remote terrains and takes up the challenges that come along the way. Despite being part of a larger family or a big organisation, she has an identity of her own. She does not allow herself to be consumed by the bigger picture and stubbornly stands out so that all else fades into insignificance and only she remains etched in memory.

The woman with the Matrka archetype will not rest in peace or let go of things. Even if it is the slightest of gestures which will perhaps make no difference to the order of things, she will still do it to make her presence felt and to remind the system that it has to take cognizance of her. It has to acknowledge her presence and her power, however trivial it might consider her. Journalists, activists, educators, lawyers fighting or pursuing truths that hardly matter in the larger scheme of things have the Matrka archetype where what matters for them is how true they have been to their cause. Even with their diminished powers after being absorbed in the Hindu pantheon, the Matrkas continue to dominate regional cultures. They have not allowed themselves to be forgotten.

Women with the Matrka archetype carry on in different fields knowing that the cause cannot be accomplished in a day, with the optimism that their presence can make a huge difference to the lives of a few, if not many. They are not looking for grand, historic victories only small, significant ones. They look at clearing the view of their patch of the blue sky for those who believe in them.

The Matrka Archetype in Brands

The manifestation of the Matrka archetype in brands or constructing femininities based on the Matrka archetype for brands will not be much different from the constructs along the lines of Durga or Kali and sometimes Parvati because the Matrkas have elements and archetypes of all three of these goddesses. They are rebels and outlaws like Kali, warriors fighting as per instructions for the devas like Durga and at times dynamic wives out to protect their husbands with their female shakti. Their transgressions and excessive behaviour matches that of Kali and sometimes Durga and they are autonomous despite being mothers and wives just like Parvati.

Progressive constructs of Matrkas can be shown in brands by depicting the foster mother aspect in women who have a change of heart and turn into nurturing mothers for random, wayside children. Or since Matrkas are also addressed as 'Mothers of the World', they can be depicted as women who are engaged in social work related to children. The advertisements could depict them as conducting classes for street urchins, rehabilitating them, getting them foster homes or parents, or taking up their responsibility. A woman with the Matrka archetype can be depicted as enabling a home for children. The product could be a brand of cement or paint that goes into the actual making of a house or a bank loan which makes the project possible.

The excessive and free nature of the Matrkas can be positively captured in women that enjoy coming together, celebrating an occasion or a success, holidaying and partying in the corporate setting. The products for this context could be a drink, a beverage, a brand of cosmetics or a car. The Matrka archetype can be equally effective in the context of women's cooperatives or other organisations where women work together and are at the helm of affairs in both urban and rural settings.

Matrkas can likewise be an all-women's band, an all-women's task force, an all-women's crew or an all-women's entrepreneurial enterprise. The message that needs to be conveyed is women empowering themselves and then moving on to empower other women. It could depict women actively engaging in the business of women's political, social and financial empowerment through activism or state-sponsored projects.

Within the domestic setting, the Matrka could be a woman or women in the joint family who eke out a space for themselves to exercise their freedom and fulfil their desires without having to deal with the prying gaze of patriarchy on them. In the 2016 black-comedy film *Lipstick Under My Burkha*, women of different social groups and ages are shown to do exactly that, each living out her fantasy or transgressing in some way or the other, whether it is secretly applying make-up or clandestinely reading soft porn literature, having illicit relationships or going for secret abortions. The contexts can be reworked in advertisements to more humorous and lighter settings with lighter transgressions. The products can be a brand of women's wear, cosmetics, a two-wheeler or a phone or even an eatable.

Matrkas are women with a reckless edge and an element of natural abandon about them. They are women who like to feel free and call the shots. They do not judge and they do not like being judged. They are difficult to bond with but once they do, they are consistent companions and confidantes. They may have their weak moments but they always come out, even out of the darkest hole. They believe in moving on, not lamenting over things that are irreversible. The Matrkas carry all shades and valences of human possibilities as they do the range of patriarchal anxieties regarding women and their lived reality. The Matrkas refers to the repressed consciousness in each woman in a patriarchal society, which seeks to be free and outside the pale of the binary of normative and non-normative. A Matrka is every woman who has kept the atom of the Great Goddess alive in her or who would like to revive the atom someday to breathe better and live more freely.

CONCLUSION

MYTHS AND ARCHETYPES, the projections of the mind, are so exteriorised and sublimated that they cease to be seen in the light of the psychic drama and acquire a significance, a dynamism, an identity and a momentum of their own as they are handed down through tradition. With passage of time, it is the image or the iconography or the ritual that remains, the meaning is elided or rather it is lost and recedes in the background. The more evolved, the more sophisticated, the more refined an image or a story, the further removed it is from individual experience.

This is why, we fail to understand myths and archetypes as projections of the human mind's innermost longings, desires, apprehensions and anxieties. And when handed down through religion and theology, this loss is even more. They are congealed, concentrated and impactful. They are also at the same time ossified. Though myths and archetypes shine and shimmer with regular and systematic use, they are polished beyond recognition so much so that they lose their texture and their initial relevance and come to serve an arbitrary function. We no longer know their relevance because they are beyond the realm of interrogation and recognition.

However, what is also undoubtedly true about myths and archetypes is that though the original sense and root of the experience is lost, there is nevertheless a familiarity when one encounters it in the outside world. There is an urge to associate, a desire to identify with them and claim them as one's own. Because they are, after all, a part of us, a part of our residual memory, just existing outside the pale of our conscious mind. Once we set about the task of unfreezing these archetypes and the myths surrounding them, they will certainly cease to be unidimensional or have a perfunctory presence. We can then start to trace and unravel them and discover the ways they impact our lives and influence our thoughts.

Many of the goddesses that have been analysed in this book are already regarded as archetypes representing often one overriding quality. Parvati is the divine mother, Durga is the archetypal feminine shakti, Lakshmi symbolises wealth and Saraswati knowledge. Guile and deceit are central to the Matrkas, bloodlust to Kali and rebellion to Sati. This book, however, has endeavoured to do something different. It has attempted to revisit these figures not as the central archetypes they represent but as figures and entities through which different archetypes manifest themselves.

The focus of this book has been on highlighting those myths that will reveal not one but a range of archetypes that will offer a more holistic understanding of a particular goddess. This means that one has to locate multiple archetypes that contribute to the construction of a particular goddess which requires going beyond hegemonic myths.

Through a discovery of the archetypes that constitute the goddesses, the book attempts to offer more empowering and multidimensional projections of them, which humanises the goddesses and makes them more relatable and interesting. The same approach is adopted while tracing the archetypes of the goddesses when they influence the cinematic depiction of female characters. Certain myths which are not that popular but that bring out a particular archetype of the goddess have been traced in a particular narrative that is part of the popular culture, to offer a holistic understanding of the mythological archetype along with how it is absorbed and projected in contemporary times and also the possibilities of projecting it in more empowering ways.

Though it is very difficult to historicise or periodise or date the appearances of the goddess archetypes in Vedic, Puranic or literary texts and epics, wherever possible, the sources of the myths have been mentioned so that interested readers can arrive at an approximation of their emergence. Along with the focus on the archetypes being analysed, in many instances the myth too is foregrounded and traced to present-day popular culture. This is with the intent to establish the extent to which myths are entrenched in our collective unconscious.

Each goddess analysis also focuses on the empowering qualities the goddess has, which the 21st century Indian woman would like to associate or identify with. By Indian woman, I do not in any way intend to homogenise women of India or treat them as one monolithic community. Indeed, there is no such thing as 'the Indian woman' and if I were to even remotely suggest this, I would be glossing over the diversity and the multicultural contexts and nuanced sensibilities that define women in India. When I refer to the Indian woman, in this context, I primarily mean the urban-bred, city-educated Indian woman from the middle class which is also largely the consumer class, the movie-watching, restaurant-going, internet-browsing, mall-hopping class with its power to decide what to buy and make informed choices. A class that is global and local at once.

It is interesting to see how consciously or unconsciously, these goddess archetypes have made their way into Indian cinema and web series and through popular culture entered modern Indian households and can often be seen in Indian women professionals who are in the limelight, in positions of leadership. The idea is for more such manifestations to gain prominence and more conscious branding to happen along the lines of these empowering archetypes.

The humanised depictions of the goddesses by allowing them to insinuate themselves beyond antithetical matrices are intended to offer positive, believable, empowering and progressive depictions of mythicised and deified women. The intention has also been to offer the general reader and readers interested in Indian mythology, gender studies, film studies, consumer behaviour, marketing, media studies and advertising more holistic and less stereotypical constructs of femininity so that they are able to incorporate these figures in their creative pursuits and perception of women.

We look at things and people in the external world, beyond

and outside of ourselves and get influenced and inspired. We look up to people as role models. We dress up like them. We behave, speak and act like them. If external models in media, academia, business, fashion, politics, television and films can inspire us to this extent, how much more could we learn if we were stimulated and inspired to look within and identify the models within, the goddesses within. These goddesses that lie unrecognised and many times dormant, are our archetypes which can inform our life trajectories.

GLOSSARY

Adiparashakti: Means ‘First Supreme-energy’. Adi literally means ‘beginning’, primal. Shakti refers to a power beyond the physical universe; the term itself comes from the root aak, m**eaning, ‘to** be able’.

Alta: Lac dye used by hindu women (especially in Eastern India) to paint the borders of their feet.

Apsara: A type of female spirit of the clouds and waters in Hindu and Buddhist culture. They figure prominently in the sculpture, dance, literature and painting of many South Asian and Southeast Asian cultures.

Ashrama: A two-fold meaning: first, it refers to the doctrine of the ‘four stages of life’ for a twice-born man laid out in the Manusmrti and later Classical Sanskrit texts; second, the word ashram may be used to denote a religious hermitage.

Asura: Asura is used as an adjective meaning ‘powerful’ or ‘mighty’. According to the Bhagavad Gita (16.6-16.7), all beings in the universe have both the divine qualities (daivi sampad) and the demonic qualities (asuri sampad) within each. Scholars call Asuras a special group of gods in one of major Vedic theories of creation of the universe. Their role changes only during and after the earth, sky and living beings have been created. The sky world becomes that of Devas, the underworld becomes that of Asuras. The god Indra is the embodiment of good and represents the Dev*as,* while the dragon Vrtra is the embodiment of evil and an Asura. During this battle between good and evil, creation and destruction, some powerful Asuras side with the good and are called Devas, other powerful Asuras side with the evil and thereafter called Asuras. This is the first major dualism to emerge in the nature of everything in the Universe, according to Hinduism.

Avataar: Incarnation.

Avatar: a manifestation of a deity or released soul in bodily form on earth.

Brahmana: A member of the highest Hindu caste, originally that of the priesthood.

Brahmanical: Following rules set/ideologies perpetrated by Brahmins, the priestly class.

Brahmastra: A weapon created by Brahma.

Danava: In Hindu mythology, the Danavas were a race descending from Daksha. They were the sons of Danu, the daughter of Daksha.

Dasamahavidyas: A group of ten aspects of Adi Parashakti in Hinduism.

Deva: A member of a class of divine beings in the Vedic period, which in Hinduism are benevolent and in Zoroastrianism are evil.

Devi: The Sanskrit word for 'goddess'

Durga Puja: Durga Puja celebrates the victory of the goddess Durga over the demon king Mahishasura. It begins on the same day as Navratri, a nine-night festival celebrating the divine feminine.

Durgatinashini: The one who eliminates suffering.

Ganas: In Sanskrit and Pali means 'flock, troop, multitude, number, tribe, category, series, or class'. The attendants of Shiva who live on Mount Kailash are also known as ganas.

Gandharvas: Semi-divine beings believed to be performing artistes, musicians; They are also believed to live on trees, such as the banyan and the sacred fig, and are entreated to bless wedding processions. Companions to the apsaras, they are handsome, possess brilliant weapons, and wear fragrant clothes.

Ghata: Mud or copper pot of big mouth.

Gramadevata: The presiding deity or guardian deity (patron deity), usually a goddess, worshipped in villages in India.

Halahala: Halahala, literally 'black mass' or 'time puzzle' is the name of a poison created from the sea when Devas (Deities) and Asuras (Demons) churned it (see Samudra Manthan) in order to obtain Amrita, the nectar of immortality

Hara: One of the many names of Shiva

Hari: Refers to God who takes away all the sorrows of his devotees; another name for Vishnu.

Hasta-mudras: Hand gestures that assist in guiding energy flow to particular parts of your brain; also used in Indian classical dance forms.

Hindu: Persons who regard themselves as culturally, ethnically, or religiously adhering to aspects of Hinduism. Historically, the term has also been used as a geographical, cultural, and later religious identifier for people living in the Indian subcontinent. The historical meaning of the term

Hindu has evolved with time. It is rooted in the word Sindhu, the river Indus.

Hinduism: Variously defined as a religion, a religious tradition, a set of religious beliefs, and 'a way of life' believed to have evolved from the early Aryan settlers as expounded and evolved in the Vedas, the Upanishads, the Bhagavad-Gita etc., having an extremely diversified character with many schools of philosophy and theology, many popular cults, and a large pantheon symbolising the many attributes of a single god. The definition of Hinduism has been shaped by the interests of colonialism and by Western notions of religion.

Hindu pantheon: The collective of gods and deities mentioned in the various Puranas.

IB: Intelligence Bureau

Imaginary: A concept in sociology: the set of values, institutions, laws, and symbols through which people imagine their social whole. It is common to the members of a particular social group and the corresponding society. The concept of the imaginary has attracted attention in anthropology, sociology, psychoanalysis, philosophy, and media studies.

Kashi: the old name for present day Varanasi or Benaras also spelt as Banaras, a city in the state of Uttar Pradesh in India.

Kauravas: Kaurava is a Sanskrit term for the descendants of King Kuru (or simply Kurava in Tamil), a legendary king who is the ancestor of many of the characters of the Mahabharata. The Kauravas are generally understood as the 100 sons of Dhritarashtra, the King of Hastinapur, and the cousins of the Pandavas.

Kotha: A rough equivalent of a brothel in feudal society.

Krrttkas: The six Krrttkas who raised the Hindu God Kartikeya The star cluster Kattika; sometimes known as Kartika, corresponds to the open star cluster called Pleiades in western astronomy.

Kshatriya: A member of the second of the four great Hindu castes, the military caste. The traditional function of the Kshatriyas is to protect society by fighting in wartime and governing in peacetime.

Kurukshetra: According to the Puranas, Kurukshetra is a region named after King Kuru, the ancestor of Kauravas and Pandavas, as depicted in epic Mahabharata. Also where the great battle between the Pandavas and the Kauravas was fought. A battlefield, believed to be in the geographical region of the modern State of Haryana.

Lasya: Parvati's dance; denotes happiness, grace and beauty. Lasya is said to be the response to the male energy of the cosmic dance of Tandava.

Linga: The male sexual organ.

Mahamaya: Literally means divine power of illusion; seen as a goddess, a manifestation of Shakti.

Marathas: Warrior clan.

Masala: in the context of the Bollywood masala movie it means a film that has elements of action, drama, romance, suspense packed into one narrative.

Maya: A fundamental concept in Hindu philosophy, notably in the Advaita (Nondualist) school of Vedanta. Maya originally denoted the magic power with which a god can make human beings believe in what turns out to be an illusion. Maya is also an epithet for the Goddess. As in Mahamaya.

Nandi: the sacred bull of Shiva. Nandi is believed to be Shiva's animal form, his mount and his most ardent worshipper.

Navratri: A Hindu festival that spans nine nights (and ten days) and is celebrated every year in the autumn; observed in the honour of the divine feminine Devi (Durga). Also marks the victory of Rama over Ravana, after invoking the Godess.

Northern invasions: Waves of northern people descending into the Near East as described by Merlin Stone and several other anthropologists; northern invaders generally known as Indo-Europeans brought their own religion with them and the worship of a father god which affected the Goddess-worshipping cultures.

Pandavas: The five powerful and skilled sons of Pandu, the King of Hastinapur and his two wives Kunti and Madri. The brothers were famously involved in the Kurukshetra War with their cousins, the Kauravas, over who would control the throne of Hastinapur, and were, ultimately, victorious. They feature in the epic Mahabharata.

Pisachas: Flesh-eating demons in Hindu theology.

Pishachinis: Flesh-eating female demons in myth.

Pretas: Hungry ghosts.

Puja: In Hinduism, ceremonial worship, ranging from brief daily rites in the home to elaborate temple rituals.

Puranas: A class of Sanskrit sacred writings on Hindu

mythology and folklore of varying date and origin, the most ancient of which dates from the 4th century AD.

Rajputs: Warrior clan.

Rakshasa: A supernatural being in Hinduism; also called 'man-eaters' (nri-chakshas, kravyads).

Ramayana: A Sanskrit epic, traditionally attributed to Valmiki but believed to have close to 300 versions.

Rishi: A Vedic term for an accomplished and enlightened person; something like a sage.

Rudra tandav: Shiva's dance of destruction.

Saat-phere/pheras: Seven circumambulations around the sacred fire; basically seven vows that bind the bride and groom into husband and wife and each vow has a significant meaning.

Sabha parva: The 'Book of the Assembly Hall', is the second of eighteen books of Mahabharata.

Sadhaka: Devotee, worshipper

Samudramanthan: Churning of the ocean of milk) is one of the best-known episodes in the Hindu philosophy narrated in the Bhagavata Purana, in the Mahabharata and in the Vishnu Purana. The Samudra Manthana explains the origin of Amrita, the nectar of immortality.

Sanjeevani vidya: One of the most powerful mantras. It was given to sage shukracharya by Lord Shiva.

Saptarishis: The seven sages of Indian mythology. In Indian astronomy, the asterism of the Big Dipper (part of the constellation of Ursa Major) is called saptarishi, with the seven stars representing seven rishis.

Sattva, rajas, tamas: Sattva is one of the three guaas or "modes of existence", a philosophical and psychological concept developed by the Samkhya school of Hindu philosophy. The other two qualities are rajas (passion, enterprise and activity) and tamas (inertia, excess, destruction, chaos). Sattva is the quality of goodness, positivity, truth, serenity, balance, peacefulness, and virtuousness.

Satyalok: the highest heaven, where Brahma and Saraswati live with Brahmins.

Shaiva: a Bhakti sect devoted to Shiva.

Shakta: A follower of Shaktism; a mother goddess worshpper.

Shakti-peethas: Significant shrines and pilgrimage destinations in Shaktism, the goddess-focused Hindu tradition. The legend behind the Shakti Peethas is the story of the self-immolation of the goddess Sati.

Shakti: The female principle of divine energy

Shaktism: A major sect of Hinduism, wherein the metaphysical reality is considered metaphorically a woman and Shakti is regarded as the supreme godhead. It includes many goddesses, all considered aspects of the same supreme goddess.

Shloka: Hymn or prayer in metered verse in Sanskrit.

Siddha: Perfected masters who have achieved a high degree of physical as well as spiritual perfection or enlightenment.

Soma: A Vedic Sanskrit word that literally means 'distill,

extract, sprinkle'; drinking or entitled to drink soma—juice.

Tandava nritya: A divine dance performed by the Hindu gods; when Shiva performs it, it is usually seen as the dance of destruction.

Tantra: The esoteric traditions of Hinduism and Buddhism that developed in India from the middle of the 1st millennium CE onwards. The term tantra, in the Indian traditions, also means any systematic broadly applicable 'text, theory, system, method, instrument, technique or practice'. A key feature of these traditions is the use of mantras.

Tantric: Of tantra.

Tapa or tapasya: Austerities (control) of the body, mind and tongue; 'tapa' in Sanskrit meaning to heat or burn.

Vaishnava: A member of one of the main branches of modern Hinduism, devoted to the worship of the god Vishnu as the supreme being.

Vamanavtar: An incarnation of Vishnu, Vaman was born as a midget.

Vanaras: Refers to a group of people living in forests, in the Ramayana and its various versions. In the Ramayana, the Vanaras help Rama defeat Ravana. It is derives from the word vana (forest), and nara (man), means, 'belonging to the forest' or 'forest-dwelling'. Although the word Vanara has come to mean 'monkey' over the years and the Van*aras are depicted as* monkeys in popular art, their exact identity is not clear.

Vasant Panchami: Also called Saraswati Puja in honour of the goddess Saraswati, it is a festival that marks the preparation for the arrival of spring.

Vedas: Any of the four collections forming the earliest body of Indian scripture, consisting of the Rig Veda, Sama Veda, Yajur Veda, and Atharva Veda, which codified the ideas and practices of Vedic religion and laid down the basis of classical Hinduism. They were probably composed between 1500 and 700 BC, and contain hymns, philosophy, and guidance on ritual.

Yajna kund: The altar of the Vedic sacrificial fire or Yajna; the fire pit.

Yoga: Protection, method, meditation, harmony and technique, union.

Yogic: Of yoga.

Yoni: The female sexual organ

Akal bodhan: Worship or invocation of Durga in an uncustomary time.

Akshay patra: Means inexhaustible vessel of food.

Ayudhas: Weapons; but, in shilpa-sastra, the term indicates whatever objects the idol holds in his or her hands.

Bahu: Daughter-in-law.

Bhartiya nari: Ideal Indian woman.

Bija mantra: A one-syllable sound used in meditation or yoga.

Buddhi: A Vedic Sanskrit word that means the intellectual faculty and the power to 'form and retain concepts, reason, discern, judge, comprehend, understand'.

Collective unconscious: A concept originally defined by psychoanalyst Carl Jung. Sometimes referred to as the 'objective psyche', it refers to the idea that a segment of the deepest unconscious mind is genetically inherited and is not shaped by personal experience.

Daityas: In Hindu mythology, Daitya describes a member of a clan or race of giants, who were the half-brothers of the Devas. Sons of Diti.

Dakinis: Energetic beings in female form.

Damru: A small two-headed drum, used in Hinduism and Tibetan Buddhism, supposed to be Shiva's musical instrument.

Devi-bhakta: Worshipper of the Devi.

Jugaad: A colloquial Hindi word, which refers to a non-conventional, frugal innovation, often termed a 'hack job'.

Kamandalu: An oblong water pot, generally carried by sages, preists and upper castes; container for holy water.

Kurmavataar: One of the 10 avataars (incarnations) of the Hindu god Vishnu in the form of a tortoise.

Maha yajna: Grand fire sacrifice.

Manavantaras: Literally meaning, the duration of a Manu, or his lifespan; the lifespan of a human being.

Masala: Spices, spicy. in the context of the Bollywood masala movie it means a film that has elements of action, drama, romance, suspense packed into one narrative.

Munis: A holy man ; sage.

Nawab: Refers to males and literally means Viceroy; The primary duty of a Nawab was to uphold the sovereignty of the

Mughal emperor along with the administration of a certain province.

Panchyatana puja: A system of puja (worship) in the Smartism sampradaya (group), which is one of four major sampradaya of Hinduism.

Parashakti: Ultimate form of the goddess

Prakriti: Primal creative or natural force.

Purana Pandits: Professional reciter of religious narratives

Rani sahiba: Her highness, the queen.

Rudraksha: A rosery bead. Fruis of Elaeocarpus ganitrus trees, used as prayer beads. Said to be Shiva's preferred ornament.

Sharodiya Durga Puja: the autumnal Durga Puja festival to celebrate the arrival of goddess Durga along with her children Ganesh Kartik Lakshmi and Saraswati particularly popular and traditionally celebrated in the Indian states of West Bengal, Assam, Odisha, Tripura and the coun*try o*f Bangladesh

Subhedar: A historical civ*il or* military rank originally relating to a *senior* official of the Mughal Empire who governed an assigned 'Subah' or region.

Thakur: A historical feudal title of the Indian subcontinent to describe a landlord or the master of an estate.

Vana parva: The 'Book of the Forest', is the third of eighteen parvas in the Indian epic Mahabharata.

Vasavi Shakti: The second weapon of Indra, inferior to Vajra. It could be used only once and upon usage, it killed the opponent.

REFERENCES

Advertising as Culture by Chris Wharton

Advertising Cultures Gender, Commerce, Creativity by Sean Nixon

Amar Akbar Anthony Bollywood, Brotherhood and the Nation by William Elison, Christian Lee Novetzke and Andy Rotman

Archetypes Who Are You? by Caroline Myss

Bhagavata Purana by Ramesh Menon

Buddhism After Patriarchy: A Feminist History, Analysis and Reconstruction of Buddhism by Rita M Gross

Companion to Literary Myths, Heroes and Archetypes edited by Pierre Brunel

Deewar The Footpath, the City and the Angry Young Man by Vinay Lal

Devi: Goddesses of India Comparative Studies in Religion and Society by John Stratton Hawley

Devi The Bhagvatam Retold by Ramesh Menon

Encyclopedia of Goddesses and Heroines Africa, Eastern Mediterranean and Asia Volume 1 by Patricia Monaghan

Film Theory: The Basics by Kevin McDonald

Fingerprinting Popular Culture edited by Vinay Lal and Ashish Nandy

Gender, Nation and Popular Film in India by Sikata Banerjee

Given to the Goddess – South Indian Devadasis and the Sexuality of Religion by Lucinda Ramberg

Goddesses in Everywoman by Jean Shinoda Bolen

Goddesses Mysteries of the Feminine Divine by Joseph Campbell

Goddess Traditions in Tantric Hinduism History, Practice and Doctrine by Bjarne Wernicke Olesen

Hindu Goddesses by David R Kinsley

Hindu Mythology: Classic Stories of Hindu Mythology by Scott Lewis

Hindu Mythology: Vedic and Puranic by William Joseph Wilkins

Hindu Myths by Wendy Doniger

How to Read a Film Movies, Media and Beyond by James Monaco

Jaya: An Illustrated Retelling of the Mahabharata by Devdutt Pattanaik

Kali The Black Goddess of Dakshineshwar by Elizabeth U Harding

Keyframes Popular Cinema and Cultural Studies edited by Mathew Tinkcom and Amy Villarejo

Leadership, Popular Culture and Social Change edited by Kristin M S Bezio and Kimberly Yost

Man and His Symbols by Carl C Jung

REFERENCES

Myth a Very Short Introduction by Robert A Segal

Mythologies by Roland Barthes

Ogilvy on Advertising by David Ogilvy

Sacred Contracts by Caroline Myss

Seeking Mahadevi Constructing the Identities of the Hindu Great Goddess edited by Tracy Pintchman

Srimad Bhagavatam by Kamala Subramniam

Symbols of Transformation by Carl C Jung

The Archetypes and the Collective Unconscious by Carl C Jung

The Collected Essays by A K Ramanujan edited by Vinay Dharwadkar

The Civilization of the Goddess by Marija Gimbutas

The Goddess as Role Model by Heidi R M Pauwells

The Goddess' Mirror: Visions of the Divine from the East and West by David R Kinsley

The Hero and The Outlaw Building Extraordinary Brands Through the Power of Archetypes by Margaret Mark and Carol S Pearson

The Heroine's Journey by Maureen Murdock

The Hero's Journey by Joseph Campbell

The Hero with a Thousand Faces by Joseph Campbell

The Language of Archetypes by Caroline Myss

The Mahabharata A Modern Rendering Volumes I and II by Ramesh Menon

The Rigveda by Wendy Doniger

The Rise of the Goddess in the Hindu Tradition
by Tracy Pintchman

The Routledge Handbook of Greek Mythology by Robin Hard

The Seven Basic Plots Why We Tell Stories
by Christopher Booker

The Ten Mahavidyas Tantric Visions of the Divine Feminine
by David R Kinsley

The Woman's Dictionary of Symbols and Sacred Objects
by Barbara G Walker

The World of Hrishikesh Mukherjee by Jai Arjun Singh
True Myth by James W Menzies

When God was a Woman by Merlin Stone

When the World Becomes Female
Guises of a South Indian Goddess by Joyce Burkhalter Flueckiger

Woman and Goddess in Hinduism Reinterpretations and Re-envisionings by Tracy Pintchman and Rita D Sherma

Women in the Hindu Tradition Rules, Roles and Exceptions
by Mandakranta Bose

Women Who Run With The Wolves by Clarissa Pinkola Estes

Why I Am Not A Hindu? by Kancha Illaiah Shepherd

You Are a Heroine: A Retelling of the Hero's Journey
by Susanna Liller

7 Secrets of the Goddess by Devdutt Pattanaik

50 Films that Changed Bollywood by Shubhra Gupta

ACKNOWLEDGEMENTS

The journey of writing this book has been a very interesting one. I felt growing as a woman, as a human being and as an individual with my writing, and the writing in turn grew on me. I need to deeply acknowledge all those who have enabled this incredibly transforming journey for me. I think if I start from the very beginning, it would be my mother and my father for their avid interest in mythology. I grew up listening to the Ramayana, the Mahabharata and a lot of other myths, imagining Shakuntala absorbed in thought and Durga astride a lion. A deeply felt gratitude would be towards my Nrityaguru Vidya Deshpande for initiating me into myths and allowing me to embody and be the goddess in body, mind and spirit.

What I owe to Saumya Chattopadhyay, my very old and special friend and Senior Vice President MullenLowe Lintas Group India, is a lot more than a thank you. He is the one who evolved the idea of this book, who believed in me when I entered into this sacred contract and who I had several rounds of discussions with before this book started taking shape. A heartfelt thanks to my very dear friend Mridula Chaudhari who is the only person to have read the entire manuscript apart from my editor and publisher. Mridula would come back to me with her observations and her deep insights and her faith in me would keep me going.

My deepest gratitude to Dr Kamala Gopalan, my PhD supervisor and a very special person in my life since, for being that beacon of light who shows how to set sail for unknown destinations and also hit the shores sound and safe, Dr Sucharita Sarkar, a friend and a scholar I hold in very high esteem, who read through several sections of my manuscript and vetted it and Dr Anjali Kulkarni, my favorite teacher from my college days and a scholar and academician par excellence, for extending her sharp observations and inputs whenever I approached her.

I thank my husband Arun for bearing with my ramblings, being a sounding board and sitting through my long readings and my son Shiv for nourishing me with his unconditional love. My sister Dr Adity for always listening with an empathetic and an interested ear whenever I had something to share. Dr Sachin Labade, of the Dept of English, University of Mumbai, one of my best friends for giving me thumbs up after thumbs up. A deep sense of gratitude to Soumya Mathew, the commissioning editor of the award winning website Feminism in India who showed such faith in my analysis of myths and lent a platform for me to take my analysis to readers. A hearty thank you to Air Commodore Nitin Sathe, a dear friend for putting me through to Vitasta. A big thank you to Papri Sen Sri Raman, my editor in Vitasta for her patience and her promptness in addressing my queries and making me do what it took to make the book an interesting read and most of all to Renu Kaul Verma for being so warm and kind and making me feel like family, but above all for believing in the worthiness of the manuscript.

And to every single goddess in this book who allowed me access, allowed me intimacy and who revealed herself to me.

SHYAONTI TALWAR

SHYAONTI TALWAR is an academician, writer and columnist.

Shyaonti married her avid interest in mythology and films with her scholarship in gender studies and started keenly pursuing readings and writing papers on goddess constructs in mythology, parallels in Greek and Indian mythology and gender in cinema. She has been working in these areas for the past several years now and has presented many papers in national and international conferences which were subsequently published in research journals.

Shyaonti's extensive research led her to conclude that there is a real dearth of books on Indian goddess archetypes and almost no in-depth work that brings together the anthropological and ethnographical details of the Indian goddesses along with their archetypes, their analysis and the tracing of the archetypes in popular culture and contemporary society which is what led to the present book.

An Assistant Professor of English in a college affiliated to SP Pune University, Shyaonti is on the Board of Studies of several universities and academic bodies. She writes regularly for *The Wire* and is a columnist for *Feminism in India* and writes on mythology, popular culture and Feminist praxis. Her areas of research interest include gender studies, women's writing, myths and archetypes and cultural studies. She is also a trained practitioner of the Indian classical dance form of Kathak.